Little Cicero

Duane Schwartz

Aberdeen Bay

Atlanta - Beijing - Harbin - Washington, D.C.

Aberdeen Bay
Published by Aberdeen Bay, an imprint of Champion Writers.
www.aberdeenbay.com

PUBLISHER'S NOTE

This is a book of fiction. Names, characters, places, and incidents are either the product of author's imagination or are used fictitiously. Any resemblance to actual persons, living or dead, business establishments, government agencies, events, or locales is entirely coincidental.

International Standard Book Number
ISBN-13: 978-1-60830-031-0
ISBN-10: 1-60830-031-5

Printed in the United States of America.

Acknowledgement

A special thank you:
To two great friends, Ed Svegal and Mike Nelson, who pre-read Little Cicero, pointed out trouble spots, then took the time to write a review. Their opinions follow.

From *Mike Nelson*:

Duane Schwartz has become one of my favorite authors. I have enjoyed "Cobb's Landing" and "Calumet", both fine novels, but the best to date is "Little Cicero."
To sum it up, within the pages of "Little Cicero", this author has achieved a great depth of suspense and compelling intrigue within the story's plot, a visual journey through some strange and unusual events on a road traveled through time by realistic characters he has managed to create in this his best story to date. What a ride.

From *Ed Svegal*:

Schwartz has produced another page turner. He grabs your attention on page one and uses captivating characters and an intriguing storyline to hold you until the end. Special note to iron-rangers, if you've wondered what's down in them old pits, here's one thought.

Other works by Duane Schwartz

Published May, 2009
ISBN 9780981907550

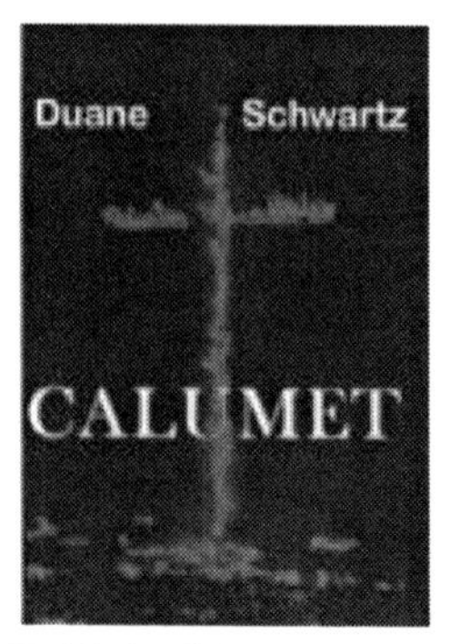

Published Nov, 2009
ISBN 9780984134298

Editorial reviews:

Cobb's Landing: From the days of prohibition to modern times, Schwartz follows the saga of Cobb's Landing, a favorite rest stop for the mob. Safe from the scrutiny of the law, gangsters are free to frolic, gamble, drink undisturbed until the rape of a teen-ager riles a placid town to take action in 2009's most exciting family saga.

Calumet: Calumet is almost too real to be considered fiction. In fact, history will show that in many instances and in many towns the scenes that Schwartz so graphically describes in his latest thriller actually did take place. Indeed, even more vicious acts took place as unions battled non-unions, Klansmen battled non-believers, all wrestling for control of the workplace. Only the second effort by Schwartz, Calumet reflects the mature writing style that one could expect from a Steinbeck or Salinger

Praise for Cobb's Landing: Cobb's Landing pleasantly surprised me and opened me up to a new genre. A book that made me laugh, cry, feel a connection to the characters, and make me unable to put it down - I truly enjoyed the story and the history that came in Cobb's Landing. I am very much looking forward to the author's next publication. VERY WELL DONE!!! KB Elk River, Minnesota

Praise for Calumet: Once again, Duane Schwartz has captured the wildness of the Mesabi Iron Range in his writing. In *Cobb's Landing,* he kept us all spellbound with his story of the very gangsters we all heard tales of in our youths. Now, in *Calumet,* he reminds us of how rough and tough our ancestors had it in settling our area. I, along with those fellow readers with whom I have shared his books, all of us fond of mystery themes based on history, anxiously await his next novel. Retta A Zufall Postmaster, Calumet and Coleraine, Minnesota.

For more information and updates visit the author's web page at www.authorsden.com/duaneschwartz

Dedication

This work is dedicated to all those loyal fans who have read my books, called or e-mailed with kind words, and left comments of praise on booksellers' sites. It is in appreciation for those kindnesses that I continue to write, striving to create for you stories that please and entertain.

Every author needs a muse. Mine is Betty. She has never bored of reading my work as many times as was necessary, until she approved of what she read. And without her skills, energy, and devotion, my work would be little more than empty pages.

My thanks:

To all of my brothers and sisters. Your support and encouragement has been invaluable.

To Pat Mcgauly. My friend and fellow author. Your generosity in reading and suggesting in my first effort, Cobb's Landing, will never be forgotten.

To Barb Linder. You placed the periods where they belonged and dotted the i's of my early work. I learned much from your kind efforts.

To Pat Andrews. You provided editing that nearly has me spelling properly. Emphasis on the 'nearly'.

To Victor Spadaccni, who took the time from his busy schedule to share with me some of the knowledge he gained in the publishing field, making it possible for my work to attract the attention it needed.

And finally, a thank your goes out to the staff at Aberdeen Bay, and especially to Jill Cline, fellow author and my contact with the publisher. We all owe you; for no one would be reading any of this if you hadn't believed in this novel.

Little Cicero

CHAPTER ONE

True gangsters? Perhaps. Roughnecks just the same filled the overcrowded streets of the mining camp in the days of flappers and illegal booze. No wonder the murders would go undiscovered for another fifty years. Everyone was smashed. And no small wonder those murders would not have a murderer for thirty more. Nothing connected: no twin teenage girls hauled off by a perverted and crazed uncle, no choir or altar boys disappearing from the streets at random, no grouping of blond beauties in their thirties found dead and mutilated in a gutter beside a country road — nothing at all that said serial killer back when it all happened. In fact, had it not been for Mother Nature, there would still be nothing telling this story. Why? Because the lives that were taken were not connected to the town. They were not reported missing. They were not looked for. Again, why? Because roughnecks filled the streets of the mining camp, not residents. This was a place where drink could be had and whores could be bought. No killing had been done to the killer's neighbors; that was saved for strangers who no one would miss.

Mitch Polovina had sought the position of police chief and got it, not for his qualifications, he had none, but because the old chief died and nobody asked for the job. "What do you want me to do about this?" he asked Ted Mayfield, the town's mayor, also new to the job and equally as unqualified as Mitch.

"Solve the crime."

"Yeah. Like I could actually do that," Mitch said and grinned. He studied the water of the mine pit and saw yet another body pop to the surface. "Christ!" he said. That made four of them so far, all still floating belly up like dead carp, bobbing in the waves. "Christ," he said again and spat tobacco on the ground. It was a habit he picked up recently, when his third wife threatened divorce. He took it up to piss her off. "Where the hell's Doc Gray Eagle?" That was Polovina's pet-name for Henry Nason, a half-breed Ojibwa who reluctantly served as local coroner.

Pop! Another body shot out of the water and splashed down, on the lake's surface sending ringlet ripples out which caused others to bob. Grotesque! "Son-of-a-bitch," Mayfield said and reached for his cell phone. "I'll get his ass out here."

CHAPTER TWO

Farwell, the name of today's village on the site of the early twentieth century camp, was nicknamed Little Cicero. Its many under street tunnels that speakeasy patrons traveled from one watering hole to another during prohibition, much like Cicero, Illinois in the Chicago gangster days — Capone days — brought that on. And as much as locals tried to move past that undertone, locating tunnel after tunnel and sealing them off for good with thick concrete walls, the nickname stuck. Farwell was rarely called Farwell. Rumors were too grand — too romantic.

"Sheriff," Henry Nason said stepping up beside him.

"Gray Eagle," Mitch Polovina grunted. "I'm not a sheriff. I'm a police chief."

"I do wish you'd stop calling me Gray Eagle, Bugsy."

"I wish you'd stop calling me Bugsy."

"At least it's your nickname. It was in high school anyway." The two of them had played high school football together, Polovina at quarterback and Nason at center. "Mine was Amazing Nase, remember?"

"I like..."

"All right you two. That's enough. We have a serious problem to deal with here," Mayor Mayfield said.

"Just what is this problem? All I got from my nurse was something about a body," Doc Nason said. "Where is it?"

Mitch Polovina grabbed Nason's face with his palms and steered his gaze lake-ward. "Jesus Christ!" Doc said. He counted — six — pop — make that seven. "Where the hell are they coming from?"

"Under the water," Polovina said and spat more tobacco in the dirt.

"No shit," Nason said. "Know any divers?"

"You mean besides me and you?" Mitch asked. "No." The two of them had dived the pit lakes in the area when they were young, but gave that up years earlier. "Think you still know how?"

"I'm sure I can manage it."

"That's right, an Indian never forgets," Polovina said, mirth in his voice.

"That's an elephant that never forgets. I told you before... you should have gone on to college with me; you might have at least learned enough to properly quote a cliché."

"Either of you still own diving gear?" Mayfield asked.

"Someplace," Nason said. "Probably."

"Someplace? Probably?" Mayfield asked.

"Hell, Teddy," Nase said. "It's been years."

"Ted," the mayor corrected. He too had played ball. He had been Teddy then. Now he was the mayor; he was Ted.

"Okay... Ted..."

"What about you, Mitch? You still got your gear?"

"It's Chief Polovina, Teddy, and yes, I still have mine. I even know where it is. And Gray Eagle, I know where yours is too. You left it in my garage the last time we dove Stillwell Pit. Remember?" The two of them used to explore the bottoms of the many water filled abandoned mine pits along the Mesabi Iron Range. In many of them, equipment had been left behind because of the speed at which the pits would fill when miners finally ran out of ore and into the water table. Sometimes pumps were used to keep ahead of the water and mining would continue. Sometimes the pit was too played out to warrant the effort. And if equipment was old, it would often be abandoned. At the bottom of Stillwell, a steam locomotive still stood proudly on its tracks. And many other pieces of early mining equipment as well. Treasures to teens — treasures worth the dive.

"Maybe that's all the bodies. Maybe we don't have to dive," Doc offered.

"What if it ain't?" Polovina asked. "What if we called it good? Then in another week, a couple of teens are parking over there on that bluff," he waved an arm across the pit, "and she comes pourin' out of the car, buck naked and screaming, just as her daddy comes looking for her, and daddy, not aware of the bodies popping out of the water, kills the boyfriend — or girlfriend — whatever? Won't we have our hands full of trouble then?"

"He sure paints a picture, doesn't he, Mayor?" Nason said.

The mayor shook his head and grinned.

"Look, Chief. Get some people out here and get those bodies out of the water," Mayor Mayfield said. "Where do you want them hauled to, Doc?" he asked Nason.

"There's a makeshift morgue in the hospital basement. Have them brought there. Say, anybody know if there might be a map of what's under this water?" Some of the mining companies had kept great records of their endeavors, including detailed maps of train tracks, buildings, things like that. "Might be something over at the mining company office."

"I'll get an officer and the EMT's out here. Then I'll see to our diving gear," Polovina said. "Gray Eagle, you get to your morgue and see to the bodies. Teddy, you see if the mine has any kind of map. We'll meet up down on the shore in an hour." Polovina pointed out a piece of sandy beach, yanked his radio microphone to his mouth and called for backup. "And bring a van," he ordered. "Go! I'll scoot down there and wait for my guys," he told Doc and the mayor.

***

The map Mayor Mayfield retrieved from the mining company office showed a large steel structure just beneath the area where bodies had been popping to the surface. Penned in on the site were the words, *COMMERCIAL LUBRICANT WAREHOUSE.* "Lucky this happened now," the mayor said.

Both Mitch and Henry (Doc) Nason shot him matching curious looks.

"I just mean the ink," Teddy said. "Another couple months and the writing would've faded to unreadable," he explained and pointed at the penned in words.

As Mitch and Doc donned their diving gear on the shore of the pit lake, one of the stiffs was hauled past them. "Remarkable," Nason said. "They must have been in sealed containers to be that much left of them, and the clothing. These people are a theatrical group or they're out of the 'thirties'."

Polovina pulled on his swim fins, strapped on his tank, positioned his mask on his forehead, and began a duck walk to the water. A stretcher passed him—a woman, young, in a flapper costume—pretty. "Twenties, they're from the twenties," he said and stepped into the water and waited for Gray Eagle. He knew better than to dive a mine pit alone. The depth alone could be the end of you. And the debris one finds down there can trap a man in the blink of an eye. He looked up at the area where they had stood — himself, the coroner/doctor, and the mayor — no more than two hours ago, watching the bizarre sight of bodies from the roaring twenties popping out of the water one by one, as though they were dancing, and he saw a lady. She was elderly, although he couldn't tell just how elderly from that distance. She wore a dress, plaid, hem at mid shin, a broad white hat, something protruding from its center, flowers possibly. He felt more than saw Doc come up on him. He waved a hand in the old lady's direction. "Who's that, Gray Eagle?"

Doc Nason looked in her direction. "Could be from the old-folks home up the street," he said. "Wonder if she saw the bodies." All of them had been loaded and hauled to Doc's make-shift morgue already.

"You come up with any guesses on cause of death?"

"I did, Chief," Nason said. "You got yourself a serial killer. Some were stabbed, some had broken necks, one of them shot, but all were women, late teens to low twenties, all pretty, and all blond."

"Christ!"

"Yeah."

"Did the mayor have any idea how deep the warehouse is?" Polovina asked.

"He didn't say. He did say though, that we wouldn't be able to stay down long, because the pressure will be considerable."

"Well… we knew that. Remember that last dive? I put earplugs in thinking it would help with the pressure." The depth of the mine pits along the Range, three or four times their average width, resulted in tremendous pressure. Most divers who wanted to reach bottom wore pressurized suits, not scuba gear. "I had to dig them back out with a tweezers."

"I remember," Doc said and chuckled. "I'm told they struck water at a shallower depth in this mine. That may help." He pulled his mask over his eyes and inserted his mouthpiece. He stepped over the drop off and began his descent. Halfway down, they both turned on their lights and looked for the old warehouse. The map was accurate. It was right beneath them.

Inside, fifty-five gallon steel drums labeled 'commercial grade lubricants' were stacked to the ceiling. Several had fallen from their prospective stack and landed, most of them on their side, likely due to some recent disturbance in the underwater current. It was from these, the metal band and clamp holding their top in place all these years having popped loose when they hit, that the bodies undoubtedly escaped. Two were sitting top down. Polovina tipped one upright and loosened the band. He pulled the lid off and a body escaped, rising until it hit the metal sheeting of the building's roof. Both divers shined a light on the new arrival, studied it in amazement for a moment then scanned the rest of the overturned barrels. No more bodies. Polovina swam to the rafters and freed the poor creature he had released from the drum. He guided the body to the door of the old warehouse and allowed it float to the surface, knowing he had men above who would retrieve it, hopefully prior to the old woman watching from above seeing it. He started to take inventory of the remaining containers — a hundred, maybe more. He motioned to Doc Nason that they too should surface.

On the shore, Mitch Polovina shook his head, wondering which course of action should be taken. Should he hire divers? Should he call in the state police, the FBI?

"I'd call on the EPA," Doc Nason suggested.

"The EPA?"

"Yeah. Those containers have to be considered hazardous material, under the water like that. Bodies? Oil? It makes no difference. It's all a hazmat issue."

Polovina slapped him on the shoulder. "You're absolutely right, Gray Eagle." They both stood as the body the chief of police had released was carried past them on a stretcher. This one was a male. Mitch Polovina guessed him to be around thirty. He looked up at the old woman — still there — still watching. "I need to see who she is," he said and began to climb the bank.

She turned and left when she saw him coming.

"Victoria Outing," a voice from behind him said.

"Excuse me?" he said as he turned to face Mayfield.

"The old woman, her name is Victoria Outing. She lives at the retirement home." The retirement home, or as some called it, the old folks home, was an aging brick and mortar building that stood a block from the overlook. "She'd be one of the few who were around when your murders took place. Might be worth an interview, Chief."

CHAPTER THREE

"I taught you two boys," the old woman said as soon as Mitch Polovina and Henry Nason approached the garden table where Victoria Outing sat sipping her morning tea. You... Mitchell Polovina, and you... Henry Nason, and that Teddy Mayfield, I taught him as well. You, Mitchell, you came from a Catholic family, lots of children. Your folks still alive?" she asked, and petted a small dog sitting on her lap.

"My father's been gone for almost ten years; mother passed away just last fall," Polovina said.

"Did she hold on to her faith?"

"She did but she failed at it."

"Really," the old woman commented. She tightened a ribbon tied into the little dog's hair, and the dog snarled and snapped at her hand.

"I'm afraid so. Nine sons and not one priest among them," Polovina said and smiled. His religion had always amused him, so many restrictions, so many superstitions.

"I'm not surprised to hear you talk like that. Even in your youth you questioned the beliefs."

"When did you teach me, Ms. Outing?" Mitch asked.

"Fourth grade," she said.

"You must be mistaken. I spent my first six years of school being taught at St. Michael's parochial school, by nuns. My fourth grade teacher was..."

"Sister Mary Elizabeth," she said and stroked the little dog again.

"Sister Mary Elizabeth," Polovina said, "with the steel edged wooden ruler for whacking kids on the back of the hand?"

"You had it coming, Mitchell Polovina. Don't even think you didn't."

"Yes, Ma'am." He studied the lines of her face for a time. He wondered how old she was. When he was in grade school she seemed old, but then, he was in grade school. Everyone seemed old. "Sister," he started.

"Miss," she corrected. I left the profession shortly after I taught you boys. A few years later, I left the convent. Finally, I left the church. Your mother wasn't the only Catholic to fail her faith."

"Why?"

"Her," she said and fluffed the dog's ears playfully a time or two. "Well… not exactly her. But it was one just like her."

"I don't understand," Polovina admitted and looked at Doc Nason who seemed just as confused by the old woman.

"It's all about little dogs and heaven. You see, Catholics don't believe these little creatures have a soul; therefore they can't go to heaven. I found myself believing that was bullshit," she said and spat in the grass beside her chair to drive home her conviction. "They have more love in them than most humans. They have a soul. Funny, it's seldom the big issues one abandons one's beliefs over. It's usually something small, something they know is crap. So… it turns out, Mr. Polovina, you and I aren't all that much different where religion is concerned, are we?"

"I reckon not, Ma'am." Polovina smiled at Doc Nason. "Mind if I ask you a few questions, Ma'am?"

"Certainly not, Chief. My guess is the first one would concern my age. So I'll save you the embarrassment of having to ask. I was born in nineteen-thirteen. It's now two thousand and nine. Did I teach you enough math to figure that out, Mitchell?" Doc smiled. "Don't laugh, Henry Nason. You weren't all that much better in fourth grade."

"Ninety-six?" Polovina asked.

"Very good," she said. "Now… I would think the next thing you want to know is if I know anything about all those bodies popping out of the water."

"Do you?"

"No!"

"No?" Mitch Polovina was confused. Why then, was she out there watching? Amusement? No. It couldn't have been. She seemed involved in some way — attached to what was going on.

"I know about the warehouse they were in though," she said. "And I know about the man who ran the warehouse back then. Would that be something of interest to you?"

"It certainly would," Polovina said.

"It's a long story," she warned. "It's time for my nap now though. You two boys come tomorrow morning and we'll get started."

"What time?"

"Breakfast is at nine. I'll arrange for you to eat with me," she said and got to her feet. She grabbed for a cane and made her way to the door of the home, little dog tucked under an arm.

"What do you think?" Polovina asked Doc Nason.

"She's spry for ninety-six. And she seems alert. I sensed no lapses of memory."

"Yeah. I noticed, especially where fourth grade is concerned," Mitch said and smiled. "I'll make a call or two, find her physician, see how much we can trust her faculties."

"That might be wise," Polovina said. "Say, Gray Eagle, you coming with me in the morning?"

"I wouldn't miss it."

***

Homer Jenkins had managed the mining company office since the nineteen-sixties. When he first took the job over, he had a crew who looked after things while he saw to the clerical side of keeping the company's holdings safe from hoodlums, scavengers and treasure seekers, campers and hunters and fishermen, and the like. Nowadays, the entire job was left to him. No one seemed to know why he was there at all, why the company hadn't released him from his duties long ago and bulldozed the remaining buildings. Two were all that were left of the original mine property anyhow, and they were so uncared for they were hardly worth protecting. In the sixties, equipment still filled the property. But by the close of Homer's first decade as manager, good equipment had been hauled off and lesser equipment had fallen into the pit lake due to its banks giving way to their tremendous weight. But Homer Jenkins still occupied the old office, and when he was in it, he was a king. "I don't have to release anything to you. This property belongs to the company, and right now, Chief Polovina, you are trespassing."

"Why in the hell don't you retire, Homer. You must be ninety years old," the chief of police said.

"Eighty-six," Homer corrected.

"Well there you go. Eighty-six then. I'd say it's high-time you went on your merry way — get some enjoyment out of your golden years."

"Golden years my ass," he shouted. "Call it like it is — old age." He eyed Mitch up, then down. "You're one of 'em," he said.

"One of what?" Polovina asked.

"One of those hoods from back in the sixties, you and all them brothers of yours. You 'bout run me ragged back then, and here you are now, badge on your chest like some big shot John-law, tryin' to do the same, run me raged, or run me off." He pushed a thick layer of dust off of the glass covered counter, unearthing a paper. He blew the remainder of the dust at the chief of police and Chief Polovina coughed. "This," he pointed at the paper beneath the glass. "This here's my authority to be here. Now where's yours."

"Are you going to make me get a warrant? Is that what this is all about?"

"That won't be necessary." The voice came from behind him. It was Ted Mayfield. "Homer, you need to let Mitch look around. He won't hurt anything, I promise."

"I ain't worried 'bout him hurting nothing. I don't want him stealing something."

"Promise not to steal, Bugsy?" Mayfield asked and smiled. Polovina shot him a manufactured and exaggerated grin in return. "Let him look at the records, Homer."

"You know, you being Mayor, that don't exactly give you authority to ask," Jenkins said.

"I'm not asking as Mayor. I'm asking as your son-in-law, Pop."

Homer held an arm out, palm up, as though to say, "Help yourself, then."

"You know anything about any of this, Homer," Mitch Polovina asked him.

"About any of what?"

"The bodies," Mitch said. He wondered if at eighty-eight, the old boy wasn't getting a bit daft.

"What bodies?" Homer asked.

Mitch looked out a window at the water filled pit. He could clearly see where the bodies had popped from the water the day before. "Were you here yesterday?"

"I was here."

"And you saw no bodies in the water."

"Nope."

Chief Polovina shook his head and looked at Mayfield.

"Pop," Mayfield said to the old man, "Seven dead women and one man were fished out of the lake yesterday. And the chief here tells me there may be more in that old lubricant warehouse at the bottom."

"Lubricant, my ass," Jenkins said. "My dad had this job before me. You know that, Teddy."

"I do know that."

"Well, he used to tell a tale about that old building, full of barrels it was, but those barrels weren't full of oil and grease like everyone thought."

"What were they full of then," the chief of police asked.

"Shine," the old man said. "My daddy swore they was full of moonshine. That was prohibition you know. The man who ran the warehouse was the biggest whisky runner in the business, or so I was told."

"You wouldn't happen to recall the man's name, would you, Homer?" the chief asked.

"Nope. Not sure I ever heard it. I reckon it might be in some of these papers around here, but I don't know that we could connect it to the warehouse. Like I said before, he was a bootlegger, not a mine employee." Jenkins thought for a moment. "You know, I think I can remember a name though, not his, his girlfriend's. It was Victoria something. Can't recall the last name but I think she's still around these parts."

"Victoria Outing?" Mitch Polovina ventured a guess.

"Yeah. That's it. She worked as a waitress over at Mick's Café — a real dish too — from what my dad told me. He had quite a crush on her. Hell… most of the men in town did. But there was something odd about her too, he always said. He could never put a finger on it though."

"Maybe it was that she became a Benedictine nun later. That'd be enough contradiction, girlfriend of a bootlegger and murderer to a Catholic nun. It must have been one hell of an internal struggle. That'd make her seem odd enough."

"Could be I suppose. Like I said, he never did say why, just that she was odd," Jenkins said.

Mitch Polovina had enough information, a good trail to begin an investigation on, and no longer felt the need to snoop through countless scraps of brittle paper from prohibition times, not for the moment at any rate. "Thanks for your help, Homer. I may need to come back later, but for now, I have all I need."

Jenkins shot his son-in-law a look, to which Mayfield replied, "If he needs to come back, Pop, you be nice. Mitch here has a job to do. You give him all the help he needs, understand?"

CHAPTER FOUR

Mitchell Polovina usually began his day early and with a big breakfast. By the time he settled into a chair in the garden of Victoria Outings retirement home, across from Ms. Outing and beside Doc Nason, he was famished. The fruit plate an attendant placed in front of him was not going to fix that. He looked at Doc. Doc winked and forked himself a small wedge of pineapple. "It's good for you, Bugsy," he said.

Polovina slid his toward Doc. "You eat it, Gray Eagle," he said and curled a lip. He turned his attention to Ms. Outing. "I'm told you had a boyfriend in your youth, Victoria."

"Arthur Shaw," she said and smiled. "I was just sixteen. I was a waitress at Mick's and he came in every morning, eight o'clock sharp. He was handsome and charming and I fell for him the very first time I saw him."

"And he was the man in charge of that lubricant warehouse that's now at the bottom of the lake?" Polovina questioned.

"He was a salesman. He sold something to the mines. That's all I know," Victoria said.

"Was he a local boy?"

"No. He came from south of here, over in the St. Cloud area," she said.

It added up. Polovina wasn't much on computers, and less in touch with the modern day when it came to exploring the internet, but one time recently, while experimenting with the laptop in his office, he managed to get online. And in his stumbling around he lit on a site which made a claim about St. Cloud being one of the largest suppliers of contraband alcohol in the state during prohibition, maybe in the country, he couldn't recall. But putting Arthur Shaw's and St. Cloud and prohibition together, and adding to those things the fact that Virginia Outing was now looking down as she regaled him and

Gray Eagle with her tale of her love for the man, indicating untruth or omission of facts, and Mitch knew he had just climbed another step on the evidentiary ladder. This police work might not be so bad, fun actually, when one begins to build a trail to follow. "I think we're done for now, Ms. Outing. I'll be in touch. Thank you for your time."

***

"What're your thoughts," Polovina asked Doc and buckled himself in behind the wheel of his squad car.

"Well… first, I'd say Dr. Benniful, her doctor, was absolutely right with his claim that Victoria Outing has the mind of a much younger person, and second, she's lying to you."

"That was my guess as well," the police chief said. "Question is, about what?"

"Well there now, you see. That's police work, not doctor work."

"How about wise old Indian work? Could it fall under that?" Polovina suggested. He smiled at the doctor. "I could really use your help, Nase."

"How about those officers of yours? Won't they help you?"

"Not likely. They were all Randy's men." Randy Newell was the former chief of police who had died. "They thought one of them would automatically slide into the lead position. They all resent my being appointed, not thinking to kick their own asses for not placing their name in the running. And… when you think about it… that says a whole lot about their intelligence doesn't it? Anyway, there's hardly anyone left. Most quit."

"Really," Doc said, surprise in his voice. "I guess I can lend a hand. This is pretty interesting stuff anyway. But I do have a condition."

"What's that?"

"No more calling me Gray Eagle."

"Can't do that, Doc. To me, that's who you are," Polovina said and smiled once more. He knew Doc didn't mind the teasing. He just liked to make an issue of it.

"One of these days, Bugsy, you'll be sorry."

"Probably, but for now, what's our next move? How do we get the truth out of Victoria Outing?" the chief asked.

"It's been my experience in dealing with patients, everyone's favorite subject to talk about is themselves. Why not dig for her early story and let the facts fall through the cracks."

***

"You saw Daddy?" Karla Mayfield asked her husband, Ted, during dinner while he filled her in on the day's peculiar happenings — bodies popping from the water, the chief and the doctor diving to the bottom of the mine pit and finding more, the old woman so intent on watching what was going on, and her father's rude behavior over Polovina asking him questions.

"I wonder. Does he have something to hide?" Mayfield more suggested than asked.

"Daddy?" his wife questioned. "What could he possibly have to do with this? If it's as you said, the women dressed like flappers, the one guy discovered wearing spats, hell, Father wasn't born until thirty-seven; he couldn't know anything about this."

"Well there is something. You didn't see how he reacted when Bugsy Polovina wanted to look around the mining company office. He became much more than simply protective."

"Maybe he's projecting."

"Projecting?"

"Yes. You know how he was when Mama died," she said.

"Yeah. He locked the house down and moved into his office."

"Exactly. And he was always so protective about Mama and his home. Now that he has neither, he could be projecting that defense instinct on the company property."

"Seems a stretch, but… okay," Mayfield said.

"So you'll leave him be?"

"I'm not sure it'll be up to me."

"Who's it up to?" Karla Mayfield asked. Perhaps she could intervene if she knew who to approach. Perhaps she could keep her father out of it. After all, he had been a widower only six months. He needed his space for a time yet.

"Mitch, I suppose," Ted Mayfield told his wife.

"Well you can handle Mitch, can't you?"

"Mitch, I can, but what if it goes further?"

"How could it go further?" she asked.

"Mitch tells me there's maybe a hundred more barrels down

there. That could add up to a lot of bodies. Somebody's going to take notice, the Feds, somebody."

"Well what if they're full of something else?"

"God, I hope not," Ted said.

"You want it to be bodies?"

"If it isn't, we'll have a real mess on our hands. Because if it's not bodies, it'll be toxic waste. We'll have the environmental people here. They'll drain the lake. Cleanup will go on forever. Crews who'll arrive here will outnumber the town's population, and they'll all be out at your dad's office."

Ted Mayfield was right; his wife Karla knew it. If this turned into draining the lake and a massive cleanup operation, her dad might as well go hide someplace because they'd be all over him, the only company official remaining out at that mine. She began to hope for bodies as well, or empty barrels.

***

"I got a plan," Mitch Polovina told Doc Nason when he picked up his telephone.

"Don't you eat dinner?" Doc asked. He had just sat down and began his meal.

"I'm too wound up for that. Besides, the bitch left me. You can't expect me to eat my cooking."

"Well you don't mind if I eat, do you?"

"No. Of course not. Did I catch you at a bad time?" Mitch asked but did not wait for an answer. "Anyway, Gray Eagle, like I was saying, I got an idea. You know anybody with a barge?"

"A barge?" Doc asked.

"Yeah. It's a big raft."

"I know what a barge is," Doc said.

"Well… you know anybody who owns one? And while you're thinking, do you know anybody with pressurized diving gear?"

"Yeah. I know. Now can I eat?" Doc asked and shoved his plate away. He knew his meal would be cold before he got rid of Polovina. Too much excitement and too little control in his voice.

"Sure you can. But which do you know, the owner of a barge, or where we can find pressurized suits?"

"Both!"

"Both? Where?" the police chief asked him.

"Old man Jenkins. Out at the mine," Doc Nason said.

"Homer? He don't have a barge, not that I know of."

"Maybe not him, but the company does. They used to send divers down to retrieve equipment years ago. The last time I was out there, everything we'd need was still there in that old shop behind his office." Doc pulled his plate back and picked at the food a bit, then he shoved it away. His excitement was growing, his appetite taking a back seat. "What you got in mind?"

"You and me. We're diving down and pulling those barrels up. We get them out of the pit before any outside help, FBI — EPA — whatever, gets wind of this, and we save a whole bunch of grief."

"Who we getting to man the barge?" Nason asked.

"We'll enlist Homer and his son-in-law."

"Teddy? Our industrious mayor? You expect Teddy Mayfield to help?"

"Oh... he'll help. I talked to Homer Jenkins today. They'll both help."

"And you know this for a fact?"

"I do."

"How?"

"Because Homer's hiding something. I know it. Mayfield knows it. I think the old man even knows I know it. And by now Karla Mayfield knows. Think about how protective she is over her father. She'll make Teddy help just so we leave her dad alone."

CHAPTER FIVE

"You're here a mite early, Sheriff," Victoria Outing said. "Breakfast isn't for another half-hour."

"I know, Ma'am, but I thought I might take you for breakfast. I thought you might enjoy getting out for a change," Polovina said.

"Where will we go?" she asked.

"I thought you might enjoy going to your old stomping grounds, Mick's Café."

"I would like that. It's been years. Has the place changed much?"

"Hardly at all. I think it still has the original paint on the walls," the police chief said with a smile.

"How dreadful," the old gal said and slapped him on the forearm.

"Let's go find out," she said and stuffed an arm through his. "Will your friend be joining us?"

"Doc Nason? You bet."

"Good. He was always such a nice boy in school, so quiet. How come you weren't more like him? You were always such a hellion."

"I never could come up with the answer to that one myself, Ma'am," Chief Polovina admitted. He helped her into the car.

"I do wish you'd stop calling me Ma'am," she told him once he had settled in and started the engine.

"What should I call you, Sister?"

"No!"

"How about Ms. Outing?"

"That or Victoria."

"You don't mind if I call you Victoria?"

"I'd rather like it. Nobody calls me by my given name anymore. I miss it."

"Then Victoria it is," Chief Polovina agreed. A more personal level might be useful given what he and Nason had to do, shake whatever modicums of truth they could out of her.

***

"Where's Ms. Outing?" an older gentleman demanded of the desk nurse at Victoria Outing's retirement home. He had visited her often. All of the employees and residents alike knew him by sight. None of them, however, knew what their relationship to each other was, be it friend or relative. Some thought nephew. Others thought former neighbor. Still more thought fellow teacher. But none knew the truth about Victoria Outing and Michael Decker. No one around the home pried.

"She's gone out this morning," the nurse told him.

"With whom?"

"I honestly don't know, Mr. Decker," she said. "She left while I was away from my station."

"Isn't it your job to know?"

"Not really," she said.

"Then whose is it?" Decker demanded.

"No one's. Hers. Look, Mr. Decker. This isn't a nursing home. The residents here aren't under constant care. They come and go as they please. Some of them even have cars."

He looked at her oddly for a moment. "I apologize. I wasn't aware of that. Would you tell her I was here to see her and ask her to call me?"

"Certainly," the attendant said and wrote it down. "I'll tell her the moment she returns."

***

Victoria Outing could not believe her eyes when Mitchell Polovina walked her into Mick's Diner. "It may not be the same paint, but it's the color I remember. My, it's been a long time," she said and wiped at a tiny tear.

"Would you prefer a booth? The counter? A table?" Polovina asked.

"I want to waitress. That's what I'd prefer," she said and smiled. "But... I don't suppose that's possible, so let's take a table, that one over there, in the back. I know you two boys will want to ask me all sorts of things, and it's no use in everyone hearing." Doc joined them as they approached the table. She sat in the chair he pulled out for her and looked around the café, her expression — sad, almost dismal. "This is the table Arthur Shaw sat at way back when I was a mere girl. At first he would place his order, then ignore me. Then he began to pay attention. I was just developing, you know, sixteen, and the more I developed, the more Arthur Shaw paid attention. It was not long before I had blossomed and he began flirting."

"So… he was a cradle robber?" Doc asked and shot her a disapproving look.

"You need to realize something, both of you boys. In my day, sixteen year old girls married. They were courted properly, and then they wed. Arthur was twenty two and handsome as the day was long, and that six years difference in our ages, well that was common. He did nothing wrong in paying attention to me." She was clearly upset by Doc's assertion.

Mitchell Polovina feared she'd clam up. "He meant nothing disrespectful toward you or your Mr. Shaw, Victoria," he told her.

"He's right, Ma'am," Doc added. "I sometimes forget different times had different rules. I apologize. Please continue."

"I got the chief of police here to address me as Victoria rather than Ma'am. I wish you'd do the same."

"I will, Ma'am, I mean Victoria," Nason told her. "Now, tell us about Mr. Shaw. What kind of man was he?"

"Oh… he was handsome, I think I told you that, he was kind, soft spoken, and he was generous. Would you boys like to hear about the first time I saw him?"

"We'd love to," Polovina said.

"Like I said, I was sixteen. I had been working for the café for only a short time and I was still a bit clumsy about serving customers. When he walked through those doors, my world lit up. And I just knew, before that episode was over, I would spill something on him. He walked past me when he came in like I wasn't even there. I, of course, saw him immediately. I rushed to his table, this table, as soon as he sat down, so that Nancy Bjorquist couldn't beat me to him. She was a devil, that Nancy Bjorquist, yearning over every man who came in like he was the last man on earth. It was the tips she was really after. She knew something I didn't know, her being older and wiser. She knew that every extra exaggerated wiggle of the hips was worth another nickel come tip time. Anyway, this time Nancy did not beat me to him. And when he sat, I was already there with my order pad ready. It was May Day. I remember it like it was yesterday."

***

May 1, 1929

"Good morning, young lady," Arthur Shaw told the waitress.

"Good morning, Sir. Coffee?" she asked and placed a glass of water in front of him. The bottom of the glass landed squarely on the thick handle of a table knife. A split second later, and its contents were spilling into the crotch of his pants. He jumped back, the chair toppling, crashing to the floor, all eyes in the place on him and on the fear filled face of the young waitress. She grabbed a cloth she had tucked in the band of her apron for cleaning tables and moved toward him, her impulse, to dab at the damage. He put his hands out to stop her.

"I don't think you want to do that," he said and snatched the towel from her. Tears began to well in her eyes. "It's fine," he told her. "No permanent damage, I'm sure. Now, if you'd be kind enough to get me some coffee, we'll simply forget about all of this." He handed her towel back, reset his chair, and sat back down at the table as though nothing had happened. He determined to spend as much of his day right there as he had to and leave with a dry crotch. That is if the girl didn't douse him with something else, hot coffee perhaps. Another man joined him as she went for coffee. "I recommend you decline the water," Shaw warned.

***

Polovina laughed openly at the old woman's account. Doc Nason looked at him curiously. He hoped the unthinking police chief hadn't hurt her feelings. "That must have been a terrifying moment for you," he said.

Victoria Outing sniggered a bet. "Didn't you find my story laughable, Mr.... ?"

"Don't mind him, Sister. He's Indian. They don't have a sense of humor."

"I asked you to call me Victoria, Mitchell Polovina. Now

please do as I asked."

"Yes, Ma'am."

"And I distinctly told you not to address me as Ma'am."

"Even in school he was a bit slow," Nason threw in and punctuated it with a kindly smile.

"You weren't so quick yourself as I recall, Henry," Victoria Outing admonished, effectively turning his kindly smile into a scowl, the look of a wounded ten year old. "I had to constantly remind you of things back then."

"And you haven't changed much," he told her.

She shot him a scolding glare.

"Sorry, Ma'am," Nason said and received a cane to the shin for it.

"Victoria," Mitch Polovina started, thinking the old gal might be tiring, "Would you like me to take you back to the home?"

"No, Mitchell. What I'd like is to continue."

The chief smiled and waved a hand — a sign of turning the floor over to her.

***

As the sixteen year old Victoria Outing hurried to the counter of the little café for coffee, close to tears, fear of having messed up in her young eyes, the more mature Nancy Bjorquist approached her. "Why don't you clean tables, dear. I'll see to those men for you."

"No you won't," Victoria said. "It's my table and I'll take care of it."

"Are you sure? I mean… you look so… so… beside yourself over all of this."

"I'm fine. Really," Victoria said.

She picked up two filled coffee cups and set out for her table. More relaxed, graceful now, she placed the hot liquid in front of each of the men while they cringed in anticipation of her turning clumsy once again. She did not. "Breakfast, Gentlemen?" And they both ordered hotcakes. They watched as she walked off toward the kitchen to place their orders.

"What do you think of that little morsel?" Arthur Shaw's companion asked him.

"A mite young, don't you think?"

"I do not think."

"You mean you'd be interested in that slight girl?" Shaw asked.

"I would. Look at that little wiggle. She might be a nubbin of a girl right now, but she's a flower just weeks away from full bloom, I tell you."

Shaw took another look. His friend was right. He'd keep an eye out.

***

Mitch Polovina took a long sip of his coffee and considered Victoria Outing. He waited for her to continue her story. She seemed in a trance. "Who was the fellow at the table with Arthur Shaw?" he asked. "Victoria?" he said when she hesitated to answer.

"Oh! I'm sorry," she said. "Where were we?"

"I was asking you… who was the fellow with Arthur Shaw?"

"He was some mining company bigwig named Jenkins," she said.

"Homer Jenkins' father?"

"I expect so," Victoria told him. "I didn't think he was anybody's father right then, but that's the man. I'm sure of it."

"Was he a particular friend of Mr. Shaw's?" Doc asked.

"Oh! Heavens no. They scarcely tolerated one another. But they were business associates."

"Business associates," Sheriff Polovina commented. "What business?"

"I'm not sure I should say," Victoria said.

"Why not? Is Shaw still alive?" Mitch thought not, and knew Homer Jenkins' father to be deceased, so wondered what harm his knowing the nature of business between two dead men could do.

"I should think you'd know he is dead, Chief Polovina. You pulled him from the water yourself," she said. Sadness seemed to cross her face as she said it.

"Are you sure?" Doc asked.

"Reasonably. It looked like him from where I watched. I'd have to look at him up close to be absolutely certain though."

"Would you be willing to do that?" Mitch asked.

Henry Nason shot him a disconcerting glance.

"What?" Polovina asked.

"Don't you think that's a little cold?" Doc asked him.

"Nonsense, Henry," Victoria said. "It may not be a desirable thing to do, but still, I never did find out what became of him. Rumors, that's all. I'd like to take a look, if you don't mind."

"When?" Polovina asked. Then he thought, maybe this was a bad idea. Maybe someone her age should not be put through such things. What would be the gain?

"Tomorrow morning," she said. "I'm tired now. Would you two boys take me home, please?"

CHAPTER SIX

Flashy cars are difficult to ignore, especially if they're parked in front of a retirement home, and even more so if you're a cop. The automobile in question, a 1967 Buick Gran Sport — bright white, black vinyl top, deep red hood scoops and wheels, baby-moon size chrome hubcaps and beauty rims — exactly like it came from the showroom floor. The cop in question, brand new police chief, Mitchell Polovina. He eyed the car when he walked Victoria Outing to her room in the home, and again on his way back out. And as he drove off, he watched a man in his rearview mirror get out of the car. He was a stocky man, not tall, thinning hair that made him look older, yet, the man's carriage told Polovina he might not be. Hard to tell from his vantage point. Polovina stopped and watched him in the mirror all the way to the door. He wondered if he should go back in and check him out. Probably not. Probably it was just the momentum of the case he was working, his first case as an actual policeman, that he was getting caught up in. It was unlikely the man he just saw was part of anything but some elderly person's family. He should stop letting things go to his head. Leave the stranger alone to visit his loved one. Trouble would be reported, if there was indeed trouble brewing. "Get a grip, Polovina," he told himself and drove off.

Mitch grabbed a cellular phone from a pocket and pulled to the shoulder. He punched in Doc Nason's number. "Grey Eagle, how long can you keep those stiffs on ice?"

"Why?"

"I do want the old gal to take a look, see if the guy is Arthur Shaw," Polovina said. "And maybe she'll recognize others."

"She tell you more?" the doc asked.

"Just that Shaw's body went missing just a couple of days before the miners struck water and the mine became a lake."

"I should check with her physician before we subject her to

viewing dead bodies, don't you think?"

"I do not," Chief Polovina answered. He did not want a delay. He had heard someplace that a case goes cold in something like ninety-six hours, or maybe he saw it on a television movie. It made sense though, so he did not want to delay.

"What if she strokes out on us from the ordeal? What then? We'll have no witness at all."

"All right, call her doctor. But do it immediately so we can get on with this."

"Mind if I finish stitching up Jimmy Newman's gash before I make that call?" he asked and hung up.

***

"There's going to be trouble."

"Why do you say that?" Teddy Mayfield asked his wife, Karla.

"Mitchell Polovina and Henry Nason dig too deep and they'll uncover a huge pile of crap. And in that pile, my father will be."

"You're kidding," Mayfield said.

"No. I'm not."

"What the hell are you talking about, Karla? What'll they find? What could they possibly find?"

"Secrets. That's what they'll find. Everyone thinks the old mine flooded because they struck water. And everyone thinks they let it happen because the ore was played out anyway," Karla said.

"And those things aren't true?"

"No they're not." She looked into her husband's eyes. She wanted to be sure what she would tell him next would be understood. She saw no sign of confusion. "There was plenty of ore. And the pit was flooded on purpose, by my grandfather. Pop knows all about it. He always has. So do I as a matter of fact. I doubt it'll cause us a problem, but my father? That's a whole other ballgame, Teddy. He has proof."

"Well… I doubt anyone's going after anybody over a mine that got flooded on purpose back in prohibition times, Karla."

"It's not the flooding, Ted. It's the dead bodies. That's what my father knows about. If the flooding was against the law, the statute of limitations ran out many years ago. But murder? That's a crime they never forget about. Pop knows. Pop's got proof. He's withheld evidence of murder. That's serious."

"You think Mitch Polovina's even capable of getting to the bottom of things? I don't. So I don't think Pop has anything to worry about. Not if everyone keeps tight lipped about all of this."

Karla Mayfield knew Mitchell Polovina. She knew how persistent the man could be; at least he had been in his high school days. Karla had been a cheerleader for Mitch's football team. She had been a real dish in those days: larger breasted than most of the other girls, long slender legs — perfectly proportioned, round little bottom that drove boys wild. Mitch pestered her from the first time he saw her on the practice field. He was relentless, claiming he wanted one date, that was all, nothing more. If she would agree to just one date, and she didn't enjoy herself, he'd go away and never trouble her again. She had his word. It took months, but she finally gave in. Their date began with a movie — in the very back row, and so came her first mistake. Mitch waited until the movie was half over before he tried to feel her up. It was a love story with steamy scenes, promiscuous for the day, capable of heating a young girl's desires to a slow burn. She could not stop herself. She let him feel all he wanted. She allowed herself to be kissed passionately time and time again. And she was, even after sharing a shake with him at the local malt shop, still on fire when they walked to the bleachers of the football field. She let him take her, right there on the bleachers. It was her first time and she was happy at the moment that it was with Mitch because, despite how she had held him off, she really did have a thing for him. She had been infatuated. But Mitch Polovina, the high school football player, was nothing but a conquistador, the hot to trot post pubescent jock out to find and fuck anything worth finding and fucking. That was not the Mitchell Polovina of today, but it was to Karla Mayfield, the jock's first one night stand in a long line of one night stands. But this was information she had never shared with her husband and she would not reveal it now. "Mitch will dig his teeth in and he'll hold on until he draws blood. You have to stop him, Teddy," she said.

***

"Look at me. I'm ninety-six years old. What can they do to me? Kill me? Lock me away? Being ninety-six is worse than both of those things."

"But mother," Michael Decker pleaded with Victoria Outing,

"What about me?"

"What about you?" Victoria asked.

"I only recently found you. To lose you now just wouldn't be right."

"Michael, Michael, Michael. Get a grip, Son. I told you, I'm ninety-six. How long do you suppose I have left anyway?"

"I hoped for a few years, Mother," Michael said.

"Think I'll know you in a few years?"

"Oh, Mother."

"Look, he was the man I loved, the only man I ever had in my life. I have to make sure it was him. It will give me some long awaited closure. I need that very much. Please try to understand."

"And if they come for you, Mother?" Michael Decker asked.

"Mitchell Polovina? Please. He wouldn't know what to do with me. I'd be in the grave by the time he and this court system around this town even decided what kind of trial to hold, criminal or domestic."

"Not the chief. The others. What if they come for you?"

"Oh. Yes. Them. Now... that is a whole other story, now, isn't it?"

"It is," Decker said. "And it's one that you might at least be concerned about. Because if they come for you, they'll see to it this town's done with, so nothing like this can ever happen again."

"Aren't you being a bit dramatic, Michael? I swear you've got a bit of your father in you. He was dramatic about things, you know," Victoria said, not because it was true, it wasn't. But because it would put her son to thinking. He always drifted into deep thought whenever she compared him to a father he had never known. It took him away from badgering her whenever she did it. And she had had enough badgering for one day. "Now you must run off now, Michael. You're old mother needs rest. Come back and see me soon, dear." And she leaned back in her recliner and closed her eyes. She kept them closed until he was gone.

***

"Michael Arthur Decker," Juliette Moore told Mitch Polovina as he entered the station. He had radioed in and asked that she run the plates of the Buick for him. "Address in Claytonville." Claytonville was a small town, even smaller than Farwell (Little Cicero), five miles to the east. Mitch thanked her and watched her walk off toward the front desk.

She was a tiny thing for a cop, slender, brunet hair she wore in a twist piled on top of her head. It framed her face, made it look rounder than it actually was, and set off her eyes — dark brown, almost black. He watched her walk, a gentle but sensual sway from side to side, and he silently thanked Randy Newell, the former chief of police who had passed away, for his foresight in making Juliette wear a uniform that included a form fitting (shorter than necessary) skirt made from a subtly soft cotton blend material that moved magically with her every step, showing off each and every fascinating curve in the girls incredible figure. Randy must have known Mitch would take over. And Randy must have known Mitch would be between wives when he did.

"Bugsy!" someone shouted, snapping Mitch Polovina out of the spell his dispatch officer had just put him under. "Back to earth, if you don't mind."

"Someday somebody's going to shoot you for sneaking up on them, Gray Eagle. You should know better."

"As should you," the doc said and leaned his head to see Miss Moore around the police chief's body. "But I can see why you don't."

"What do you want?" Polovina asked.

"I thought you'd like to know, the old woman's doctor called back. He says she's tough, probably tougher than us. He says viewing bodies should have little effect on her health."

"Well… then we have her look, I guess."

"When?"

"She originally wanted to do it in the morning. Let's let her. That work for you?"

"Perfect. I have a light schedule tomorrow."

"Not many sick? Or too many sick of you?" Mitch asked.

"Blow me," Doc Nason said and left.

***

"What the hell was Karla talking about, Pop? Tell me about this evidence you're sitting on that could cause the kind of grief she imagines?" Mayor Ted Mayfield asked his father-in-law.

"I don't know what you're talkin' 'bout, Boy." Homer Jenkins said.

"Maybe you'd better start leveling with me, Homer. Mitch Polovina isn't going to go away, not until he gets answers. And if he gets answers from you that don't add up, he'll be all over you and all over this place. And he'll dig into all of our lives, me and Karla included, until he's satisfied."

"Think there's that much to the boy?"

"Pop, you think in terms of yesteryear. You size everyone up and come up with the way you saw them way back when. Mitch for instance, and me, and Doc Nason..."

"You mean that Indian kid?"

"You see? That's exactly what I'm talking about. Take Mitch. I could tell when he talked to you the other day, right here in your office. You treated him like he was out here to do some damage, perhaps steal something. You treated him like the kid who gave you fits in high school. Goofing off. Kid stuff. And as for your question, Yes, I think there's that much to him. I think there's a whole lot more. You need to give the man credit for maturing. This isn't some high school boy you're dealing with."

"Well, I still ain't scared of him." Pop Jenkins said.

"Stop fucking around with this, Pop. This is serious. Let me help. Please!"

CHAPTER SEVEN

Chief Polovina sat in the lobby of the of Victoria Outing's retirement home from seven a.m. until eight-thirty, his squad car running out in the parking lot. He thought sure all old people were early risers. Apparently he was wrong. Miss Outing was nowhere to be found. He approached the front desk. "You might want to check on her. She could be dead," he told a nurse who rolled her eyes at him and went on about her business.

"I'm not dead, Mitchell," the voice of Victoria Outing came from behind him.

"Good morning," he told her.

"The town must have extra money these days," she said in a complaining fashion.

Mitch looked at her questioningly.

"Your car," she explained. "It's been running for hours."

He checked his watch. An hour and a half, maybe a few minutes longer. Certainly not hours. "What time did you get up?"

"Quite some time ago," she said and studied him for a reason for the inquiry. "What? Did you think I should come-a-runnin'? — no shower, in my pajamas, just because you arrived? Why… you're almost as silly as you were in fourth grade."

"Of course, Ma'am." She took aim with her cane and he corrected to, "I mean Victoria."

"Do you think that Doctor Nason is up and around yet?"

"I'm sure he is," Mitch said.

"Well?"

"Well, what?"

"Well let's go see him before you run out of the town's gasoline."

***

"That's him." Victoria Outing brushed a tear from her cheek as she looked down on the body of the beau of her youth. Mitchell Polovina and Henry Nason both moved close to her, to comfort her. She pushed them back. "I'm all right. He was a long, long time ago, and the slight moment in which we knew one another was just that— slight. I don't know where the tear came from, but it certainly wasn't for him, not the way he treated me, always running off in the middle of the night like that, like some coward." And she wound up and slapped him across the face.

Mitch grabbed her arm and stopped her from doing it a second time. "Jesus Christ, Victoria!" he said. "You're slapping a corpse."

"Well he had it coming," she said. "Kindly let go of my arm, Mitchell."

"Only if you're done," the chief said.

"Oh, have it your way. He's long past feeling it anyway," she said. She started toward the door, stopping at each of the other bodies along the way, shaking her head in dismay at each stop. "I wonder," she said, "did he do all of this?"

"I don't know," Mitch said. "But I intend to find out." He looked her over to see how she was faring. He looked at Doc Nason for approval. When Nase nodded, he asked her, "Would you like something to eat?"

"I would."

"Mick's?"

"That would be fine, Mitchell. Will you be joining us, Henry?"

"I'll catch up with you. Mrs. Coldwell awaits me in my office. Shouldn't take long. She seems to have a sniffle or something," Henry explained.

***

"You think that sexy little ass of yours is going to get you someplace, don't you," Royal Parker said. It was a statement — not a question. Parker served as Deputy Chief by default, not as Head Honcho like he thought he would be when his former boss passed away, and he hated Mitch Polovina for stealing that position out from under him. And now he hated Juliette Moore. Hell… he had looked at her in the same way Polovina does since day one of his takeover. Why hadn't she paid him the same attention she pays the new chief? Was it because he had been beat out of the position? Probably.

"This ass will take me a lot further than that sour attitude of yours will get you, Parker," Juliette Moore insisted. She turned away and smiled, pleased with her quick comeback.

"He ain't even a lawman."

"He'll learn," Juliette defended.

"Hope somebody don't die while he's learning," Parker said.

"Now there's a stretch," Juliette said and smiled. "This is Farwell. Population 6242. Whoever dies will probably go by natural causes or in a car or industrial accident. When's the last time, or the first time for that matter, someone died suspiciously around here?"

"How about those bodies popping out of the water?"

Juliette Moore laughed aloud. "You're kidding, right?" Parker made no response. "I suppose that wouldn't have happened if you were chief."

"I... ah... I," he stammered.

"Right," she said and left the office.

***

"You do know, Chief Polovina, this is not the first such happening in this town, don't you?" Victoria asked Mitch as he held a chair for her at Mick's Café.

"I'm not sure I understand," Polovina told her.

"It was back in 1966. Two girls popped out of the water. I should have said something to the police then, but I'd have only been guessing. I'll bet they came from that old warehouse of Arthur's as well."

"You don't say."

"I remember it well. Everyone thought they must have been two young ladies passing through, took a little dip in the lake, probably in the middle of the night, probably full of booze. The police investigated but came up empty. The whole thing just faded away as if it were nothing."

"I remember that," Henry Nason said as he approached the table. "I was in medical school, home for the summer. Wasn't Homer Jenkins' dad on the force back then?"

"Homer, Sr.," Victoria said. "He was about five years older

than me. He had forty years in with the company when he retired in '65. That's when Homer, Jr. took over as manager; of course, he had been with the mine for some time before that. But old Homer felt he was too young for retirement, so he joined the police force. Actually, he was Police Chief when those two girls popped out of the water like that."

"Well... let me see if I understand all of this," Polovina said. "Two girls appeared in the lake, just like those bodies the other day, only they popped out at night, or at least at a time when nobody actually witnessed it."

"Witnessed it. Good one," Henry Nason said and smiled. "Police talk."

"Shut the fff..., shut up, Gray Eagle," Polovina said. He did not feel like being made fun of over his inexperience. "Go on, Victoria."

"I can't. That's all I know. The rest you'll have to use your investigative skills to find."

"And I'll do that. But one question you'll probably have the answer to is, what were the two girls in the water wearing? Were they dressed like the ones we found? Because, it seems to me, someone would recognize the costume of a roaring twenties flapper as out of the ordinary."

"They were both naked," Victoria said. "Likely skinny dipping. Although, there was some talk of, oh, let me think. I believe... yes... they never did find any of those two girls' clothing."

"Interesting," Doc Nason said.

"Damn right it is," Polovina agreed. "I think we need to talk to Homer, Jr."

***

"I don't know how you expect me to do anything about anything, Karla, unless you and your father are willing to give me some information," Mayor Mayfield told his wife. He was tired of arguing with her, with him, with both of them. They could either fess up, or fight the battle on their own. Hell, he knew where he stood with her anyway, and, frankly, he was getting tired of it. She had the hots for Mitchell Polovina, not him, and he knew all about it. The goddamn woman talked in her sleep. "Now I'll be at my office. If you or your father should decide to share a little, you know where to find me."

In his car, Ted Mayfield thought things through. Mitch

Polovina was his friend, never out of line, never open to the advances of married women, his wife or anyone else's. Mitch was a good man, despite two and a half divorces (he was presently going through one with his third wife). No, Mitchell Polovina had nothing to do with Karla's attraction to him and Ted knew it. It was all in Karla's head. Just the same though, he would not tell Mitch anything about this. Never know. Sometimes a man isn't interested until he knows the lady is open, especially a man in the middle of losing his wife. Ted poked at the numbers on his cell phone. "Mitch," he said when the police chief picked up. "When you get some time, stop by my office. Would ya?"

"Will do. Soon as I drive Miss Daisy home. Ouch," he said when Victoria Outing's cane made contact with his shin. Then, "Mind if I drag Gray Eagle along with me?"

"Certainly not. Matter of fact, I'd like to see him too. It has to do with the bodies. I know he's helping you with the case."

"Yeah, it makes the poor devil feel useful. We'll be by sometime this afternoon," he said and hung up.

"Now, Miss Victoria," Mitch said returning to the company with whom he was dining. "Care to tell us a bit about your old boyfriend, Arthur Shaw?"

CHAPTER EIGHT

Victoria Outing closed her eyes. "I believe I was telling you about serving Arthur that first cup of coffee." She let her mind drift all the way back to 1929. Then she began to talk as if she was an outsider, telling someone else's story.

***

"At least you didn't burn him with hot coffee," Nancy Bjorquist told young Victoria Outing. "You going to risk it again? Or do you want me to step in and serve them food. Wouldn't want hot syrup all over that fine looking gentleman, would we?"

"I can handle this, Nancy," Victoria said and walked past her with a tray of food. This was her tip, and she'd not give it up. Maybe Nancy would get more out of them with that bottom of hers swinging back and forth like a pendulum, but she'd not share it with Victoria anyway. But wait. What if she swung her bottom a bit? She tried it and nearly lost the tray. She vowed to practice later, when no one was around to get injured. For now, though, she felt fortunate that there were only two men at the table. It left her with room to set the tray down and slide the plates in front of her guests. No chance of spilling that way.

"What's your name?" Arthur Shaw asked Victoria.

"She's the Outing girl. Victoria, I think," Shaw's friend said.

"Did I ask you, Jenkins?" He looked at Homer Jenkins, Sr. with irritation. He didn't give a shit what the girl's name was, not at that point in the conversation. It was conversation itself he sought. "Is he right? Is that your name?" He smiled at Victoria.

"Yes, Sir," she said.

"Well… Victoria Outing. You sure are a pretty thing."

Victoria blushed and slid a plate in front of him, tapping

his coffee cup with the plate as she did. She began to turn red as he steadied the cup. "Thank you," she said. She wasn't certain whether she was thanking him for steadying the cup, or for the compliment. She looked into his eyes. Suddenly she couldn't breathe. She gasped for air.

"Are you all right?" Shaw asked, an expression of genuine concern in his eyes.

"Fine," she said and coughed a couple of times, covering her mouth as she did — like mannered folks would.

"My name is Arthur Shaw, Miss Victoria," he said and offered her his hand.

"I'm glad to meet you, Mr. Shaw," she said, but she did not take his hand.

"Call me Arthur," he said.

"I don't know that I should, Sir," she said and smiled sheepishly. "Can I get anything else for you gentlemen?" she asked.

"No." Jenkins said. "This'll do fine."

Victoria Outing could almost feel the nasty glare Arthur Shaw used on the other man as she walked off toward the kitchen.

***

"You know," Victoria Outing told Police Chief Polovina as she returned to the modern day, "I'm getting a bit tired. Do you suppose we could continue this at another time?"

"We certainly can," Mitch said. "When would you like to continue?"

"Are you going to buy my breakfast as long as I talk to you about this?"

"If that's what it takes, Victoria," he said. He knew this was all about a case, a real police case. But still, even if it wasn't, he'd continue. It was interesting the way she spun a yarn. And her topic sparked his curiosity. Whether Albert Shaw had anything to do with those bodies popping out of the water or not, he wanted to hear the story. "I'll take you home, and I'll pick you up in the morning. What time would you like me there?"

"Eight-thirty. Don't be late."

***

"I can't just tell the chief of police to not investigate a crime, not if you and your father aren't going to talk to me," Mayfield told his wife once again. He thought he owed her, or his father-in-law, one last opportunity to let him in on the big secret before Mitch and Henry showed up at his office, so telephoned her.

"It isn't a crime, Ted. It's ancient history."

"Karla, really. Bodies popping out of the water — six or seven at a time? That doesn't spell out crime to you? I don't care if they came from this century or the last, it's illicit at best. Now… give me something or I'll have to let Mitch look into it. No? Nothing? Then, suit yourself." And he hung up.

***

Mitch Polovina spotted Michael Decker's '67 Gran Sport parked on a side street near Victoria Outing's retirement home. He radioed Juliette Moore in dispatch, and asked her to send Royal Parker to the location, and question the car's occupant.

"Royal is out to lunch," she told him.

What's new? He thought but did not ask. He disliked Parker nearly as much as Parker disliked him. Maybe more. For he also distrusted Parker. He thought of telling Juliette to interrupt Royal's lunch, but then decided on another plan. "Remember that plate you ran for me?" he asked.

"Mi…" she started to ask but was cut off by Mitch keying the mike. He did not want Victoria Outing to know who he was after.

"That's the one. What I want you to do, is go to Park and Third and keep an eye on that car for me. If it moves, follow it and radio me. I need to talk to that driver. I'll join you in just a bit."

"Who will watch dispatch?"

"Give Paula Bloom a quick lesson, then get over there." Paula was his secretary, not trained in police matters and procedures, just clerical help. "Take my personal car so you won't be spotted. The keys are on my desk and there's a hand-held radio on the seat."

"Will do, Chief. See you there."

"Here we are, Miss Victoria," Polovina said as he pulled the squad car up to the front doors of the home. He got out and walked to the passenger's side and opened her door. "Now tomorrow," he said as he walked her to the door, "I'll want to hear all about Arthur Shaw."

"You will," she said. *The hell you will,* she thought. *If you only knew. All I have for company these days is that son of mine. And he's making less sense than me. You'll hear as much about Arthur as I desire to tell you, Mitchell Polovina, a little at a time, until I tire of telling the story.* "You'll learn all about him."

Mitch bade her good day and set out for Park and Third to hook up with Juliette Moore. He would approach from behind and hope that the driver of the observed car would not see him and take off. And when he pulled to the curb near Juliette, (she was parked a half-block away from the car she watched) she opened her door to get out. As she did, her skirt rode up to reveal the tops of her thigh high stockings and even some bare leg above them. Mitchell Polovina brushed at sweat forming on his forehead, and enjoyed the view, all of it, until she stood beside the car. Then he got out. "I see he's still here," he said. Just then, the car took off. Mitch jumped back in his car, shouted for Juliette to join him, and threw on the emergency lights. More distance came between him and the pursued vehicle as he watched her settle into the seat beside him and stretch to pull the seatbelt around her.

"We're going to lose him, Chief," Juliette warned. She looked at him. He appeared confused. She smiled, knowing what was confusing him. "Drive," she said. And he sped away from the curb, to the intersection, and left, the direction the Buick had taken. Six blocks of high speed driving, siren blaring, and it was over. The pursued car was parked at the curb.

"License and registration," Mitch said as he approached the driver's window.

The driver obliged him.

Mitch read the license. "Mr. Decker, mind telling me why you've been hanging around the retirement home lately?" He looked at Decker's date of birth — June 27, 1930. *Christ, it's a wonder he isn't in the retirement home.*

"I visit my Mother there," he said.

"Your mother?" Mitch didn't think folks this old had mothers anymore. "And who's your mother?"

"Victoria Outing," Decker said.

And the plot thickens, thought Mitchell Polovina. *And the plot thickens.* "Sorry for the inconvenience. You can go, Sir." Mitch said;

then he made his way back to his car, his head shaking from side to side in disbelief. "Not a total loss. At least I get to watch Juliette Moore get back into the car," he whispered to himself.

***

Deputy Chief Royal Parker was fuming when Juliette Moore walked into the station. "Who the hell told you to run off and leave the secretary to watch the shop?" he demanded.

"That would be me," Mitch said as he walked in behind her.

"Look, Chief, I know you're supposed to be the one in charge around here," he said.

"That's correct," Mitch agreed.

"But I also know you're a bit green at this police business."

"So?"

"So I think you need to follow procedure, or let me run things until you learn how it's done," Royal Parker said.

"Well, Royal, that's not gonna happen. I tell you what though. I do think we'll initiate a change around here," Mitch said.

"And what would that be?" Parker asked, his chest puffed out, his stance, that of a high school bully.

"You and Juliette will be changing duties. You'll dispatch. She'll hit the street."

"Well… I ain't standin' for that!"

"You will, Royal, or you'll go home." He stared eye to eye with Parker for a time, long enough to see that Parker was backing down, despite further words to the contrary which Mitch Polovina let go in one ear and out of the other. "Juliette, you spend the remainder of the day training Royal, and tomorrow, you show up in long pants, sidearm and knight stick on your hip. Clear?" No one spoke. "Good. Now I'm off to a meeting with the Mayor. I can be reached at his office if I'm needed."

***

"That policeman you've been hanging out with pulled me over, Mother," Michael Decker told Victoria.

"What of it?" she asked.

"He'll dig. I know he will. And once he's dug far enough, he'll find out about you."

"I suppose he will, that's if he's clever enough."

"He is," Decker warned her.

"Maybe."

"Doesn't that worry you?"

"Why should it?" Victoria asked.

"You'll be in serious trouble if he uncovers all of the truth," Victoria's son said.

"I suppose I will," she agreed.

"And that doesn't worry you?"

"Michael, I'm ninety-six years old. Soon I'll be ninety-seven. Why should I worry? How much longer can I live anyway?"

"Good point. But what about me?"

"Michael, you're eighty. Far as I'm concerned, neither one of us should be alive."

"Well we both are, so I beg you to reconsider what you're doing before it's too late."

"The truth should have been told long ago. I aim to see that it's told before I die. Now run along, Michael, and let your mother get some rest. My mind's made up and you'll not change it." She lay back on her pillow and closed her eyes.

CHAPTER NINE

"I just got off the phone with my father-in-law," Mayor Ted Mayfield told Mitch Polovina and Doc Nason when they entered his office unannounced. "And next time, go through my secretary. Don't just barge in on me."

"You told us to come," Polovina complained. "So... what did Homer have to say?"

"He says you're not to have use of any mining company equipment."

"Why not?"

"He claims you don't have jurisdiction out there."

"Is he right?" Mitch asked. He had no way of knowing these things. All he had done was get the mayor and the city council to appoint him after all, and that wouldn't have happened had he not been the only one to apply. But his lack of knowledge about police work in this instance gave him an idea. In the future, instead of traveling with Gray Eagle Nason, maybe he'd stick like glue to his new street cop, Juliette Moore. She'd know the ropes. She had been with the department for years.

"I don't know, but I think we should find out before we step on toes that'll take us off this investigation," Mayor Mayfield suggested.

"And just how do we do that, Teddy?" Doc Nason asked.

"I've told you not to call me Teddy, especially in public."

Mitch Polovina went to the mayor's office door and closed it. "How's that, Teddy?"

"Good one, Bugsy," Nason said.

"Thank you, Gray Eagle." The two of them eyed each other for a moment. "Who do we ask, Teddy?"

Mayor Mayfield picked up the phone. "Get me the county attorney, Edith." Then he waited. When County Attorney Rick

Monson picked up, Mayfield explained their situation and asked for an opinion of their rights and responsibilities in this circumstance. He put the conversation on speaker.

"My... don't you boys have your hands full. You sure you shouldn't call in the State Police, or the Feds?"

"We'd rather not," Mayfield said. "Mitch here, Mitch Polovina is our new police chief,"

"I know. You're the guy who doesn't know what he's doing?"

"Excuse me?" Mitch said.

Monson laughed. "I got a call from Royal Parker. He's the one who told me you don't know what you're doing."

"Royal Parker is a royal pain in the ass," Mitch said.

"Yes, but he is stupid. You can't argue that, now can you, Chief?" Monson said. "Anyway, moving on. Didn't you boys move the city limits of Little Cicero, I mean Farwell, recently?"

"Just prior to the last election," the mayor said.

"And doesn't the town now surround the old mine?"

"Technically, yes," Mayfield said.

"Well... in the case of a criminal investigation, and you certainly have cause to declare one, you are within your rights, Chief Polovina, to close down the entire area and let no one in until it's no longer a crime scene despite the fact the land itself is not public domain. You got enough crime scene tape for that?"

"If we don't, we'll get it." Polovina said. "But what about Homer Jenkins?"

"Who the hell is Homer Jenkins?" Monson asked.

"He's the old timer the mining company keeps onboard to watch over the place. He claims to be the manager, but really, he's just a caretaker."

"The mining company? I thought they deserted the place years ago. I'll look into that for you as soon as we get off the phone. I think though, Chief, you'll be on sound legal standing to remove this Homer and go on with your investigation. Just make sure you let only officials on the site so some judge doesn't deem the scene contaminated somewhere along the line — the mayor, his deputy, police personnel, myself and the district attorney, a city attorney if you have one, people like that."

"Mr. Monson, I'm new on the job as you know," Mitch said. "I don't exactly have the full loyalty of my staff. You know that too from talking to Parker. So I've been using my friend, Doc Nason, as my assistant and he's a civilian."

"Gray Eagle? Are you there too?" The two of them had attended college together.

"Right here, Rick."

"Swear him in, Chief, put him on the force," Monson said and hung up.

"Well…" Teddy Mayfield began, "Somebody's got to get Homer off that property. Want me to see to it?"

"No. No offense, Mr. Mayor, but where your wife or her father are concerned, you seem to have as much pull as I have with my ex-wives. I'll go out there. You call Karla and maybe she can make some arrangements for him. Then if you wish, you can come along with me."

"I want to go with you," Nason said. "I've never been on anything like this before. Swear me in like Rick Monson told you. I want to be there if there's an arrest."

"Nobody's getting arrested," the mayor said.

"We don't know that yet, Teddy," Mitch said. Then he turned to Nason. "Hold up your right hand, Gray Eagle." Doc Nason did. "You're sworn," he said. "Teddy, you're a witness."

***

The sound of a shotgun blast told Mitchell Polovina this would not be easy. Ted Mayfield had obviously gotten a hold of his wife, and she in turn had obviously alerted her father. "Jesus Christ!" Mitch shouted and slammed on the brakes.

"What? You thought being appointed Chief of Police wouldn't get you shot at now and then?" Nase asked.

"Not in Farwell," Mitch said.

"But this is Little Cicero. Went back to that the moment bodies began popping out of the water."

Polovina grabbed the mike and switched his radio to PA. "Homer, don't shoot again or I'll have to shoot back. You don't want that, do you?" Another blast. Then another.

"He's not listening," Nason said.

"I can see that, Nase."

"What'll we do?" Henry Nason asked.

"I'm going to sneak around behind the building. Maybe I can

get on him before he sees me. He can't be too tough to take down; he's in his eighties for Christ sakes."

"He shoots like he's in his twenties, so watch yourself. Oh, and come at him from the right side if you can."

"Why?"

"I'm his doctor. His vision is impaired in his right eye, and he's totally deaf in the right ear. Stroke," Nason said.

Mitch Polovina gave Doc a thumbs up and disappeared into the underbrush beside the squad car. Moments later, Mayor Mayfield and his wife, Karla drove up in time to see Mitch stuff the disarmed and handcuffed Homer Jenkins into the backseat of the police cruiser. They were told by their police chief who was in no mood to argue with anyone, that they could have Homer back just as soon as the judge says so, and not a moment sooner.

***

"Am I still Deputy Chief?" Royal Parker said as he booked Homer Jenkins on the charges of firing on an officer and resisting arrest.

"Why did you call Rick Monson?" Chief of Police Polovina asked him.

"I'm sorry, Chief. I was a little hot under the collar. It won't happen again."

"No. It won't." Mitch said. Mitch stood nearly half a foot taller than Parker, and outweighed him as well, a typical ex-football hero, while Parker looked more… swim team. "At least no more than once more." Mitch found himself both surprised and impressed by his own words. Until now he hadn't pushed. He was a gentle soul where dealing with his new office was concerned, never raising his voice, never demanding, not sure of himself at all. But now, now that he had been fired upon and had his first arrest under his belt, things felt different. "And the office of Deputy Chief no longer exists. Little Cicero…"

"Farwell," Nason corrected.

"All right, Farwell then. Farwell isn't big enough to need a deputy chief."

"So, what will my job be?" Parker asked.

"Your job, if you still want one, will be whatever I tell you to do. For now, it's dispatch. You go against me again, Parker, and it won't even be that."

***

Juliette Moore stood outside Mitchell Polovina's front door still dressed in her uniform, the short skirt uniform she had worn every day since Mitch took over as police chief. It was dinner time and Mitch had just thrown a fifty-cent chicken pot pie in the oven. He invited the pretty officer in. "What's that smell?" she asked him, her nose wrinkling a bit. He explained and offered her some. "Pass," she said. He went on to explain that he was a bachelor now, and his cooking skills were pretty much nonexistent, but that with his constant eating out with Victoria Outing for the purpose of extracting information from her, he was beginning to dislike restaurant cooking nearly as much as his own. He wouldn't have had to tell her he was a bachelor; she already knew that. Small town. It had come on just recently, and, the way she saw it, far too slowly. Mitch's ex-wife, everyone knew, was a real bitch. He could have done so much better. She thought of offering to cook for him; then she thought better of it. Then she reversed her position. "How about I fix you something edible?" she offered.

"Well you just come on in, Miss Moore," he said.

"Juliette," she corrected. Might as well be on a first name basis if she was to cook for him. She wondered if he knew she was interested in him and had been since the first day they worked together. It didn't seem to her though, that he had even noticed her, at least she hadn't seen him notice her. And she had hemmed her skirt twice since he took over. It had to be an inch and a half shorter now. "We have a slight problem, Chief."

"Mitch," he corrected. Might as well be on a first name basis if she was going to cook for him. "And what would this problem be?"

"Actually there are two," she said as she dug around in his refrigerator, then his cupboards. "First of all, you have no food."

"Should we order in? Pizza? Chinese?"

"Pizza," she said.

"What's problem number two?" he asked her.

"Randy (she spoke of Randy Newell, the deceased police chief Mitch replaced) didn't supply me with anything but skirts for uniforms. I can't wear pants tomorrow. Don't have any."

Mitch was on the phone ordering pizza and listening to her at the same time. When he hung up, he said, "That's a shame." But what he was thinking was, *all right!* "We'll have to do something about that real soon. Can't have you out on the street looking like that now, can we?"

"You don't like the way this looks on me?" she asked as she stretched to reach plates in an upper cabinet. She smiled to herself, knowing she was giving him an eye full.

"Oh, yeah. I like the way that looks on you. I just think pants might serve you better on the street."

"Okay, but I'll miss the skirts."

"As will I," he said. "As will I."

CHAPTER TEN

Breakfast with Miss Victoria and Chief Polovina, Doc Nason had to miss out on. Old Edith Cherry, one of his elderly patients, not as old as Victoria Outing and not living in a retirement home like her, passed away in her sleep. She died from a massive heart attack. Without a physician present at the time of death, an autopsy was required by state law. Doc would spend his morning performing that procedure. Mitch would have to fill him in on Miss Outing's account of a life long ago lived at a later time.

"We're all alone this morning, Mitchell. Where's Henry?" Victoria asked.

"He couldn't join us today. Doctor business of some sort."

"I don't ever recall teaching you to communicate in incomplete sentences. Do you?"

"No Ma'am… ah, Sister… ah, Victoria. I'll watch myself."

"You do that," she scolded and frowned at him. Good thing she didn't have a steel edged ruler on her.

"You were going to tell me all about your Mr. Shaw today," Mitch reminded her.

"Was I now?"

"You were."

And she began, just as she had before, telling the tale like it was being told by another person.

***

Arthur Shaw was a regular at Mick's Café and he always chose to be waited on by Victoria. Several times Nancy Bjorquist tried to horn in, but Arthur Shaw always ran her off like she was a hound with fleas. "I want that Outing girl," he'd say. And one day when Victoria's mother took sick and she couldn't make it to work for caring for her, Arthur Shaw refused to eat breakfast at all.

"I missed you yesterday," he told her on the next morning. "Is everything all right?"

"My mother is ill. I had to stay around and look after her."

"Nothing serious, I hope," Shaw said.

"She's dying," Victoria said and a tear came to her eye.

"Oh, no, I'm sorry. Here, sit a moment," he said gesturing at a chair.

"I can't. I'll get fired."

"No you won't. I won't let them fire you. I'm a powerful man around this town you know."

"You are?" Victoria asked.

"I am."

"How so?"

"It's a side business of mine. I sell oil to the mining company, that's for sure, but that's not all I do. Come with me, Victoria, I'll show you something."

"But I'll get fired," she objected as he stood and took her by the hand.

"Mick," Shaw shouted out to the proprietor. "I'm going to take your girl away for a moment. You don't mind, do you?" Victoria's employer waved a hand at Shaw, a sign of his approval. "You see, Victoria, your boss is one of my better customers."

"He buys oil?"

"No. No. Not oil, but he buys. Come. I'll show you." And he led her through the kitchen and into a pantry on the back wall. Inside the pantry he pushed a button near the ceiling where most folks, especially folks her size, couldn't even reach. A piece of the floor slid away revealing a set of stairs. They walked down them and passed through a small room, its walls lined with shelves from floor to ceiling filled with bottles, some empty, some full of a light colored liquid. The room narrowed into a hallway that seemed to go forever.

"Where are we?" Victoria asked after walking fifty steps in the dark, damp tunnel.

She heard a clattering noise from above and stopped. She began to shake.

"It's all right," Shaw assured her. "That's just a wagon and team."

"A wagon and team?"

"Yes. We're under Main Street."

"Where are we going?"

"To the other side," Shaw said. "That's where it is."

"Where what is?" Victoria asked and turned around. "I want to go back to work, Mr. Shaw."

"You can call me Arthur," he said. "We're almost there, Victoria. Just another twenty feet or so. Don't turn back now. It's worth seeing. I promise."

They came to the end of the tunnel and to another door. Arthur Shaw opened it and what Victoria saw beyond it was a whole other world, one which held fascinations far beyond belief. "What is this place?" she asked.

"It's called a speakeasy. It's your boss' other business. Folks can come here safe from the laws of prohibition for an enjoyable night of dancing and partying. And I supply the beverages. And so long as prohibition exists, that makes me an important man in this town and several more around this part of the country."

Victoria looked the place over. A long, polished-wood bar filled a full wall, behind it shelves almost to the ceiling packed with fancy glassware and bottles reflected in a mirror beyond, a sink in the center, an ornate brass cash register at each end. It was spectacular. The stools lining the bar were like nothing she had ever seen — padded on the seat with rich leather, backrests that looked as though they'd reach up and touch the neck. "May I sit on one, Mr. Shaw?" she asked.

"You certainly may, but call me Arthur, won't you please?"

"All right, Arthur," she said and slid into one of the stools. "These are magnificent," she said.

"Aren't they, though?" he agreed. "But look at the rest of the place," he said and grabbed the arms of her stool and spun her to face the room, a wide open and lavishly decorated area filled with tables right up to a dance floor and a stage. The sudden turn gave her a start. "It's okay. The stools swivel."

Victoria Outing stared in awe. Never in her young life had she seen anything like it. She was a farm girl, accustomed to barns and chicken coops and for luxury, a small parlor to entertain visitors in. That was her life. This all left her speechless.

"Victoria, it'll come as no surprise I'm attracted to you," Arthur Shaw said. "Would it be all right if I kiss you?"

She looked into his eyes but did not speak. He took her silence as a yes. He leaned in and kissed her softly on the mouth. She didn't know what to do, this being her first kiss, so she kissed him back.

And she was frightened and excited all at the same time. "Open your mouth a little," Arthur Shaw suggested.

She did and the taste of his sweet breath filled her with anticipation. *What was next? Did she dare find out?* "I… ah… better get back, Arthur. Thank you for showing this to me," she said and slid off the stool.

"Of course," he said. He did not want to ruin this by moving faster than the young lady might want. True, she was just a girl, but she was old enough to marry. And if a girl's old enough to marry, she's old enough for lots of things. She was a prize, one he would win. He would give it a few more days, then invite her here at night, for dancing. If this all made the impression on her he had hoped for, in a few days, after dwelling on what she had seen, she'd be ready for more. "I'll take you back."

***

Mitch Polovina watched the now silent Victoria Outing. She seemed distant. "Are you all right, Victoria?" he asked.

"Yes. I'm fine, Mitchell. Will you take me home, please?"

Mitch did not object. He wanted to get out to the crime scene this morning anyway. He and Nase were to take a look for the company's old barge and whatever else they could find that might help them retrieve the rest of the drums from the warehouse at the bottom of the water-filled mine pit. He drove her home and made arrangements for him to pick her up the next morning. She promised more of the story than she had told him today. Her eighty year old son, Michael Decker, awaited her at the retirement home. Polovina shot him a nod. Michael Decker ignored it and helped his mother into her home. Mitch wasn't sure who was helping whom. "Like a dog walking his master," he told himself and smiled.

***

One of the city police cruisers was parked at the entrance to the old mine property when Polovina arrived. Juliette Moore got out as he pulled close. He was delighted to see her uniform had not changed yet, despite the fact he had located a few pair of surplus trousers at a neighboring town's police department and sent her to pick them up. He knew she had gotten over to get them because that police chief called to thank him for sending her. Mitch could almost hear him drool on his phone as he spoke. "Jesus Christ," he had said. "Where did you get her, and where can I get one?"

"No pants yet?" he asked as she approached his window.

"I got them, even tried them on, but I swam in them. The tailor shop is reworking them as we speak. They'll be ready in the morning."

"Doc Nason is supposed to meet me here. Seen anything of him?"

"He phoned the station about a half-hour back, said he'd be late, something about an autopsy gone bad. Who died, anyway?"

"Edith Cherry. Heart attack in her sleep."

"I guess that's better than cancer, or one of those illnesses that take forever to kill you. No good way to go, though, is there?"

"Sure there is. Boots on and guns blazing," Mitch said and smiled.

"I don't know about blazing guns, that don't seem to fit you. But boots on? I can see you doing lots of things with your boots on," Juliette said.

"How about you? You wouldn't happen to have a thing for guns and boots, would you?" Mitch asked. He was killing time — waiting for Nase. A foolish conversation spoken in light hearted fun with a pretty girl he had his eye on, seemed a good way to do that.

"I do like guns, or I wouldn't be a cop," Juliette admitted. "But boots; now there's something I'm really into. I have a collection."

"A collection! Sometime you'll have to show them to me."

"Maybe. Most of them anyway," she said.

"Most of them? Why not all of them?"

"Okay, all but one pair."

"Describe them," Mitch said.

"Do you recall watching me get plates out of your upper cabinet for the pizza?"

"Yes," Mitch said and looked down in embarrassment.

"Did you see the tops of my thigh high stockings, the lacy part?"

"Yes," he answered without looking up.

"Well picture this. Picture boots that cover the lace and have four inch stiletto heels on them. Can you picture that, Chief?"

He looked into her big brown eyes. "Not without breaking into a sweat, I can't." He considered her for a moment. It was time to dump this conversation before it turned into something more serious, something Gray Eagle would probably catch them at when he arrives. "What are you doing out here, Juliette?" he asked.

"Two things," she said.

"Is it always two things with you?" he asked, thinking of the night before when she had two problems, no long britches to wear to work, and no food in his house other than chicken-pot-pies.

"I try to make it that way. It's more interesting, don't you think?"

"You couldn't be uninteresting if you tried. Now tell me what brought you out here."

"I wanted to invite you to my house for dinner tonight. I'm a real good cook, I promise. Will you come?"

"I will," he said. He hadn't had good home cooking since his first wife left him. That was fifteen years ago. Man that woman wasn't much in the sack, but could she cook. "Now what's the second thing?"

"I thought I might be able to help on this case."

"Dressed like that?"

"I thought you liked this uniform."

"I do. I like it a lot. But there might be climbing to do," Polovina explained.

"Who'll climb first? You? Or me?" she asked and donned a coy, flirtatious smile.

"Let's go," Mitch said and tore the police tape form the entrance to the old mine. "We'll walk in."

***

"Bugsy, we've got a problem here," Doc Nason said as soon as the chief answered his cell phone.

"What kind of a problem, Gray Eagle?"

"Mrs. Cherry. I found traces of arsenic in her blood. Someone was poisoning her."

A long silence followed while Polovina thought things through. "Bugsy you still there?"

"I'm here. I'm thinking. Officer Moore," he said turning his attention to Juliette. "Is Royal Baker capable of starting an investigation? Doc thinks Mrs. Cherry may have been poisoned."

"You got that foxy little cop out there with you? What's she wearing?"

"Never mind that," Mitch said.

"Lucky bastard," Nason said.

"Royal's a trained investigator. Randy used to turn things over to him when it got busy. He did all right," Juliette said.

"Nase, wait there. I'm going to send Parker over. Stay with him. We'll see to this for now." He hung up. "Radio him. Have the secretary take dispatch and send Royal over to the morgue," he told Juliette.

What the hell's next, Mitchell Polovina asked himself.

CHAPTER ELEVEN

Pop Jenkins, Homer, Jr., Karla Mayfield's father and the mayor's father-in-law, would not go back into the house where his wife had died when the judge turned him loose. It was too painful, too many memories for him. He looked at the old house as a tomb, not just for his deceased spouse, but for him as well.

"He can't stay here," Ted Mayfield told his wife.

"He can stay here," Karla Mayfield insisted. "He's my father and he'll always be welcome in our home."

"I'm the mayor for Christ sakes. And he's somehow mixed up in all of this business out at the mine: bodies popping out of the water, murder, God knows what else.

"How do you know he's involved?"

"Evidence, Karla. You've admitted he's sitting on evidence. That says involvement, not just knowing. And shooting at the police? Come on. And you know what else gives him away, Karla?"

"What?"

"Silence, Karla. If he didn't have something to do with it, he'd talk. Silence says a lot sometimes."

"Maybe he knows something, but he didn't do anything."

"Well… that can be a crime too. Maybe he's not a murderer, and I don't think he is, but if he knows something and he won't tell it, he's an accessory to murder. That's just as bad. At least it will be for us."

"How the hell could that be?" Karla snarled.

"How? Either way, we would be harboring a criminal."

"Well… either way, he's not going anywhere," Karla Mayfield snapped.

"Then I will."

"Fine! I'll help you pack."

Homer Jenkins came into the room to offer his counsel.

"Teddy, Son, calm down. Everything will be all right. You'll see."

"Tell me what your involvement is in all of this, Pop. Tell me what you know."

"I can't do that, Teddy. I wish I could, but I can't."

"Homer," Ted Mayfield said.

"Yes?" Homer Jenkins answered.

"Fuck you!" And Ted Mayfield went to his and Karla's bedroom to pack a few things. He'd stay at his office if necessary, and he vowed never to return to his home.

***

Royal Parker stepped into Doctor Nason's morgue to see Doc stuffing organs back into Edith Cherry's chest cavity.

"Jesus, Doc," he said.

"Next time knock, Parker. I'll throw a sheet over whoever I have on the table and you won't have to see."

"I will. Could you throw one over that now?"

He did.

"Thanks," Parker said. "What do you got?"

"I got arsenic."

"How much?"

"Enough to get the job done. This is murder, Royal, it isn't a heart attack," Doc said. "You'll need to question the family."

"You were her doctor, sense any trouble?"

"Her and the old man argued. Some years back, she showed up in my office with bruises and a broken wrist, said she fell down the stairs. The bruises looked like hand prints on her wrist, but, she never came back in with anything like that, so, after awhile, I believed the whole falling down the stairs story. Might want to start with him."

"Anything else?"

"Never met any of the rest of them until last night when she turned up dead. Can't tell you anything more. I'm afraid you're on your own there." He flipped the sheet back, not so much to get back to the task of organ stuffing as to get Royal Parker to leave. It worked.

Nase called Mitch back and informed him that Parker was on the case. "Still need me out there? Because if you have everything under control, I still don't here."

"You finish up with what you're doing. Juliette and I can sort through this place and find what we'll need for the dive. Hopefully, it'll all be useable and we can make that dive tomorrow."

"Juliette? What happened to Officer Moore?"

"She's here too," Mitch said and hung up. He turned his attention back to the massive hunk of machinery they had been busily digging out when the call came, the barge once used for retrieving equipment from the bottom of the pit. The bad news was that it seemed enormous. The good news was twofold: it was on tracks which ran all the way to the shore of the lake, and it seemed in good enough repair to float. No vandals, like Mitchell Polovina and his brothers and friends and his brothers' friends, had filled its floats full of bullet holes target practicing. He pulled on the tarp covering the craft for a further investigation. It hung up atop the thing.

"Want me to climb up there and free it?" Juliette Moore offered.

Mitch looked her up, then down, then back up again. He eyed the short skirt. "Do I ever," he said. "But... I think you best leave the climbing to me."

"I can do it. Honest. I grew up an only child. They thought I should have been a boy the way I could climb."

He sized her up. God, she was gorgeous. "They were wrong," he said.

"Who was wrong?" she asked.

"Whoever thought you should have been a boy. They were wrong." He began to climb up to free the tarp. "You pull when I tell you." It might be just as entertaining to watch her from above as from below. He located the problem and freed the tarp. "Pull," he said. He was right. Her shirt tail pulled out of the skirt and rode up her back to reveal a tattoo, which ran all the way across her lower back, just above her waistband — black, ornate. "Aerosmith?" he asked.

"Close, but it's just a design. No meaning whatsoever. You like it?"

"I do," he said. "Pretty girls with cool tattoos are kinda hot." He wondered why he said it. Might he be moving too fast? But what the hell could he do? She was hot. With or without the sensual artwork in just the perfect location she was hot. "So... what are you fixing for dinner tonight?"

"I make mean Italian spaghetti and meatballs, if that suits you."

"Are you kidding? That's my favorite." It wasn't, but tonight it would be. These days anything home cooked by someone other than him was his favorite. And Juliette Moore? He didn't care what she cooked so long as he could watch her doing it. "My absolute favorite."

She pulled on the tarp the final few feet and let it drop to the ground behind the barge. She coughed a few times when dust rose. "Then spaghetti it is," she said.

Polovina looked over the barge from bow to stern. "She seems in good shape," he said. "I think she'll do."

"You talking to me or about me?" she asked and smiled up at him.

***

Henry Nason, having finished his autopsy of Edith Cherry and satisfied that the poor old gal had indeed been a victim of foul play, decided he could take no more of the repugnant odor of his morgue and set out to find Bugsy Polovina. He wondered if Officer Moore would still be with him.

His answer came as he drove up to the entrance of the old mine. Two squad cars, not one, sat at the side of the narrow roadway. He parked third in line and set out on foot as Mitch and Juliette must have done. There must have been cause for them walking in: path too narrow or muddy (it had rained a lot recently). Maybe driving might have contaminated the crime scene or something else along that order. "Christ, Nase, get a grip," he told himself. "Maybe you've been watching too much television."

"It's my guess you have," Chief Polovina said as he walked around a bend in the path just in time to hear Nason's comment to himself. Juliette Moore followed close behind. She looked a mess: twist on top of her head half in and half out of its band, blouse hanging out in the back and along one side — still tucked in on the other, top button unfastened, soil darkening her short skirt, an outlandish run in one of her thigh high stockings, and serious scuffs on her high heel shoes. Messy, yet still somehow enticingly sexy.

"What have you two been up to?" Doc asked.

"Investigating," Mitch said.

"You look it," Nase said

Polovina let the remark go. "We found all we'll need to make the dive."

"What condition?"

"It all looks good to me, but I think you should check the underwater gear," Mitch said, knowing Doc was the better choice for such things. Gray Eagle had always been the one to take care of their diving gear when they were young, much more conscientious than Bugsy when it came down to technical shit like that. "Here," he handed Nason a black leather wallet-sized item."

"What's this?" Doc asked.

"Your badge. Carry it with you at all times while we're on this case."

Doc opened it, looked at the badge and smiled, then rubbed it on the leg of his trousers to shine it. "Do I get to keep it after this case is over?"

"Hell no."

"Why not?"

"Because you're not a real cop."

"You mean like you," Nase said, reminding Mitch that he was merely a man off the street who knew people in power, not exactly a trained policeman himself.

"Okay. Make you a deal. We solve this case, you keep the badge — we don't solve it, and you give it up."

"Fair enough," Doc Nason agreed. It was a good bet they'd solve the case. Even when they were youngsters, playing football together and hanging out exploring and diving the pits, they never failed at anything. They always were a good team, complementing one another — any talent lacking in one always seemingly a strength of the other's.

"I thought all you wanted out of life was to be a doctor," Mitch reminded him.

"I do," he said. "I want to be a doctor-coroner-cop." He checked his watch. Five-thirty. "You guys done for the day?"

"Unless you need something," Mitch said.

"I'd kinda like to look at what you found," Nase said.

Mitch looked at Juliette, then at his own watch. "Why don't you go on ahead? I'll show Gray Eagle the loot and catch up with you in a bit. That'll give you time to clean up." He reached out and flipped a strand of fallen hair and smiled.

"You know where I live?" she asked.

"Of course I do. I'm the police chief you know." He smiled at her. She stuck out her tongue flirtatiously. "Run along," he said and began his walk back toward the mining company buildings. Doc followed.

"So… the two of you got a thing for each other?" Nase asked once they were out of earshot of Juliette Moore. Nase's objective wasn't to embarrass, but merely to find facts. He and Mitch Polovina had been friends for many years, and Henry Nason had grown tired of seeing his friend taken to the cleaners, so to speak, by women. Where women were concerned, Mitch seemed to make poor choices. Juliette, though, Nase had to admit, seemed different from Mitch's regular conquests. Much different.

"That alright with you?"

"Hey… it's none of my business." He threw his hands in the air, his sign of surrender. "Just curious."

"Damn right, it's none of your business." Mitch took a few more steps, then asked, "So… what do you think of her?"

"As far as what?" Nase would not answer the way he wanted to. He would not tell his friend that he wouldn't mind a shot at her, lest his friend took a good shot at him.

"For me. You think she might be right for me?"

"Look at her. How could she be wrong?" Nase said and smiled. "But, seriously, that's something you'll have to decide for yourself. She's a fox, but is that what you need, a playful fox, or should you go find yourself one more sophisticated, look down her nose, radical and politically and career motivated super-bitch like you always seem to go for?"

"You saying she isn't motivated and career minded?"

"Nope. She's motivated. She's always been motivated." Nase had known her for a long time. He was her physician. "And until now, she's been a real career girl. It seems to me, though, her motivation might have gotten off track lately."

"How's that?" Mitch asked.

"She seems to be entirely too motivated to conquer you."

"Really!"

"Really," Nase affirmed. "You seen her naked?"

"No."

"You're missing out," Nase said, and smiled. "I am her doctor, you know."

Chief Polovina shot Doc Nason a curious glance. "Here's the barge," he said.

"Rails, that'll help," Nase said. "That is if rust hasn't frozen everything up."

"It hasn't. Juliette and I were able to roll it back, just the two of us."

"Why didn't you shove it into the water?"

"I thought you might want to look her over first," Mitch said. "You're the equipment specialist."

Mitch was right. Nase had always been the one to check out their equipment. He wondered why that was. He walked around the craft, examining each piece as he passed it, paying particular attention to the floats, grasping nuts and bolts checking for anything which might need tightening or adjusting. After all, get her in the water and she sinks, where would they find another barge big enough to retrieve her? "Looks pretty sound to me. Shall we?" he asked and took up a pushing stance on the end away from the water. Mitch joined him and seconds later, they heard the splash at the other end as the floats hit water.

"Hope she don't sink tonight after we leave," Mitch said as he tied her off to a nearby tree. He didn't trust the post sticking out of the ground at the shoreline, the one used many years ago to prevent the craft from drifting off. It looked iffy at the base — rotted, maybe — where wood meets earth.

"Me too," Nase admitted. "I'd rather she did tonight though, if she's going to. Once we're out there depending on her, well... that's a whole lot worse time for sinking."

The two of them waded out, one man on each side. They checked for bubbles, signs of leaking around the floats. Nothing. Then Mitch showed Nase the other equipment he and Juliette had found: air tanks, hoses, and a small gas powered compressor.

"I want to take this unit," he said, gesturing at the compressor, "and all of these hoses into Walt Brink, let him check everything out for us." Walter Brink owned and operated a repair shop, and was generally considered to be a genius with small engines the likes of which powered the compressor, and one of the best along the entire Mesabi Range at repairing anything he got his hands on. "If Walt can't fix it," folks around said, "it can't be fixed."

"Let's get it all to your car." Mitch said.

CHAPTER TWELVE

The aroma of Italian spaghetti: sausage and beef, garlic, onion, and many exotic spices Mitchell Polovina could not put a name to, flooded through the open door of Juliette Moor's home when he arrived. His appetite accelerated to a height where he scarcely noticed that the girl wore denim shorts with rolled cuffs, which lacked all length, and a light spaghetti strap cotton top over bare skin, nipples hardened and trying to poke their way through the material as if they searched for him, wanted to greet him in some way. He scarcely noticed — not didn't notice. He stepped in and shut the door behind him. He took her in his arms and kissed her passionately.

"I wondered if you'd ever get around to that," she said. "Was it all you dreamed of?"

"More," Mitch admitted. "Smells wonderful in here?"

"Me or the food?"

"Both."

"So… which would you like first?"

"Do you like motorcycles?" he asked.

"I don't know much about them," she told him. "Why?"

"I have one."

"Then I love them," she said and smiled.

Mitch had made up his mind when his last wife filed for divorce. He had never been with anyone who would ride with him, all too stuffy, too proper, too good for biking. The next time, he had vowed, she would have to like motorcycles and most other things he liked. He was pleased to hear her make such a commitment. That was two off of his list of prerequisites, the other a good piece of ass often, something he already felt sure of even though he hadn't tried it out yet. And the kiss at the door told him tonight might just be the time for that tryout. "Mine's a big one," he told her.

"Your motorcycle?" she asked. "Come. Let me feed you.

Then you can show it to me."

***

Karla Mayfield pounded on her husband's office door for all she was worth.

"Go away," Ted Mayfield shouted through the closed door. He had no desire to continue the fight that had been brewing for… well… for all of his recent memory it seemed. He had had enough. And today, having been treated like a goddamn outsider in his own home just because his father-in-law, a man he had always respected and cared for, had some secret he did not wish to share, well… that was the last straw — that pushed Ted Mayfield over his own personal edge. "Leave me alone, Karla."

Karla was determined. Her husband was right. He needed to know what was going on within the walls of his own home, and in the past, he always did. This was a first and it would be the last. She would repair the problem. And if it takes sleeping outside Ted's office door until he allowed her to do that, then that is how it would be. "Please talk to me, Teddy. I love you."

"You speak Mitchell Polovina's name in your sleep. Did you know that?"

She did. She woke up one night, half asleep yet half awake, and she heard herself speak his name. "Not in fondness," she said.

"What does that mean?"

"Let me in, Teddy, and I'll tell you all about it." It was time anyway, time for her husband to know the truth about her and Mitchell Polovina, and time for her to let it all go — put it behind her. And she knew the only way for her to do that was for her to share that little piece of disgusting history with someone she loved — and that would be Ted. "Please, Teddy?" she begged.

"What about your father?"

"We talked. He's decided he must trust you. Please, Teddy. Let me in. I promise you nothing like this will ever happen again. Please."

Ted Mayfield turned the lock on his door.

"Is it bad?" he asked facing her in the open door. "What your father's hiding, is it bad?"

"It's bad."

***

Victoria Outing tossed and turned. Her dreams, vivid and terrifying, were of a night she never wished to relive, for in it, someone she truly admired died. Perhaps had she shared the events of that time with someone years ago, someone she felt comfortable with, a friend—a loyal friend. Perhaps then it would not be her ever-haunting dream. But there had not been such a person. Who would she call upon? A priest? Mother Superior? One of the other nuns with whom she lived and served all of those years? Not no but hell no. They couldn't be trusted, not one of them. And so… she tossed and turned — just as she always did. But tonight it would be different. Tonight, given her advanced years and weakening heart, the dream would be too much. Victoria Outing suffered a heart attack—a severe heart attack. The on staff nurse at the retirement home found her around seven-thirty in the evening after being alerted by the kitchen help that Miss Outing's evening meal had returned to the kitchen untouched.

Miss Outing's regular physician, the doctor who had assured Henry Nason that her heart was as sound as a teenager's, was not available to take the nurse's call, so Doctor Nason was summoned. A brief examination and she was in an ambulance on her way to the local hospital. Nason was in his car, on his way to the same.

***

"Do you think you could be our top-side man tomorrow?" Mitch asked Juliette as she stood in front of her sink readying herself to do the dishes dirtied by what Mitch thought was the best meal of his entire life. It was hard for him to concentrate, his being able to see the bottom inch or so of her magnificently well rounded and tanned butt-cheeks each time she bent slightly or stretched even enough to turn on the faucet.

"Do I look like a man, topside or any other kind?"

"No."

"All right then."

"I guess what I'm asking is, can you man the equipment on the barge while Gray Eagle and I dive tomorrow."

"I'd be the one to do it," she told him.

"Why is that?" he asked.

"Because there's no way I'll let something happen to you, not before I get to find out if you're a good lay or not." She had grown tired of waiting for him — thought it time to push a little.

He came up behind her. He put his arms around her middle, palms gently touching her stomach, soft to the touch yet flat and firm. He slid one hand slowly upward until it touched the bottom of her braless breasts. She turned her head and leaned back, their lips making soft contact, two gentle kisses, then her tongue searching out his. His other hand crept gently up, and when it arrived at her breasts, both began cupping and massaging, her nipples hardening immediately to his touch. He let one of his hands slide down, reaching the waist of her shorts, fingers fumbling to unbutton the top button, then the second, then the third. Soon his hand slid into her shorts, gently stroking soft pubic hair, searching lower and lower, his mind excited to find no panties beneath the denim shorts.

The obnoxiously loud and persistent tones of his cell phone announced an end to their foreplay and some unwanted caller's need to speak with him. "This better be goddamn important," he said into the phone and stepped back from Juliette.

"It is."

"What the hell do you want, Gray Eagle."

"Miss Outing's had a heart attack, Bugsy. She's been comatose most of the evening. She's come around for now though. Thought you'd want to know about it."

"Where is she?"

"Hospital. I.C.U."

"I'll be right there."

***

"I thought you said he was willing to trust me."

"Goddamn it Dad. Tell Ted what he needs to know," Karla Mayfield told her father.

"Question is, what does he need to know?"

"I'm the Mayor, Pop. If you're hiding something that might give me a problem, I do need to know about it. Besides, Karla says you need my help."

"I've changed my mind," Homer Jenkins told his son-in-law. At his age, in his eighties, Homer felt he could change his mind, and no one younger had any right to prevent that. "I doubt there's anything you can do anyway, unless you can get your buddy, Mitch Polovina, to close down that investigation of his."

"How could I do that? Bodies popped out of the water and floated around the lake like bloated fish. He's the chief of police. He has to investigate something like that. You gotta know that, Pop. Oh, and here's something you might keep in mind for the future. Never shoot at someone you might want or need the help of later. You only made him know there was something you're hiding. He wouldn't quit now if I fired him."

Homer Jenkins looked first at his daughter, Karla, then at his son-in-law, then he hung his head. "What I did, they'll have me in jail for it, Karla. You know that."

"Dad, I think you better tell Ted. He might be able to help with it. He might be able to do something." She had no idea how serious her father's transgressions might have been, but trusted that they couldn't be all that bad. He hadn't been the type.

"Son, will you give me your word you'll not tell anyone if I tell you the truth?"

"If you've done something that'll ruin my career by my knowing and not telling, you'll have to move to your own house until this is over. If you can live with that, Pop, you can tell me, and I'll do everything I can to protect you," Ted Mayfield said. After all, he knew Karla's father and had known him since he and Karla were just kids, just after she broke up with Mitchell Polovina and the two of them started dating. He was a kind and gentle soul, not easy to rile, happy for the most part, not the kind of man who could do something outside the law — not on purpose. Perhaps he had done some foolish thing like steal money from a storekeeper, a kid prank. So what? Whatever it was the statute of limitations, in all likelihood, passed by years ago. "Anything short of murder, we can probably fix."

"It's just short. They'll call me an accessory to murder."

"Don't say more. I can't know," Ted Mayfield said excitedly. "You'll have to move to your house, Pop. I'm sorry."

***

Doctor Henry Nason met Chief of Police Mitchell Polovina at the main doors of the hospital. He quickly ushered him into Victoria Outing's intensive care room where she laid, tubes hooked to her, IV hanging from a mobile stand, the beep-beep-beep of a heart monitor sounding steadily in the background. "She's been awake and waiting to tell you something she would only tell *you* for a half-hour or so now," Nason told him.

Mitch dragged a chair to her bedside. He sat. "Sure you wouldn't rather have a priest for this?"

"For what, dear boy?"

"Are you going to confess something?"

"No. And if I was to confess something, it would be to God himself, not to you, and most assuredly not to a priest."

"Then why did you call for me?" Mitch asked.

"I sense time is short, Mitchell. I wanted to make arrangements."

"Make arrangements?"

Mitch wondered what kind of arrangements. Funeral arrangements? Why him? "I'm afraid I don't understand, Victoria," he said.

"The story I'm in the process of telling you, you know, the story about me and Arthur Shaw, it has to be finished. I wanted to make sure you and I did that. But I do think we need to pick up the pace a bit, don't you?"

Mitch agreed. The old gal looked as though she might not last the night, but he did not feel right in saying so. "Nonsense, Victoria. There's plenty of time," he assured her.

"Kind of you to say so." Then she looked at Henry Nason. "What time do they serve breakfast around here, Henry?"

"Yours is pumping into your vein right now, Miss Outing," Henry said.

She looked at the IV. "So it is." She smiled a weak smile. "Isn't that convenient?"

"Well… let me put it this way. I want Mitchell here in the morning. What time shall I tell him to arrive?"

"Victoria," Henry began, "how about I check you out first thing in the morning. Once I've done that, we can decide what time and for how long. Then I'll call Mitch Polovina. How would that be?" Henry thought about what he had just offered and felt there was something to add, just to keep from stepping on the wrong toes. "But I imagine your regular physician might have some input as well. I'm only filling in, you know."

"Myron Benniful? If you don't object, Henry, I'd rather you took care of me. That old quack, I'm afraid, has outlived his purpose. He's nearly my age you know."

***

After saying goodnight to Victoria Outing, Mitch and Henry met in a waiting room at the hospital. "What's up with her?" Mitch asked. "Will she make it long enough to get the story out of her?" Mitch surprised himself. He had never been cold or unemotional about something like an old woman's illness and probable death. That wasn't him. Maybe he was becoming a real policeman, tempering a bit around the edges, creating a shell he could encase himself in whenever he was wearing the uniform, realistically or metaphorically. Then again maybe he was tired and reading way too much into this.

Henry looked him over with a professional eye. "Go home. Get some sleep. I'll call you in the morning."

CHAPTER THIRTEEN

Homer Jenkins could still feel his wife's presence as he lay in their bed staring at the ceiling. She was the reason he lived at the mine, this business of her sticking around. Why couldn't she move on — heaven or hell — like everyone else he had ever known who died. His mother moved on. Even his father had gone, malcontent rebel that he was, never satisfied with anything in life: his marriage, his career with the mine, with his job afterward with the police department, and especially with his son, Homer, Jr. Yes, he had moved on, and without fanfare or the kind of constant haunting Marion seemed compelled to do to Homer. But Marion had loved her husband and Homer supposed that to be her reason for not leaving him in peace. His father, on the other hand, was done with Homer long before his death. He was done with him soon after he made him help strip and dump those two girls' bodies back in '66, except of course, to threaten him about what would happen if he didn't keep quiet about it. Homer's father made him feel like a teen most of the time, unable to say no, even if he knew it was wrong. "Maybe I should have told Chief Polovina about that night," he told the ghost of Marion Jenkins.

"Maybe, Homer," Marion's ghost said back. "But you were never the kind to violate a trust, now were you, dear?"

"I suppose you're right," he said and shut his eyes.

***

"You will do what you can to steer Mitch Polovina away from my father, won't you Ted?" Karla Mayfield asked her husband lying next to her in their bed after they had moved Homer back to his own place.

"I will do all I can." Ted agreed.

"You won't say too much, will you?"

"I can't say too much. I don't know too much. I stopped Pop from telling me more so I couldn't say too much, Karla. Now… it's been a long and trying day. I suggest we get some sleep." He reached for the switch on the lamp beside the bed, shut the lamp off, and laid his head back on the pillow. He closed his eyes and let his mind drift through the day's activities. He hoped for a calmer tomorrow.

"Will he be all right over there by himself?" Karla Mayfield asked about her father.

"He'll be fine. He's probably talking things through with your mother right now."

***

Mitch Polovina ran by his office. He wanted to retrieve his personal car. But as he pulled to the curb, he remembered he had asked Juliette Moore to take it to the stakeout of Michael Decker's 1967 Buick that afternoon. She didn't return the keys. He would have to do something he did not like to do and didn't want anyone else doing — take a squad car home.

As he pulled up in front of his home, he noticed the front porch light on and another inside the house — odd. He was especially assiduous when it came to wasting electricity, not that he was environmentally conscious or anything of the sort. He wasn't. He simply hated the power company and avoided giving them one penny more than absolutely necessary.

He walked to the door. He inserted his key. The door swung open. He came face to face with Juliette Moore and nearly passed out from the shock of it. "What?" he tried to speak but could not.

"Really, Chief, a key under the flower pot? How television of you," she said and pulled him the rest of the way in. She threw her arms around his neck, pushed the door shut with a bare foot, and kissed him a long, hard, passionate kiss. "Now… where did we leave off?" She was talking about her at her sink — his hand down her short-shorts.

Mitch grabbed her by the shoulders and pushed her back to arms length. He searched her up and down. She had traded the tight denim short-shorts for a blue jean skirt that wasn't much longer. The top was the same. "You changed." he said.

"I had to trade the shorts in. They were wet."

"From doing dishes?"

"They were wet. That's all."

"What're you doing here?" It wasn't that he objected. He didn't.

"I wanted to see that big motorcycle of yours," Juliette said. "I hope that's all right."

How could he object? Every couple of years since he hit his twenties he bought a new one, each time bigger, more powerful, fancier. She was the first woman in his life to pay attention. "Not at all," he said. "Come on. I'll fix us a drink. Then I'll take you in the garage."

"Take me ... in... the garage?" she asked and smiled a seductive smile.

"Sorry. Take you to the garage... to show you... my big... ah... motorcycle." He led her to his kitchen, and there, found a surprise. The room was spotless, everything in its place, sink and appliances scoured to like new condition, floor swept and mopped.

Drinks already prepared and sitting on the counter. "That's a real time saver," he said.

"I thought you might be later. I didn't want to lose out if you were."

"Lose out on what?" he asked and took a sip of his drink. His lips curled a bit as the bitterness of the sour mash whiskey awakened his taste buds. "Good," he said.

"A ride. It does work doesn't it?"

He placed his glass, only half gone, on the counter and took hers. If he had a woman willing to get on the bike with him, the drink could take a hike. "It works. Let's go." He made his way through a laundry area in a hallway to a service door which led to his attached garage. "Did you bring pants?" he asked her.

"No."

"How are you going to ride in that?" he asked, surveying the skirt.

"Don't worry yourself about it. I'll show you."

Mitch flipped the switch and the garage lit up. It was spacious and neat, surprisingly so, she thought, considering his kitchen. The only vehicle in it was the bike, a late model Gold Wing, full dress, decked out with every available chrome piece, polished to a foot deep shine. "She's beautiful," Juliette said.

"He," Mitch corrected.

"Alright, he."

Mitch pushed a button on the wall of the garage and the automatic door opener kicked into action. "Climb on," he said anxious to see how she would do it and still maintain her dignity.

She sat on the passenger's seat, side saddle, then swung one leg quickly and smoothly over the cycle's gas tank. "See? Not so tough."

"I'm impressed," he said and mounted the bike in front of her. He fired up the engine, fully choked. It ran at a high RPM for a time until he backed the choke off. "It's warmed up. We can go. Ready?"

"Yeah," she said excitedly. It wasn't her first ride, but this bike was definitely bigger and better and more comfortable than the one Billy Roberts had when they dated fifteen years earlier. This one had a seat that was not only made of soft, subtle leather; it rode up around her hips cradling her bottom like a recliner. And when Mitch pulled out of the garage, closed the garage door, and turned on the radio to an oldies station playing a Bob Dylan tune, she felt she had passed on and gone to heaven. She leaned up and kissed Mitch on the middle of his neck, near his hairline, just as he turned from the driveway onto the street. He shivered. "Sorry," she said.

"No. Don't be. I liked that, just wasn't expecting it." She did it again, and once again he shivered, she giggled. "Where do you want to go?" he asked.

"Parking," she said.

"Parking? On a bike?"

"Can't it be done?" she asked.

"I suppose. That is if you're innovative."

"Find a place that's dark and out of the way. I'll show you innovative," Juliette told him.

"Really!"

"Really. What do you think the skirt is all about?"

***

It was Ten o'clock at night and Royal Parker was still pestering Edith Cherry's family. "Somebody administered arsenic to her. I aim to find out who."

"I hope you do," one of Edith's sons, the eldest, Arnold, said. "But you can't seriously suspect one of us, Officer Parker."

"These things usually turn out to have been done by someone

close to the victim," Parker insisted.

"Tell me, Parker," Arnold said, "just how many of these things have you investigated? How often does something like this happen in our town?"

"Never that I know of, but…"

"But, nothing." Arnold snapped. "I think that's one statistic you collected from too many hours in front of your television. Those aren't real cops you're watching, you know. And what they're saying has been written by some writer, and all writers are liars. Everyone knows that. Now, my father has been through enough for one day, so you get your ass out of his home and leave him alone." Arnold stood to remove Parker if he showed signs of not leaving on his own. Parker unfastened the snap on his holster. "You pull that out you son-of-a-bitch, and I'll feed it to you barrel first." Arnold was a big man, half again Parker's size, and was reputed to have been a Green Beret in the Army. Parker fastened the snap on his holster and excused himself.

***

Juliette Moore must have kissed Mitchell Polovina a hundred times on the back of the neck as they rode along in the peaceful night air, and each time he shivered. One would think he'd get used to it, but no, not Mitch. Every kiss came as a surprise. But all of them reminded him why he had always wanted a woman who would ride behind him. He turned the bike, after more than an hour of touring the streets of the town and the surrounding countryside, onto the drive leading into the old mine and, being cautious of loose sand and puddles of water, rode them all the way to where they had found the barge. Just as they got there and as he was setting the kickstand, Juliette reached around him, unfastened his trousers, and unzipped his zipper. "Sit right there," she ordered.

He sat. He was far too curious not to. Juliette slipped off the seat behind him and, almost in the same motion, slid a slender leg across the gas tank in front of him. The move was so sensual that Mitch, already erect from all of the other playfulness and indications of more to come, grew larger than he had ever grown before. He knew he had. Not even back in high school when he was a jock and popping cherries like he couldn't get enough of them, had he felt a high even remotely equivalent to this experience. She slowly, deliberately, teasingly, moved her face to his, brushing her sensual lips on his several times, then kissing a brief, soft kiss and pulling back, then doing it again, this time with the tip of her tongue parting his lips. She repeated the action until he could take no more. Mitch grabbed a handful of hair at the back of her head. She winced, but did not object. He pulled her pretty face to his and kissed her passionately. Giving up the grip he had on her hair, his hands floated around to her breasts, bare under the thin material of her top, and began a passionate massage of them. Her hands floated to his privates, her grip tightening as though something might somehow escape. She pushed up, her still bare feet using the rear foot platforms of the bike for support, and settled onto him. She hadn't been wearing panties under her denim short-shorts earlier in the evening, and she didn't put them on when she changed into the skirt. She slid him easily into her and began moving slowly, sensually, deliberately up and down, using the magnificent muscles of her slender legs, in time to a softly sung love ballad from the 'sixties playing on the radio. Neither of them cared what song or what artist, their breathing escalating with each pump of her legs, their bodies filling with sweat, their lips locked and tongues probing as deeply as they could reach into each other's mouths. And they climaxed the likes of which neither of them had felt before. Then, with him still inside her, she leaned back on the handlebars of the motorcycle, her spaghetti strap top pushed up and exposing her round firm breasts. She sighed. He sighed. "Wanna go again?" she asked him.

And they did.

CHAPTER FOURTEEN

Mitch Polovina's phone rang and rang. He and Juliette Moore made such a night of it that when they arrived back at his house and settled into a comfortable position on his sofa in front of the television, they were asleep so fast neither of them knew what hit them. Popcorn remained in the microwave, an electronic beep now and then letting them know it was done. The blue screen of the television left behind by a movie no longer playing lit up the room in an eerie glow. Mitch looked at Juliette, still asleep on his shoulder, and gave no thought to the waste of electricity. He reached for the phone on the end table beside him. "Hello," he said.

"You got any idea what time it is?"

"Who the hell is this?"

"Henry."

"Good morning, Gray Eagle."

"Have you lost your watch, Bugsy, or your mind?"

"Just my virginity," Mitch said. That's how he felt anyway, like last night's excitement had been his first piece of ass. Juliette stirred and moaned softly.

Nason heard her. "So that's how it is," he said.

"So… what time is it?"

"Ten."

"Ten?"

"Ten. And Walt Brink's been calling me every half-hour since seven-thirty. The compressor's in good shape and the hoses check out fine. We can dive."

"Christ!" Mitch said and jumped. He had forgotten all about the dive. "Oh, sorry Baby," he said and hauled Juliette back to a sitting position. "Give me an hour, Nase," he said into the phone. "Get the equipment from Walt and meet me out at the pit."

"Should I get ahold of Teddy Mayfield and his father-in-law?

Won't we need them topside?"

"Juliette Moore will run the top. I don't want Homer out there, and until I find out what he's hiding, about having Mayfield around," Mitch told Henry Nason. Then he hung up the phone. "C'mon, Sugar. We need to get you home so you can change clothes."

Juliette stretched and yawned. "I'm hungry," she said.

'We'll grab a muffin on the way. C'mon."

***

Ted Mayfield paced in his office. "Christ," he complained. He was Mayor. He ought to be able to handle his father-in-law's secret, or he shouldn't be Mayor. "Some leader I turned out to be," he told himself. He suddenly felt obligated to alter the situation. He needed to know. He had a right to know. He realized he had told the old man he didn't wish to know anything that might bring trouble to his own doorstep, but what's the difference, sooner or later, the trouble would come, and sooner or later he would have to choose. And when trouble does come, he should not let it be an out and out surprise. So… what would he have to choose? Sides, of course. This whole thing had sides — no middle — just sides and he could pick only one. His dilemma? As Mayor he had a responsibility, and that responsibility should be to stand on the side of the law. As Homer Jenkins' son-in-law and Karla's husband, he should stand with family. The internal struggle needed resolving before he made any contact. He sat down at his desk to think.

Mayor Mayfield was nearly asleep when his desk phone rang. Doc Nason and Mitchell Polovina were in gear, and ready to dive when Mitch thought it might not be in bad form to call the mayor after all, and invite him to look in on this operation. "Can you hold up a few moments, give me time to collect my thoughts and get out there?"

"Collect your thoughts? You weren't asleep at your desk again, were you Teddy?" Mitch asked.

"Of course not, "Ted Mayfield said. "I'm just tied up in work, that's all. Give me twenty minutes," he said, and hung up.

"He coming?" Nason asked.

"Yeah," Polovina answered. "Twenty minutes, but we ain't waiting." He spread a large net out on the deck of the barge, secured each corner with a heavy nylon rope which he tied to a single round steel hoop, three inches in diameter. He locked the cable of the barge's winch to the hoop and threw the net overboard. "Go ahead and let the cable out, Juliette," he said. And Juliette lowered the net.

Doc leaned close to Mitch and asked, "Does she have to dress like that?"

"It's a bathing suit, Gray Eagle. What'd you want her to wear on the water? Thought you said you've seen her naked anyway."

"I did, in my office, many times."

"So why should this trouble you?" Mitch asked.

"As a physician, it isn't the naked female form that's exciting, it's the scantily dressed one," Nase explained.

"You're twisted," Mitch said. "I think it has something to do with being Indian."

"What're you boys talking about over there?" Juliette asked. She couldn't hear over the sound of the winch's motor.

"Diving," Doc Nason shouted. "Just diving." And when he was sure she had been satisfied with his answer, he turned the conversation back to Polovina. "The old woman's made remarkable progress just overnight. I don't think we'll be losing her too soon. Just the same, you might want to pick up the pace. She's a tough one, but, you never know."

"If we find what I suspect at the bottom of this lake, we'll be doing just that, picking up the pace."

"What are you expecting? More bodies?"

"I got me a feeling, Gray Eagle. I think we may have hit the proverbial tip of the iceberg. We'll see soon enough. Now… I see you also brought tanks. You thinking we should forget the hoses and compressor?"

"Nah. The tanks are for just in case. The helmets and hoses will protect us better; keep us from popping our eardrums. Lots of pressure down there."

Polovina yanked the recoil starter of the compressor a couple of times and it fired like the day it was new. He smiled at Nason and asked, "Ready?" Nase had already pulled the diving helmet over his head, so gave Mitch the thumbs up and lowered himself into the water. Mitch followed.

At the bottom of the pit, the two divers located the net Juliette Moore had lowered, spread it out on the lake floor, and cautiously, so that no hoses would tangle, cut, or be caught on something, entered and found an ancient two-wheel cart designed for moving drums. As luck would have it, the thing still rolled freely. They began moving drums, one at a time, bringing them to the net, until the net would take no more. Then they would return to the surface to pull their load up and deposit it on the barge. They worked at the task the remainder of the day and just as dark was settling in on them, they finished, the last of the drums finally on the barge. Now to get them in a warehouse where they could explore their contents, something neither man, or Juliette Moore or Mayor Mayfield for that matter, cared to do. But it would need doing. Ted Mayfield, while the rest of them diligently saw to the drum retrieval, arranged for a truck and flatbed trailer to be on hand. The original dock for the barge allowed for forklift operation on and off, so moving the drums from barge to truck was something the others had only to supervise.

"Royal," Chief Polovina said to Officer Royal Parker when he picked up the phone. "I have a little nightshift babysitting for you to do." He gave him the address to the warehouse Mayfield had secured for their use and told him to be there by the time he got there — within fifteen minutes.

"But I'm in the middle of Mrs. Cherry's murder investigation," Parker complained.

"Bring your notes. I want to take a look myself," the chief ordered.

Parker thought to argue, but recalled Polovina's warning from earlier. He had gone from Officer Parker to dispatcher, and by circumstance, the coroner having found arsenic in Mrs. Cherry's blood, he found his way to investigator. He wasn't going to argue with the new chief and end up back on dispatch. Not this soon. "Will do, Chief," he agreed.

Chief Polovina knew Parker wanted to argue with him over the notes on the Cherry case, and gave Parker credit for holding his tongue, well... not so much Parker as himself. It showed progress in gaining the respect of his staff. Now he could move in the right direction — forward. His staff, after all, if it could even be called a staff — most of it having flown the coop the moment he took office — consisted of Juliette, Parker, and Paula Bloom, the secretary. He needed to smooth things over with Royal Parker, or lose him as well. Now that he had been able to usurp authority without argument, he saw that as possible. "And Parker, before you leave, put a note on the Paula's desk. Let her know that we'll all be out here in the morning, and tell her to place an ad in the paper. We need more officers — a dispatcher and a couple of night cops — so *we* don't have to do it all."

"Will do, Chief," Royal Parker said. Chief Polovina could sense the excitement in his officer's voice. More progress. "See you in fifteen. Say, any of you eat?"

"Nope."

"Want me to call in for pizza?"

"Do that. We could all use it. Get a large. Doc and the mayor are out here too. And Royal… bring a sleeping bag. There's one in my office." Mitch kept one on hand for emergencies, for times when he might work into the wee hours and not have the energy to go home. He had developed the habit initially, when he was nearing the end of his second marriage. That woman was forever throwing him out. He never broke the habit. Came in handy with his third wife too. He wondered if he'd get serious with Juliette Moore and someday need it again. He hoped not — about the sleeping bag that is.

"You want to start opening them?" Royal Parker asked Chief Polovina. They had all arrived, pretty much simultaneously, at the empty warehouse on the edge of town, the one Mayfield had secured for their operation. The place had gone back for back taxes, so technically, was now owned by the city. Parker had ordered pizza's delivered, so ample time for unloading the drums passed while they waited.

"You spend the night. Use the office. You should be comfortable there. Just make sure no one comes in here. We'll start finding out what's in the drums in the morning," Polovina said.

"But, Chief," Parker complained. "I thought you said there might be more bodies in them." He gestured toward the drums.

"Might be," Polovina confirmed.

"I don't want to sleep in a warehouse with dead bodies."

"They're sealed in drums, Parker. They can't get out."

"But…," he started to further his complaint. A harsh look from Polovina detoured him. "Never mind."

***

He didn't know what made him do it, but Mitch took a pass at the home Victoria Outing lived at on his way to take Juliette back to her place. He pulled the car to the side of the street and looked at the front door for a moment. "Look at that," Juliette said, pointing a finger at the corner of the building.

Mitch looked where she pointed, a little dog ran back and forth skittishly, obviously lost and frightened. "It looks like Victoria's dog," he said and got out of the car. He approached the poor thing cautiously so that it would not be frightened and run off. And when he got within diving distance, he dove. The dog peed. "Shit, he said and picked it up anyway. He went to the front door. Locked. He went to the car, got in, and handed the animal to Juliette.

"How adorable," she said. She sniffed the air. "What's that smell?"

"The little bastard pissed on me. It's all over my sleeve."

"Is she Victoria's dog?" Juliette asked and snuggled her close to quiet her shaking.

Mitch flipped the dome light on. "Is it a she?"

"She is."

"Has she got a tag?"

Juliette felt around the animal's collar. She found and read the tag. "Sister Mary Elizabeth, it says. Who would name a dog Sister Mary Elizabeth?"

"An ex-Benedictine nun," Mitch said and started the car.

"What'll we do with her?"

"Take her home with us, I guess."

"With us?" Juliette asked.

"Well… to my place then," Mitch said.

"Why not mine?"

"Are we about to have custody issues over a dog we don't even own?" Mitch asked and smiled.

"No. Take her to your house if you want to, only I'm staying with the dog."

CHAPTER FIFTEEN

The time was five a.m. Mitch Polovina had just finished digging through a closet, had located a tall work boot, took one of the laces out and tied it to the little dog's collar, and he and Sister Mary Elizabeth were in the back yard exploring. Sis, as Juliette had shortened the unusually long name to, could not seem to find just the right place to do her business. It took forever. But, alas — success. "How does one little tiny dog like you shit that much," Mitch asked the animal upon seeing a pile that could have been left behind by a Labrador. She looked up at him pitifully and stood, her front paws on his leg. She scarcely reached his knee. He stooped and picked her up and carried her back inside. In the bedroom, he sat her on the bed, and Sis immediately crawled on top of Juliette, her back legs hanging on one side of her, front paws on the mattress on the other side, draped like a floppy furry rug. Mitch wanted to get the camera. But he imagined Juliette might object to having her picture taken, along with the dog, sleeping in the raw. So Mitch went to the kitchen to make coffee instead. He would let Juliette sleep for a bit.

***

It was an important day — solidly booked — so Doctor Nason made rounds early — 5:30 a.m. Victoria Outing was awake and alert. "I didn't realize you rose this time of the morning," he told her.

"Only a fool gets up this early," she said.

"Then I guess I'm a fool," Nason said. "Did you sleep well?"

"I did until you came stomping in here."

"Oh, come now, Victoria. As Mitchell Polovina is so fond of telling everyone, I'm part Indian — almost half. How noisy could I walk?"

"I guess you're not that loud, Henry. I just don't sleep well in a hospital bed," Victoria Outing complained. "I'll be much better off once I get back to my home."

Nase held two fingers to her wrist and checked her pulse. He didn't have the heart to tell her it was unlikely she'd be going home. Along with the heart attack, something that probably should not have been survived by someone her age, she suffered a mild stroke, which will limit her motor skills long into the future. And a hairline crack in her hip showed up in x-rays, probably from a recent fall, maybe even hitting the bed with this episode. It wouldn't take much at her age. "You seem to be getting along just fine," he said.

"Then, when can I go home?"

"Oh, don't be in too big a hurry, Victoria," was all he would say.

"Will Mitchell Polovina be in to see me today?"

"I can't say for sure. We pulled the remainder of those drums out of your Arthur Shaw's warehouse. We'll be opening them this morning. I imagine it will depend on what we find."

Victoria Outing shut her eyes and shook her head slightly.

"Something wrong?" Doc Nason asked.

"No. Nothing.

***

"Michael?"

"Mother? Is that you?" Michael Decker asked.

Victoria started her phone calls the moment she heard Doctor Nason giving instruction to the nurse at a station down the hall from her room. She tried Homer Jenkins at the mine first, and when she got no answer, chose to call her son. "I need you to run an errand for me," she said.

"What time is it, Mother?"

"Don't concern yourself with that. You just get up, drive over to Farwell, and find Homer Jenkins for me. He'll be at the mine, or at his daughter's home, or at his place. Look in a phone book. His address will still be listed. His wife has been gone only six months. The daughter is married to Ted Mayfield, our mayor. You find Homer and get him over here as quick as you can. Understand?"

"Get him where?" He hadn't been informed about her heart attack yet.

"To the hospital, the intensive care unit."

Michael Decker sat bolt upright in his bed. "The hospital," he said excitedly. "What's happened?"

"I've had a heart attack, just mild, but you know how those doctors are. They smell a buck, and suddenly everything is life or death. Just you get Homer Jenkins for me," she said again and hung up before she had more explaining to do — more questions to answer.

***

Seven a.m. and everyone was on the job: Chief Mitch Polovina, Mayor Ted Mayfield, Doctor Henry Nason, Officer Juliette Moore, and Officer Royal Parker who had spent the night. Everyone was anxious to see what goodies lay sealed inside the drums that had been retrieved from the bottom of the mine — excitedly fearful that is. One after the other they were opened and inspected. More than fifty were found to be exactly what they were said to be, full of lubricant of one kind or another. Drum number fifty two was not. But it also was not a body like Chief Polovina thought it might be. Inside the outer drum was a wooden keg — contraband whisky, imported, according to black printing on its exterior, from Canada. Several more of the same were located. A number of drums contained moonshine in clear gallon jugs, old newspaper packed around them to prevent breakage in shipment. Then came one that contained what they all assumed they would find — another body, this one different from those found earlier. It was a woman, mid thirties Mitch Polovina guessed and Doc Nason agreed to, but unlike the others they had found, this girl was not dressed in roaring twenties party attire. She was dressed in common street wear.

"Man, this just keeps getting better and better," Mayor Mayfield said. He wondered if she was the secret his father-in-law hid. "What do you make of it, Mitch?"

"Don't know," Mitch said and studied her for a moment longer. "But I intend to find out. Parker, call for a van. Get her to the morgue. Then you take the day and get some rest. I imagine you were up most of the night. Juliette, you and I will talk to old Miss Outing."

"What about me?" Doc Nason asked.

"Get to work, Gray Eagle. Tell me who she is," he said and pointed at the latest victim.

He considered Mayor Mayfield for an instant, and then said,

"Teddy, do you suppose you're going to get Homer's secret out of him, or do you want me to get involved. I feel whatever he doesn't want to tell us has a great deal to do with this case, don't you?"

"I do. But let me take another shot at him first."

"Okay, but you fail, and you bring him around this afternoon. Let's get to the bottom of this mess."

***

"You helped!"

My daddy was Chief of Police and he made me do it."

"It won't matter, Homer. All Mitch Polovina will see is that you helped undress two girls and dumped their bodies in the lake, and that'll make you as guilty as anyone," Victoria Outing told Homer Jennings in her hospital room.

"He's not even looking into that," Homer said.

"Polovina is no dummy, Homer. He'll connect the dots, and soon, he'll figure out that those two girls are an extension of the rest of this."

"What am I supposed to do, Victoria?" Homer was asking as he heard Mitch's and Juliette's footsteps coming down the hallway. Victoria shot him a look that silenced him. Homer looked down and brushed by the two officers as they entered the room.

"He seemed in an awful hurry," Mitch said. He gave Juliette a glance and nodded his head, almost unnoticeably, in Homer Jenkins' direction, his sign that she should catch up with him and learn whatever she could from him.

"I don't think he likes you," Victoria said and smiled.

"I didn't know you knew him, I mean, not so well that he would visit you here." Mitch knew from his past few days with her, and a few well asked and well placed questions of the staff at her home, that she received few visitors. Mitch and Henry had visited; Michael Decker did so quite often, Mrs. Cherry had paid her brief visit only days before she passed away, but no Homer Jenkins. "Did you teach him too?"

"Oh, heavens no. He's too old for me to have taught him. I taught only fourth grade, and I didn't teach at all until I was in my mid-thirties. Mitch's mind was too caught up in the newest addition to the case, the girl they found in a drum earlier in the day, to do the math and find out if everything added up all right, Homer's age, the age of a fourth grader, Victoria's age — information that would tell him if she had just lied to him. "Are you here to listen to more of the Arthur Shaw story?"

"Do you feel up to it?"

"I do. Will Henry be joining us?"

"Not today. He's tied up on something else, some medical business. He may drop in on you later, I'm told. He is in the hospital someplace," Chief Polovina explained. He thought a little extra detail might keep her from asking questions.

It did not. "Is he in the morgue?"

"I believe he is."

"Then you found more bodies."

"One."

"A girl?"

"Yes."

"Nancy Bjorquist."

"How would you know that, Victoria?" Mitch asked. Juliette entered from her short and not very informative visit with Homer Jenkins. Mitch looked at her and she raised her hands, palms up, in a sign of defeat. She mouthed, "Sorry."

"She went missing. No one ever heard from her again. And no one ever came up with her body. Will you take me to the morgue? I'd like to be sure. She was my friend."

Polovina went to the nurses' station and asked to be connected to the morgue. When Doc Nason answered he asked his opinion of bringing Victoria Outing down there for a look at the body they had found, explaining that the old woman thought she might identify her for them.

"Absolutely not. She can't be moved, not today anyway," Nase answered.

"How about a picture? Could she hold up to looking at a photograph of the body?" A long silence followed. "Nase?"

"Yes, yes. I'm thinking."

"Well… think fast."

"I tell you what. I'll arrange to have a photo printed and bring it up to her room. She can take a look, but only after I check her over thoroughly and find her fit enough for the stress it'll most likely cause her. Now, that's the best I can do. I don't want to get up there and have you snatch the picture from me and show it to her. Is that clear?"

"Clear," the chief agreed. He wouldn't have to be told. He

wouldn't put the old gal in harm's way right now. There was far too much he needed to learn from her. He hung up and went back to Victoria's room.

"Doc says he'll check you out and, provided you won't croak on us, he'll let you identify your friend from a photo." Juliette gave him a strange look, as did Victoria. Perhaps the term (croak) might have been too strong under the circumstances. "Maybe we should wait until after he clears you to continue," he offered.

"Nonsense, dear boy. I can still tell you a story. What could that possibly hurt? And I promise you, Mitchell Polovina, I won't croak on you. Now… who is the pretty young assistant you have with you today?"

"I'm sorry. Victoria Outing, this is Juliette Moore. Miss Moore, this is Miss Outing."

"Tell me, Miss Moore, are you from Farwell?"

"No, Ma'am. I moved here ten years ago."

"What do you think of our new police chief?" Victoria asked.

"I like him just fine," Juliette said and smiled. It was her downward look that gave her away.

"I should say you do," Victoria observed.

"Victoria, can we get on with the story?" Mitch asked.

"Of course," she said and began.

***

Three weeks had passed before Arthur Shaw got around to asking Victoria on an actual date. She thought, perhaps he had lost interest, found himself a prettier girl to court. He had, after all, missed several days' breakfast at Mick's. But she had been wrong. Arthur was only busy. And those days he hadn't shown up, she would later learn that he had been away. Saint Cloud was where his home office was. That was where his people lived and his superiors operated from. He would go from time to time over the summer months and late into the fall, and he would be gone for days at a time, once for more than a week. But when he finally did find the time for Victoria, it was a time she would never forget.

It was just past dark. Arthur had sought and received approval from Victoria's father to take her with him whenever he wished and for as long as he wished, on his word that the girl would always be protected and treated with total respect. Victoria thought the lax boundaries her father had set had something to do with her ailing mother's condition. They did not. They had to do with Arthur Shaw's position in the community, his influence, his connections among the business and legal community who could rain down disparity on Victoria's father's head at will. The poor man, dying wife not even a consideration, had been intimidated and threatened into submission to Arthur Shaw's will, and that was all there was to it. Sure, Arthur agreed to certain conditions. He was not, after all, an animal, nor were his people. But those conditions, just the same, were something he intended not to keep anyway. So their first date began just past dark, and just after a nod of approval from a father with a worried look on his leathered face.

"I'll be fine, Father," Victoria said and pulled her mother's shawl over her shoulders as she had promised she would do.

"I will take good care of her, Mr. Outing. You have my word." And this time he would be telling the truth, his plan for conquest of this sweet young thing, one of a slower pace.

***

Doctor Nason's entrance into Victoria's hospital room broke the momentum she had been gaining on her story. He handed a print of the latest victim in a barrel to Mitch Polovina?

"What's that you have there?" Victoria asked.

"We were hoping you could tell us," Polovina said.

"But not before I check you over," Doc Nason said. He shot Mitch and Juliette a glance, then without looking at them, "You two can wait in the hallway if you want."

"It's getting on toward lunch. We'll stop later in the afternoon," Mitch said. He folded the picture and stuck it in a pocket. "Call me, Nase. Let me know what time will work."

CHAPTER SIXTEEN

Ted Mayfield finally caught up with his father-in-law — alone — at the old man's home — no Karla around to interfere. "I know I told you I didn't want to hear your story about those bodies the police are finding, but I think I'd better change my mind. I doubt that I can protect you, not much anyway. Mitch Polovina is going to find out the truth one way or another. It appears that he's been underestimated. Who would think a green cop could get this far? But it occurred to me, Pop; I can't even try to help you without knowing what'll be coming at me. So... start at the beginning and tell me everything.

Chief of Police Mitchell Polovina and his assistant, Juliette Moore, stood listening to Teddy Mayfield's one-sided conversation with Homer Jenkins. "Yeah, Homer," Mitch threw in as he pulled the screen door open and entered, "start at the beginning as Ted suggested. We'd all be interested." It was only moments, Homer refusing to talk to anyone, and Mitch Polovina had him in cuffs and in the back seat of the police cruiser. "Sorry, Teddy. But this is an official investigation, and with Homer calming up on me, it makes him the number one suspect, don't you agree?"

"No. I do not agree."

"Then it's a damn good thing you're not Chief of Police."

"But I am Mayor," Mayfield said, "and I could have your badge for this."

"Don't lock horns with me, Teddy. You can't fire me for doing my job here. You do, and well..."

"Well... what, Mitch. You plan to arrest me too?"

"Interfere with this investigation, and I'll do just that, Mister Mayor. Then I'll go see Orin Hobbs and get whatever paperwork I need to keep you in jail until this is over." Orin Hobbs played football with Mitch, Henry Nason, and Mayfield in school, and now served the community as Judge Orin Hobbs. In high school, Orin had been good friends with Mitch and not so good with Ted. Things hadn't changed much since those days. The threat was valid. And Teddy Mayfield backed down.

Juliette Moore was impressed with her boss' exacting use of authority over even the mayor almost as much as she had been impressed with his skills as a lover. Two questions popped into her mind: why hadn't he been police chief all along, and why had three wives dumped him? She smiled at him approvingly. Then she walked to the squad car to look after their prisoner in case the chief had more to say to the mayor — perhaps something he needed to say privately.

"She looks almost as good in the tight trousers as she did in the skirt," Mayfield, who had been watching her walk away, commented.

"She certainly does," Mitch Polovina, who had been helping the mayor watch, agreed. "Look, Ted, he'll be treated with respect — kid gloves — you know what I mean. But it's better this way. I know that he hasn't told you anything. I heard that much before I came in on the two of you. And I came in to stop him from telling you anything, because if I know what I think I know about all of this, well... let's just say you're better off not knowing... career wise I mean," Polovina said and began to walk away. He stopped suddenly. He turned to face Mayfield. "You threaten to take my badge away again, and next time I'll give it to you."

"I apologize, Mitch. I had no right."

"Chief!" Juliette Moore shouted. "Come quick. Homer's stabbing himself." She pulled the back door of the squad car open and reached in to grab Homer's arms. Mitch Polovina made a mad dash for the car, Ted Mayfield right on his heels.

By the time they got to him, Homer had done a job on himself and was bleeding profusely from a stab wound to a thigh. Lucky his hands had been cuffed behind him limiting his movements or he might have slit his wrists. Still, Mitch blamed himself. Someone should have searched Homer, and that someone was him. A jackknife — in his pants pocket — *Jesus Christ.*

Juliette successfully relieved Homer of the knife without getting cut herself, but just by luck. She was applying pressure to the worst of the bleeders as Mitch and Ted got to her. "Radio for an ambulance," she told them.

"Pop, what the hell did you do that for?" Mayfield asked his father-in-law.

"Those who'll come for me won't be this nice," was all he would answer.

As the ambulance pulled away, Mitch asked the mayor, "What did he mean those who'll come for him?"

"I haven't a clue."

***

Royal Parker waited in Chief Polovina's office for over an hour. When he heard the call for an ambulance to Homer Jenkins' address, he set out for the hospital. He knew he would be needed, if only to stand guard over Homer, although he did not know yet whether Homer needed guarding, or Homer needed protecting. With this whole fresh batch of shit coming down lately it was difficult to tell. Bodies floating in the lake, another in a barrel for Christ sakes, and there was Mrs. Cherry. Sweetest little old lady, good wife and mother, Christian woman who'd never done anything to anybody, poisoned like a trash eating dog. Just like that. No reason that Parker could tell, and no suspects. Maybe the chief or Juliette could see something he was overlooking, but he doubted it. A real mystery, that's what it was. And the town of Farwell hadn't had a mystery since the days it was commonly called Little Cicero. Parker was stumped.

Parker pulled up in front of the hospital, walked in, approached the receptionist, and flashed his badge at her. He loved flashing his badge. It was never necessary since it was a relatively small town and everyone knew him, but he didn't let that stop him. "Official business." He loved saying that too. "Where'd they take Homer Jenkins?"

"Emergency room. They're stitching up his wounds now. But the chief is already there," the nurse yelled after him. She doubted he even heard the last part — about the chief being there. He was too far down the hallway by the time she got it out. She shook her head and went back to what she had been doing, filing her nails and reading *Calumet* by Schwartz. Pressing work.

"Learn anything about the Mrs. Cherry case?" Polovina asked Parker as soon as he stepped up beside him.

"Nothing worth knowing," Parker said.

"Well... suppose you tell me what you learned and we'll decide if it's worth knowing."

"All I found out was it wasn't any of the family. Nobody had motive or opportunity, and everyone had an iron clad alibi. Like I said, nothing worth knowing."

"Depends on who you are."

"How's that, Chief?" Parker asked, thinking he was missing something.

"I'm sure to the family of Edith Cherry it's worth us knowing that."

The two officers stepped to one side to let an orderly wheel Homer Jenkins' gurney past them. "Follow," Mitch told Parker. "Set up outside his door."

"He under arrest? Or are we protecting him?"

"Both." Chief Polovina began to leave, then, "Parker. Cuff him to the bed."

***

Arnold Cherry, the eldest son of Edith Cherry, awaited Mitch Polovina's return to his office. He had been sitting, sipping the same cup of coffee for more than an hour, listening to the receptionist/ dispatcher as she tried to raise anyone from the department without success, and getting more and more annoyed as that hour passed until he was fit to be tied. The cold coffee spilling on his clean shirt was all he could stand. He jumped to his feet, yelled at the poor dispatcher — words that implied if she was anything at all it was inept at her job, Chief Polovina's entrance catching him in the process. "What's this, then?" Polovina asked.

"What the hell kind of police department is this — no cops in the place, a dispatcher who can't find any?"

"A small one, I reckon. What can I do for you, Mr. Cherry?"

"You are aware your Officer Parker has been harassing my father," Cherry stated.

"I'm aware he has been investigating your mother's death," Polovina said.

"Murder," Cherry corrected.

"That hasn't been fully established."

"She's been poisoned, hasn't she?" Arnold Cherry said.

"She has… according to the coroner."

"Well… don't that kinda tell you it's murder?"

"Not at all. Plenty of folks are accidentally poisoned every year, although it's a little uncommon in a small town like Little Cicero," the chief insisted.

"Farwell," the receptionist corrected. "It's the town of Farwell, not Little Cicero."

"I know. I know. It just seemed to fit, what with all the bodies we're finding these days. Look, Mr. Cherry, we're going to keep looking into your mother's case until we get to the bottom of things. I promise you that. But you need to keep something in mind and keep a cool head about it. If we find that the poisoning wasn't accidental, the law of averages says the culprit is someone close to her, generally a family member, usually it's the husband. Officer Parker is barking up the right tree if it's murder. So… that having been said, how were your folks getting along lately? Any fights?"

Arnold Cherry shook his head and stormed out of the police chief's office.

"That's it. That's keeping a cool head, Mr. Cherry," Mitch yelled after him. Then he looked at Paula Bloom, the secretary filling in as dispatcher. "Any response to the ads?" he asked.

"None."

"Nobody in this town wants to be a cop, or a dispatcher?" Polovina asked.

"I wanted to talk with you about that, Chief," Paula Bloom said.

"What? You interested in becoming a cop, Paula?"

"Well… dispatcher. I wouldn't mind having the job on a more permanent basis. And I think it'll be a whole lot easier to hire a secretary. Lots of girls around town who'll snap up that position."

Paula was right; Polovina knew it. Just the title, dispatcher, could frighten most away because they'd have a tendency to think it was a job needing qualifications, maybe even experience. "Change the ad. You're the new dispatcher, Paula," Mitch said. "Now, any ideas on where we'll find some cops?"

"Willy Hobbs mentioned wanting his job back," Paula told him. Hobbs, Judge Orin Hobbs' nephew, had been a hard-ass when Mitch took over, declaring he'd sooner mop floors than work under an inexperienced chief who had the job because of connections rather than qualifications, and who was likely to get everyone in the department killed because of it. Mitchell Polovina's first reaction was to let him mop floors. But after a moment of thought, "Have him give me a call. Anyone else?"

"I called the county sheriff. It seems they had a layoff a while back. Might be a couple out of work deputies looking for something," Paula reported.

"Call him back."

"Her," Paula corrected.

"Her?"

"Her. The sheriff is a her. Marion Kuhn."

"Well… call *her* then," Mitch ordered and rose. "I'm going home. Lock up when you leave. Send a meal over to Royal Parker. Tell him his relief will come at midnight."

***

The '67 Buick Gran Sport belonging to Victoria Outing's son pulled away from the curb in front of the police station as Mitch Polovina and Juliette Moore were getting into Mitch's personal vehicle, a nondescript Japanese midsized. "Now how do you suppose an old coot like him gets his hands on a car like that?" Juliette asked.

"A better question might be… why?" Mitch suggested, thinking about how that car had been a prize in his day: Buick's GS, Olds' 442, Pontiac's GTO, Chrysler Corporation's Super Bee and Road Runner, not the car of a man in his eighties. When one collects a classic, generally he'll go for a vintage of his early years of driving or of his birth year. Almost always. "It don't fit him. That is unless he's much younger than he looks."

"He is what his driver's license says, and you ran that," Juliette said.

"I did. And it agreed. Only thing is, there was nothing on him. Strange."

"Maybe he's never had a ticket, never been in trouble."

"He was speeding when we pulled him over," Mitch said. "You know anything about running a background check?"

"A little. I could give it a shot. Why? What are you thinking?" Juliette asked.

"I'm not sure, but something isn't adding up. Not quite. You start that check in the morning while I get with Victoria. I bet something shows up."

"I'll get right on it, Chief. Now… what about dinner? You got plans?"

"Let's meet up at my place," Polovina suggested as he pulled to the curb in front of her house. "Wear your uniform, the skit uniform," he said. She got out and began to shut the door. "Juliette," he said while she could still hear him. "Bring your gun and handcuffs."

***

"No, Karla," Mitch Polovina told Homer Jenkins' daughter at the hospital when he came at midnight to relieve Royal Parker from guard duty on Homer's room. "We can't take the cuffs off. Try to understand. You're dad tried to kill himself. You don't want that now, do you?" Karla Mayfield made no effort to argue with the police chief. "Well, then, are you staying through the night?"

"I am. And don't think you'll be stopping me either."

"Then we won't stay. I doubt he's in danger other than from himself, so… with you here, we're not needed anymore tonight. Royal, you can go home. Get some sleep. Show up here in the morning."

"Boss," Parker said. "I'd rather stay here and sleep in a chair in case I'm needed."

"Suit yourself," Polovina said and left. On his way to the car, he called Juliette on his cell phone. "Tired?"

"No."

"Still got the handcuffs?"

"Left them at your place."

"Still got the skirt?"

"Left *it* at your place."

"I'd say you best get to my place then," he told her and hung up.

***

The aroma of fresh popcorn filled Mitchell Polovina's nostrils when he opened his front door; the annoying bark of Victoria's little mutt trying her best to chase off an intruder filled his ears. He had forgotten all about her. He had forgotten about the key beneath the flower pot on the steps that Juliette used to let herself in. Had he married again? That's what this felt like. But the hour was late — well past midnight, it had been a demanding day, and his reasoning seemed a bit off because of all of it. He had to admit though, if only to himself — little woman in the kitchen, little dog, its ferocious bark turning itself into a wiggle of excitement that seemed to almost turn her inside out — the whole scene held a certain comfort after a harsh day. "She's made messes for you," Juliette said and kissed him on the cheek.

"Did she shit all over the living room?"

"Nothing like that. I took her out first thing when I got here. It seems she's well trained. No poop — no wet spots in the carpet."

"What, then?" Mitch asked, and the little dog jumped into his arms.

"I seems… she's a bit of a shredder. Want your paper?" Juliette asked and smiled.

Sister Mary Elizabeth licked him on the end of his nose. It tickled. It made him grin. He patted her head and sat her back on the floor. "What'll we do with you?" he asked her.

"We?" Juliette asked.

"Nason doesn't think Victoria will be going back home. I have no intention of keeping her little critter by myself."

"What about Michael Decker? Won't he want Sis?" Juliette asked.

"I don't think Michael Decker is Victoria Outing's son."

"Is that what you think I'll uncover in a background check on him?"

"I don't think you'll find anything. I suspect you'll find no Michael Decker, other than on a tombstone of course."

CHAPTER SEVENTEEN

Henry Nason made an appearance in Victoria Outing's hospital room at just past six a.m. The old woman had been awake for sometime but pretended otherwise. "I saw your eyes open when I entered, Victoria. The light from the hall, it reflects in them."

"So it does, Henry. So it does."

"So why close them when I come in?"

"To make you think me still asleep, of course."

"Not up to company yet?"

"Not up to being prodded and poked yet."

"No prodding — no poking," Doc Nason promised, and sat on the edge of her bed.

"Then what do you want with me so early, Gray Eagle?" Victoria Outing asked.

"Gray Eagle... why... I do believe you may be spending too much time with Bugsy Polovina," Nason said and squeezed her wrist, looking to take her pulse.

"That's prodding," she said.

He let go. The machine would tell him what he needed to know anyway. He only took patients pulses the old-fashioned way to give them a doctor/patient sense of personal care. Apparently she did not desire such things today. "How are we feeling this morning, Victoria?"

"I have no idea of how you feel, Henry, but as for me, just peachy." She pushed a button on a hand held remote and her bed raised her to a sitting position. "Will Mitchell be coming in to see me today?"

"I'm sure he will."

"Will you be joining him?"

"Yes."

"Will you show me the picture?" she asked.

"The picture?" Doc Nason was puzzled. He had forgotten about the photo of the latest corpse they had pulled from the lake.

"Yes. The picture of Nancy Bjorquist."

"Now how would you know who it is?"

"I told Mitchell and that floozy yesterday."

"Floozy?"

"Yes. That floozy, the girl in the police uniform who was here with him yesterday when you should have been. The girl who was hanging all over him like grease on bacon."

"Hanging?"

"With her eyes she was. Anyway, I told them about Nancy Bjorquist and how she disappeared one night and was never seen again. Everyone thought her dead at the time. It's her you found. I'll bet on it," she said and began a stare down with Doctor Nason.

"What?" he finally asked.

"Do I get to see the picture or not."

She was far too demanding this morning for anyone, even a physician, to think her weak. "Mitchell Polovina has it. I'll tell him it's fine to show it to you."

"Good," she said and lowered her bed. "Now, go away and let an old woman sleep."

***

Down the hall, an argument between Karla Mayfield and her father, Homer Jenkins, brought Royal Parker out of a sound sleep, yet his eyes did not open. He listened. He learned. "No one is coming for you, Dad," Karla had been telling Homer.

"You don't know them, those Jews from St. Cloud. They'll come. The originals, the brothers, they're probably too old or too dead by now, but you don't know how it is."

"So tell me."

"They're Jews. They're family like mafia. That's how it is. What's happened won't be forgotten until they make it right. Count on it." Homer looked over at Parker. He saw his hairline raise a touch at the mention of Jews from St. Cloud. He was awake. "No more talk. Not here," he said and motioned toward Parker.

"No more trying to kill yourself," Karla told him.

"It won't matter," Homer said and rolled onto his side, his eyes fixed on Royal Parker. "Does he have to be in the room? Can't he sit in a chair outside the door and read a book like they do on television?" He picked up a glass of ice water from the stand beside his hospital bed and hurled it at Parker. Lucky for plastic, Parker would not be injured, only moistened. But soon, he would be in a chair in the hall, reading a book.

***

"She needs toys," Juliette Moore told Mitch the following morning. Victoria Outing's little dog looked on curiously as he took everything paper and moved it out of her reach. "She'll find something to chew, maybe your shoe."

"Get her some." Mitch said and pulled his boots on. "I'm going directly to the hospital. Let me know if you find anything on Michael Decker." He patted the dog on the head, kissed Juliette on the lips, and headed out the door.

In his car, he called Henry Nason. "Gray Eagle," he said when Henry answered.

"Bugsy?"

"Yeah. How's our girl this morning?"

"Belligerent, but healthy enough to talk," Nason said.

"Will she be able to return to her home? Or is this it for her?" Polovina asked.

"I'm afraid living on her own is no longer an option. This is her fourth such incident and she needs to be where there's a full time medical staff available. This time it has left her unable to do too many essential things without assistance."

"What kind of things?"

"Make it to the bathroom for one."

"Damn. What a pity," Polovina said. He hadn't liked her much when he was young and she was Sister Mary Elizabeth leaving thin red lines on the back of his hands with a steel edged ruler, but now, in this later day, the lady calling herself Victoria Outing, he had grown fond of, almost close to. "No chance of you being wrong, is there?"

"Some. Not much."

"Can I spend some time with her today?" Chief Polovina asked Doc Nason.

"You can show her the picture if you want to. But I'd like to be in the room, just in case it turns out to be too much for her. Where are you now?"

"I'm in the car, just blocks away from you."
"We'll meet in her room."

***

"That's her. That's Nancy Bjorquist," Victoria said, the photocopied likeness of the stiff from yesterday's barrel shaking in her hand. Mitch reached to take the paper. Victoria gripped it tighter and pulled it close to her chest. "I'd like to keep it, Mitchell, if it's all right with you."

Polovina looked at Doc Nason who nodded his consent, and he let go. "I don't see why not, Victoria. Would you like us to leave you alone for a while?"

"How would I tell you more of my story if you did that?" she asked.

Mitch smiled and asked, "Where would you like to begin, Victoria?" He pulled a chair from the wall of the room, slid it to the edge of her bed, and sat down. Doc Nason did the same.

A nurse came in and asked if Nason was going to make rounds and was told to let the interns do it this morning and to have them call if there was anything that might need his *immediate* attention. Then she was told to shut the door on her way out.

"I would think… that the most reasonable place for us to begin would be exactly where we left off." And she took up the story from the evening Arthur Shaw came to her home and collected her for a night out in the speakeasy at the other end of the tunnel, which began beneath the little café in which she had served him his morning breakfast. As was her way, she told it as though it happened to a stranger, not her.

***

Young Victoria felt all grown up. Her brothers had, that evening before Mr. Shaw came for her, rolled cigars from newspaper and had nearly set fire to the piano, a transgression for which they had received a stern whipping with the sharp edge of a piece of pine kindling wood. Their pitiful cries for mercy had barely subsided before Mr. Shaw's arrival. But now that memory faded from her mind as she listened to a vehicle pass over the top of them on the street above, string lights bobbing and swaying from tires passing over rumble strip like flaws in the un-graded earth. Arthur Shaw yanked his derby from his head and held it over Victoria to shelter her from particles falling from the concrete ceiling. "I told them to grade the street. They're supposed to do it every Friday afternoon, so such as this doesn't ruin pretty dresses. Forgive me, my dear. It is my fault."

"It is nothing, Mr. Shaw," Victoria said and brushed away a tiny spot of soil. "You see? Just like new."

"Please call me Arthur. This is a date, Victoria. We should be on a first name basis."

"Where does that go, Arthur?" Victoria asked as they passed a corridor centered under the street and heading to the right. She had not seen it when he took her down here the other day to show her the speakeasy. Perhaps it had not been lit up like it was now. Perhaps it did not exist then.

"There are six more establishments down here. I told you, I'm a rich and important man, Victoria. I supply to all of them."

"Are they all as lavish as the one you showed me?" she asked.

"Heavens no. Some — most — are absolute dives, and full of misfits — dregs dredged from the very bottom of society."

"Oh, my!"

"Yes."

She stood still and looked up the corridor. At the far end a body appeared to be lying in the dirt. "Will you show them to me sometime?"

"They're not a pretty sight," Arthur Shaw warned.

"I don't care. I want to see anyway," Victoria insisted.

"Very well. I will one day show them to you."

"Not one... day. At night. I want to see them in action."

He looked at her curiously. She was a pistol for a girl so young, not afraid of anything, an explorer's disposition. "So... you will see them in action if you so choose."

"I so choose."

"Shall we continue," he asked gesturing toward the saloon at the end of the tunnel. And they continued.

Their entry to the speakeasy held disappointment for Victoria Outing. When Arthur had first shown it to her, the place was empty, it was spotless, it was quiet, and she could see the lavish carvings in the wood of its fine furniture and fixtures. Tonight she saw none of those things through the heavy smoke filled air inside. And the noise of the crowd's chatter and laughter, boisterous and shrill, drowned out the excitement she felt on her way through the tunnel to get there. But still, her curiosity led her. She overcame the disappointment. She adapted.

"There's an empty table over there," Shaw told her and pointed to a table she could not see. "Come. I'll get you settled in and then I'll get us something to drink," he said as he led her across the crowded room. He pulled out a chair for her and someone objected, noting that he had been sitting at the table. But when Arthur Shaw turned to look into the intruder's eyes, the stranger apologized and went away. Victoria was indeed impressed with his authority over the man and the degree of respect shown him by others. "What will you drink?" he asked her.

"Why… I don't know," she said. "What do they have?"

"They have moonshine that will blind a horse. I don't suppose that will suit a young girl like you. They have a whisky that comes all the way from Canada — smooth if you're accustomed to it, but for you, it'll probably take your breath away. And they may have a sarsaparilla of sorts, sweet and not harsh."

"I'll have the whisky all the way from Canada," she said. Why not? She was here; she might just as well try it.

A fiddler, a man with a guitar, another with a banjo, and a fat lady at the piano played ragtime as patrons danced delightfully. Victoria, although she had never learned how, wanted to dance with Arthur Shaw when he got back with their drinks. "Will you teach me that?" she asked and pointed at the dancers.

"I don't know what kind of teacher I will be. I scarcely know how myself."

"You don't dance much?" she asked.

"I don't date much. That leaves me with no one to dance with."

"Then I will teach you," she said as she stood and took his hand.

"But I thought you didn't know how," Shaw said.

"Then we shall teach each other," she insisted. She did have the heart of an explorer, the spirit of a pioneer. Arthur Shaw admired that in her. He was fascinated by it.

He followed her to the dance floor and they danced until they learned how, her watching those around them, him executing moves he already knew, but clumsily. And as the evening progressed, they danced, they talked, they sipped at their Canadian whisky, and they enjoyed each other and both vowed silently that they would do this again and again. Victoria was a natural at holding her whisky, odd, but welcomed. She would have to guide him, not him guide her, at the end of the evening back through the café and onto the street where the fresh cool evening air would sober him. "When will you show me the rest of the places?" she asked.

"We'll start next time. We'll visit one briefly, and then we'll go to where we just came from," he promised.

"When will next time be?" she asked.

"Next Saturday night, and every Saturday night after that until you get tired of me," Shaw told her.

"I shall never tire of you, Arthur," she told him on her doorstep and kissed him on the cheek. Then she disappeared into her house.

***

An orderly rolled a cart into Victoria Outing's hospital room. Lunch time had come.

"We'll let you eat, Victoria," Mitch Polovina told her.

"Will you return?" she asked.

"In the morning. I have some police work to attend to this afternoon, but I'll be back in the morning."

"Mitchell, would you look in on my little dog for me?" Victoria asked wondering if anyone at all was checking on Sister Mary Elizabeth.

"I have her at my house. She's fine. Juliette Moore helps me take care of her," Mitch told her.

The floozy, Victoria thought. Did she want Sister Mary Elizabeth in the hands of a floozy? What would the effect on her be? *Oh well, really no other choice.* "That's nice of her," she said and smiled.

CHAPTER EIGHTEEN

"You were right," Juliette Moore told Chief Polovina when he walked into the office.

"I generally am. But what am I right about?"

"Michael Decker," she said and slapped him on a shoulder for the smart remark. "The man doesn't exist."

"Except on the registration of the car," Mitch said. He had seen the man's license and the car's registration when he stopped him a few days earlier, and unless he was going senile, he was pretty sure the name on both documents was Michael Decker.

"Maybe, but not according to the Department of Motor Vehicles. Even though the car is registered to him, they have no information on a license issued to him."

"How can that be?" Polovina asked. "I always have to show them a valid driver's license to get plates for mine. And they know who I am."

"I just report 'em, I don't explain 'em," Juliette said

Mitch Polovina sighed and looked down in confusion. Then he looked at Juliette Moore. Then he looked down again, turned, and headed to his office.

"What do you want me to do?" Juliette asked after him.

"I need to think," he said and made a few more steps in the direction of his office.

"Willy Hobbs is in there, Chief," Paula Bloom called out. Hobbs was the ex-officer who walked out when Mitch took over, claiming that he would never work for him as he was untrained, inexperienced, and therefore dangerous. Now he wanted his job back, those things — apparently — no longer an issue with him.

Polovina looked at her questioningly and poured himself a cup of coffee.

"You told me to have him see you," she defended herself

against his look.

"I remember," he said and entered the room.

Willy Hobbs stood to face him. "Got your hands full, do you?"

"Not so full that I need you," Mitch said.

"I didn't mean to imply, Chief, I'm just trying to start a conversation."

"It'll be a short one, Hobbs. I'll put you back on. If you cross me," he said as he got up and closed the door, "I'll shoot you. That only leaves you with two choices. Want the job or not?"

"Yes, Sir," Hobbs said.

"Suit up," Mitch said. "I want you over at the hospital in less than an hour. Send Parker back here. And Willy, don't lose Homer Jenkins." When Hobbs opened the door, Polovina added, "Hobbs, welcome back."

Juliette Moore leaned against the doorjamb of Polovina's office and sipped a cup of coffee. She smiled. "What about Decker? Want me to bring him in?"

"Not just yet. Let's have Parker tail him, see where he leads us. And if he's able, get some prints. We'll run them through whatever data base we have available. Let's see if we can identify him first. Maybe we'll get lucky and his prints will tell us something that will allow us to hold him."

"That's real police thinking, Chief. I'm impressed," Juliette said. "Where did you learn that?"

"Television," he said and smiled. "Wanna get some lunch?"

"I brought something with," she said.

"Something from my place?" He was surprised. He didn't think there was anything to make a lunch from at his place.

"Yes."

Paula Bloom looked over the top of her glasses at the chief.

"That's right. We're an item, might as well know it, Paula. There's no law against it that I know of," Polovina said.

"No law. That's true enough. But it is against policy."

"Well… then the policy needs to be changed," Mitch said.

"I'm not sure how to do that," Paula Bloom said.

"Look, Paula, you get right on that and find out how. I'm doin' her, and I'm going to continue doin' her, so you get that changed. That clear?"

"Yes, Sir," Bloom said and began looking for the city attorney's phone number.

***

Royal Parker was a clever sort. He followed the classic Buick driven by Michael Decker until it stopped in front of Mick's Café. He waited until Decker was inside, then he pulled a tire iron out of the trunk of his squad car and smashed a taillight lens with it. He knew classic car drivers. He knew that the moment one of them discovered damage of any sort the car would be driven to the first shop to repair that damage. And Decker would not be the exception. Parker met him on the walk outside the café and pointed out the broken lens, and Decker drove the car directly to Paul Drummond's garage, less than a block up the street.

"You've got an hour," Drummond told Parker. And Parker took out a crime scene kit and began lifting prints. He also tested for unusual chemicals in the car, and searched through its trunk. No chemicals showed in his tests, but the search provided him with a container of rat poison — arsenic based.

He called Chief Polovina. "Should I take him in?"

"Not yet," Polovina said. "He's not going anywhere until he's figured we're on to him. Bring in the poison so Doc can try to match it to what he found in Mrs. Cherry's blood, and bring the fingerprints. Let's find out who the hell this guy really is. Maybe *then* we'll haul him in."

***

Henry Nason had no idea of how to match one compound with another. "I'm not a chemist, I'm an MD. Tell Bugsy Polovina that," he told Royal Parker.

"Bugsy?" Parker quizzed.

"Bugsy. That's his name you know. I suppose you thought it was Chief."

"No. I just didn't know it was Bugsy. Say, wasn't he a football hero?" Parker was much younger than Polovina, but Mitch's reputable senior year yielded records that were never broken, and his name remained on the tips of tongues of local fans for decades. "That's who that old guy is?"

"Old guy? Be cautious. I played on that same team, and so did the mayor and Judge Hobbs." They were the class of '68 and proud of it. And they were not as ancient as a youngster like Royal Parker would have them be. Any one of them could tear Parker and most of his kind apart limb from limb if they so chose. The more Doc Nason thought the more red his face turned and the closer he came to showing the youngster what old guys could do to him. "Bugsy Polovina wasn't so old he couldn't snatch that enticing piece of ass right out from your grasp now, was he?" he said referring, of course, to the lovely and shapely, and from what he gathered, limber and amorous Miss Moore, the short skirted and tight pantsed police officer hottie Parker tried and failed at since the day he first saw her. Everyone knew.

Parker's face now turned red, and he left the room... quickly.

"Jesus Christ," Doc Nason said. "How the hell does Mitch put up with that moron?" He shook his head in disgust, and then phoned an associate to find out how to go about proving or disproving a match between the two poison samples.

"You can't," the associate said. "But the state police lab can. Package it up and courier it to them. Save some just in case it gets lost."

"How long will that take?"

"About a week, sooner if they're not too backed up down there. Just a caution for you Nase. Don't try to rush them or it'll take two weeks," the associate warned and hung up.

Nason called Mitch Polovina on his cellular and apprised him of the situation. "Hold up for a bit on sending that out. Juliette and I are in front of Victoria's place right now. We're going to take a look around. If I find rat poison in her apartment, I'll want to include another sample. I'll let you know shortly," Mitch told him.

***

The obstinate attendant at the front desk of Victoria Outing's retirement home nearly ended up in handcuffs. She was unwavering about policy concerning who could and who could not enter the private quarters of the home's guests. And strangers, badges or no badges were not on the list. "I'm sorry. I simply cannot allow you entry without the consent of Ms. Outing or without a warrant."

"I'll tell you what I'm going to do, miss, ah..."

"Missus... Thomas," she offered.

"Mrs. Thomas. I'm going to get that warrant. And when I find something in that apartment, I'm going to arrest you for interfering with a criminal investigation. How's that?"

Mrs. Thomas turned a shade of white — fear. Mitch knew that. Anger would be red. She would soon offer to let them in. He knew that as well. But Juliette stood on her tiptoes and whispered in his ear. She told Mitch that any evidence they found might not be of value without a warrant that allowed them entry. He telephoned his old friend, Judge Orin Hobbs, and requested a warrant. He had Parker pick it up and deliver it to him. While he waited he checked in with Doc Nason. The day was growing late and the week was at an end. He made sure Henry had sufficient backup samples of the poison found in Michael Decker's trunk, and then told him to ship his off. He would send another next week if need be. He did not want a delay on the first.

The inside of Victoria Outing's apartment was in shambles. Someone had beaten the police to it. Drawers had been emptied, cabinets stripped and food containers poured out on the floor, even cleansers and dish soap had been dumped. Cushions from sofa and chairs had been pulled from their covers and the bedding had been stripped, mattress and box spring overturned and sliced open. Someone thought something of value was to be found. But what? And who? "Christ," Mitch Polovina uttered.

"Exactly," Juliette Moore agreed. She sifted through the mess with a foot, uncovering a few small stuffed toys in the process, those too, sliced open and their cotton stuffing pulled from them. "Sister Mary Elizabeth's," she guessed.

"Probably," Mitch agreed. "If you didn't buy plenty for her, you might wanna add to them. From the look of this, she was accustomed to having plenty." Mitch felt more for Victoria's little dog at the moment than he did for Victoria. The poor animal had been booted from her home, probably set free by the culprit who did this, no more master and no more toys. "Look around to see what kind of food and treats she kept on hand."

Juliette pushed aside another pile of trash. She stooped and picked up something. She handed it to Mitch.

"Rat poison," he said. He placed the container on the counter and called Doc Nason. "Gray Eagle, how much powder will you need for a sample?"

"I'm not sure. Why?"

"We found the container, but some bastard made a mess of the place. Dumped everything," Mitch explained.

"What's the brand name?"

Polovina picked the container up and read the label. "Rat-B-Gone."

"Clever. Not the same as the one Parker brought me though," Doc Nason said.

"Good catch, Henry," Mitch said and hung up. He turned to Juliette. "Let's call it a day. Maybe Paula Bloom has found us those out of work deputies and we can put them on this." He studied the room a moment, then stepped into the hall and locked the door behind them. "See if there are duplicate keys at the desk. I want them all. I don't want anyone in here. And whoever we send, let's make sure they question anyone and everyone until they find out who got in the place and how. I'll tape it off while you see to the keys."

On his way to the squad car for crime scene tape, Mitch stopped at the main desk. "You have a rat problem?" he asked the attendant.

"Certainly not," she said indignantly.

Mitch Polovina placed his palms on the counter, leaned closer to the attendant, and peered questioningly over the top of his sunglasses.

"Mice," the attendant whispered. "Mice have gotten into a few of the units."

"Ms. Outing's?"

"Hers was one of them."

Mitch walked to his car for the tape. His cell phone rang. It was Willy Hobbs. He wanted to know how late he was to stay outside Homer Jenkins' hospital room. "How's Homer?" Mitch asked.

"Awake. Alert. He seems fine to me."

"Is Karla Mayfield there with him?"

"She is."

"Remove the cuffs and cut him loose," Chief Polovina said. "You see me in the morning and we'll get you on the schedule." He hung up.

"Why'd you do that?" Juliette asked. She handed him two keys she had acquired from the front desk.

"Homer's not part of this. He's guilty of something, and we'll eventually find out what that is, but he's not part of this."

"How do you know that?" Juliette asked.

"Gut feeling," he said and smiled.
"Learn that from television too?"
"I did."

CHAPTER NINETEEN

Gone to see Victoria outing… already took Sis out… see you at the office, the note pinned to Mitchell Polovina's pillow beside Juliette Moore read. She looked at the clock — six a.m. She sat up and swung her legs over the edge of the bed, Victoria's little dog still draped over her lap. She petted the dog and moved her to one side. Shower time, and without him. She'd put a stop to this and she knew just how to do it. Their next shower together would yield entertainment for him sufficient enough to make him never again consider showering alone — so long as he could have her in the water with him at any rate.

***

Mitch sat in a chair alongside Victoria Outing's hospital bed sipping a cup of coffee as Victoria awoke. His presence startled her. She jerked back and took a hard look at him. "Today… you're going to tell me what happened to Nancy Bjorquist," he told her.

"Not before breakfast I'm not," she said.

"Would you like coffee?"

"Tea this morning."

Mitch rose and went to the nurse's station. He demanded they serve Ms. Outing her breakfast, along with a piping hot cup of tea — immediately. He was told only her doctor could order such a thing, so he telephoned Henry Nason, told him what he was up to, and then handed the phone to the nurse. Doctor Nason approved the order and Mitch Polovina returned to Victoria's room. "Breakfast and tea will be along shortly," he told her.

"Then we shall begin shortly," Victoria told him.

***

Doctor Henry Nason quickly showered, shaved, and dressed.

He would grab something to munch on at a local drive through and hope it did not give him cancer. He hated it when an old friend like Mitchell Polovina took on the job of a younger man, pushed himself overboard trying to do it, getting *him* out of bed earlier than *he* felt necessary in the process. What the hell was Mitch doing it for in the first place? He was wealthy. It wasn't for the money. And feeling younger? Hell... Juliette Moore, that sensational piece of tail he was now waking up to each morning—she was a full fifteen years Mitch's junior—can certainly do the job of making him feel younger. That is, of course, if she didn't kill him first. And if she did? *What a way to go,* Henry Nason thought. But Mitch was already on the job this morning, and if Henry wanted in on the splendid and nostalgic tale being spun by Victoria Outing, he needed to be on the job with him. He was, after all, a genuine badge carrying officer of the Farwell Police Department himself.

Henry pulled in line at the drive-up window and spoke to a clown. And when he had told the clown what he wanted, the clown gave him a price. "Christ," he told himself, "I can feel my arteries hardening just sitting here."

"Excuse me?" the clown asked.

"Nothing. Just get that sandwich for me."

***

Ted Mayfield was delightfully surprised to find his wife, Karla, snuggled close to him as he awoke. He had scarcely seen her since her father, Homer Jenkins, had been hospitalized with Mitch Polovina's handcuffs securing him to his bed. And he hadn't heard that Homer had been turned loose the evening before, so wondered what she was doing there. She would never leave Homer alone in the hospital; at least he hadn't thought she would. He nudged her and she moved closer. He nudged her again and she nibbled at his ear. Her hand slid down his stomach to settle at his crotch. To hell with Homer. It had been far too long since a morning started this way around the Mayfield house.

***

Homer Jenkins curled into a fetal position inside the musty smelling sleeping bag he preferred to standard bedding, on the worn sofa in his son-in-law's study beneath the master bedroom. He pulled a pillow over his head to block out the sounds of moaning, groaning, and spring squealing emanating through the floor from whatever was going on overhead, until a scream of ecstasy in his daughters voice caused him to toss the pillow across the room knocking over a lamp in the process. "Good God," he said and sat up, the sleeping bag falling around his waist.

***

"I certainly hope we can get to your request today," Victoria Outing told Chief Mitchell Polovina upon the last bite of hospital breakfast she could force into herself. "But, I do think you'd get more out of the story if I tell things in order."

Polovina felt it best, recalling his youth when she had been a nun and his teacher, along with those recent days in which she exhibited an authority over him as she had when he was in the fourth grade, to let her do this her way. The alternative, he sensed, was that it may never get done. So she began as was her way, regaling from an outsider's perspective.

***

Young Victoria, despite her being raised in a time of national economic depression, knew that she would never be poor. She had a job when most did not. And she had herself a beau in Arthur Shaw who possessed power and money, and so long as she followed him wherever and whenever he wished, that power and money belonged to her as well. Night after night they toured the speakeasies beneath the town, in the basements of buildings ranging from Durmont's Dry Goods to Gordon Lipschitz's livery; the latter being the dive of dives where the fifty-cent misfits gathered, drank shine, and beat each other bloody at the slightest provocation. Victoria Outing was one of the few females in town to ever step foot in the saloon beneath the livery. It wasn't considered safe. But in the company of Arthur Shaw, the man who supplied the establishment with moonshine, safety should not have been an issue. But it was.

It was on their fifth night together, she, having made him promise to show her all such places off of the tunnel below the street, and him doing what she asked in an attempt to please her, that, after considerable argument over the issue, Arthur Shaw finally gave in and took her to the dive, the final place on the tour. When they walked in all eyes turned on them, and whispers, cynical chuckles, and intoxicated disgusting dirty old man grins glared at them through yellowed and sparse teeth. "Have you seen enough?" Arthur asked her.

"No. We're already here. I'll want to come back if we don't have one drink here," she told him.

"Of course you will," he said, well accustomed to her bravery, curiosity, and unreasonable determination by now. So… he led her to a small table in serious need of scrubbing in a dark corner of the room.

"The floor is dirt," she observed.

"As is the ceiling, at least much of it."

"How does it stay up there?" she asked.

Shaw stood. He pounded knuckles on the low ceiling of the pub. "Clay," he said and pounded again. "They wet it, and then heat it, and it turns hard like cement."

"Where are we?" she asked.

"Just below the livery stable."

"Why doesn't it cave in with the weight of the horses?"

"It's twelve feed below ground. There's rock bed between us and the surface."

"It doesn't smell good in here."

"Do you desire to leave?" Shaw asked her.

"After one drink," Victoria said. Shaw got up to get them a drink from the bar. While his back was turned, an inebriated derelict in filthy bib overalls with snuff running out of one side of his mouth and down his chin, staggered toward their table, fell on Victoria, and began pushing a hand under her dress. She screamed out for Arthur Shaw. She heard the shot from Shaw's pistol and felt the drunk go limp. Then she felt Shaw push the dead drunk from her onto the dirt floor. Shaw turned, his six-gun cocked and ready to fire, waving from dirty patron to dirty patron as they made their way to the door and out into the tunnel.

"My goodness," Victoria said and went limp.

"I think you've seen enough," Shaw told her. She did not hear him. She had fainted. He picked her up and hurried back to a more suitable saloon for a lady to be in, somewhere he could get salts to bring her back around.

***

Henry Nason's entrance into Victoria Outing's hospital room did not slow the story, but when Mitchell Polovina's cell phone began its electronic music in a tune that no one recognized because it had been programmed by the much younger Juliette Moore, the story stopped suddenly. The tone signaled it was her calling, as did the photo showing on the screen. It brought a smile to Mitch's face when he flipped it open and saw the picture for the first time. She was topless. "I hoped you'd answer your own phone," she said when he picked up. "You like the picture?"

"Is it legal?" Mitch asked her.

"Lewd, maybe, but not illegal. Not in this day and age. Just check out the billboards and the television shows nowadays — breasts everywhere."

"I only watch cop shows," he said.

"That's right. Training."

"What can I do for you?" Mitch asked her, walking into the hallway and out of earshot of Victoria and Gray Eagle Nason.

"I thought I might take you to lunch, this being Saturday and our seventh day running on the job."

"We didn't take a day off this week?" he asked.

"You haven't taken one since you took over. I think it's just about time you did."

"We'll discuss it over lunch," Mitch promised.

"Come get me," Juliette said and hung up.

Mitch Polovina went back to Victoria's room. As he entered he saw the lunch cart headed her way.

Doc Nason stood and checked his watch. "I think I'll make some rounds," he said. "You taking lunch, Bugsy?"

"Yeah."

"Victoria, enjoy your lunch," Doc Nason said. Then he turned to Mitch. "Coming back?"

"I'll be a couple of hours. I need to see about getting some help at the office. Nobody's been able to take time off. There's grumblings of mutiny or ship jumping coming down the pike. I need to head it off. Look for me around two."

***

Mitch Polovina tapped the horn a couple times in front of the police station and Juliette Moore appeared.

"Where to, Miss?" he said.

"Mick's Café, of course."

CHAPTER TWENTY

"I wonder if the tunnel opening still exists under this place," Polovina said as he held a chair for Juliette Moore at Arthur Shaw's favorite table in Mick's Café.

"I don't know. Let's ask the waitress," Juliette suggested. They did and were told that the stairwell existed yet, but only a cement wall could be found at the bottom, history sealed in forever.

Mitchell Polovina said little during lunch. Juliette wondered if it was due to a lack of sleep. She didn't know what time he had gotten up, only that he wasn't there when she did. "Are you all right?" she asked.

"Of course. Why?"

"You're so… so distant," she said. "Tired?"

"A little."

"You need a day off," Juliette said.

"Can't."

"Sure you can. Parker's fresh. He took Thursday. Willy Hobbs is back with us. He can do his share. And Paula tells me a couple of those out of work deputies called. Let's get them here for the weekend, team them up with Parker and Hobbs to chase teenagers for a day."

"What'll we do?"

"How about another ride on that motorcycle of yours?" Juliette suggested.

"Which kind of ride?" Mitch asked her and smiled, thinking back to their evening at the mine.

She smiled and blushed a bit. "You choose," she told him.

"Alright. Tell Paula to call the deputies and have them report in the morning. Tell Parker and Hobbs to take one each, and start training them in."

"Will you be coming back to the office?" Juliette asked.

"Nope. I'll be spending the rest of the day at the hospital with Gray Eagle and Victoria Outing. I'll meet you at my house after work that is…"

"Yes. I'd love to spend the rest of the weekend with you," she said and smiled. I have a surprise for you anyway."

"You do? Where is it?"

"It's in the shower," she said.

***

"You've told us, Victoria, that Arthur Shaw was not on his own, that he worked for people from… I forget… down south somewhere," Mitch said when he returned to her room after his lunch with Juliette.

"St. Cloud," Victoria reminded.

"That's right. St. Cloud. Do you recall the name?"

"Cohen," she said. "It was the Cohen brothers, Allan and Abe I believe. I don't know which one was the eldest; I only met them once — briefly, and they looked so much alike they could have been twins. I remember very little about them other than their eyes."

"Their eyes?"

"Yes. Their eyes. Pitch black. Cruel looking — mean. Of course they might have just been upset about something at the time," Victoria said. "I don't know. Like I said, it was a brief visit."

"Why brief?"

"They made Arthur take me away. They wanted to talk about something they did not want me to hear, I suppose. I recall it so clearly. It happened one night in our favorite club, the first speakeasy Arthur had taken me to. The one directly across the street from Mick's Café. The Cohen brothers came in just before midnight."

***

Victoria found it curious that, as the two men approached their table Arthur Shaw's facial expression changed at the sight of them. It was as though Arthur was afraid, and she had never before seen Arthur afraid, not even when he had to shoot the drunk in bib overalls in the dive with the dirt floor and clay ceiling. He stood, almost at attention, and introduced Victoria to them. They both smiled pleasantly, but their cold glare sent chills down Victoria's back anyway. Little was actually said; just a swing of the head, and Victoria was deposited in the care of a couple Arthur knew for a time while the Cohen brothers seemed to discuss something with Arthur Shaw heatedly. Soon, Arthur got up and followed the brothers into the tunnels. It was the first and only time he left Victoria unguarded. It frightened her. And when Arthur returned, he held a cloth to his lip and walked slightly bent over. He told Victoria he had slipped in the Tunnel on some moonshine whisky someone had spilled. She never believed that story; the Cohen brothers had done something to him. She knew they had.

That experience seemed to change Arthur Shaw. He became harsh, not so harsh that Victoria became disinterested, but no longer the gentleman, no longer placid. If something upset him, which it did from time to time, he became given to fits of rage and cruelty. And he found no personal boundaries when it came to what he wanted. He just took it. That was all. And that was how Victoria Outing came to be pregnant.

There was a tunnel Victoria had been told led nowhere, one that had been started because there was to be one more pub, which, for one reason or another, never materialized. One night, a few weeks after the Cohen brothers' visit, Arthur took her to that tunnel. She was surprised to find that it led to a secret passage. Beyond a door, the tunnel continued until it came to the top of a long stairway. Beside the stairs, a contraption Arthur called a conveyor belt had been constructed and at the bottom of the stairs was Arthur's warehouse on the floor of the mine. And it was there, in an office at the rear of the building, that he took her.

She had been comfortable with Arthur Shaw, her summer having been filled with dining out, dancing until the wee hours of the morning, drinking that smooth Canadian whisky and watching others fall comically and entertainingly down from the effects of bootleg moonshine. She felt safe, despite his more harsh nature near the end. She supposed she had adapted to him because she had, somewhere along the way, come to love him.

Until that night, Arthur had only kissed her at the door when he returned her to her father at the end of an evening. But tonight it would be different. He fed her too little that evening, and pushed drink on her constantly. By the time they reached his warehouse, she had little fight left in her. Soon she was on a small cot, both her clothing and her dignity stripped from her, her virginity cancelled forever by an act she could scarcely bear at her young age. She wished, all the while he was on top of her, that her mother hadn't been so ill, that she had had the time to warn her of such things — prepare her. But she had not. So Victoria Outing, a child of sixteen, learned of sex the hard way. But it would not be her solitary experience with it.

The horrors of Victoria's night would not end with her return to her father's home this time. For it was when she walked in the front door at half-past two, tears flowing freely down her tiny cheeks, her pretty dress stained beyond restoration and her spirit along with it, in drastic need of a woman's guidance and sympathy, that she was told her mother had passed away and no one could find her to be there to hear her last words.

No one asked her what the matter was. No one cared.

***

Victoria Outing lay in her hospital bed, a single tear as testimony to a memory gone wrong.

Mitchell could think of nothing to say. His single thought, *No wonder she tells the tale as though it was about someone else.*

Henry Nason could not bear it all. He left the room, insisting he had patients to see to before the end of the day.

CHAPTER TWENTY-ONE

Chief of Police Mitchell Polovina pitched rocks into the water filled mine pit for nearly an hour after he left Victoria outing. Her sad story required think time — alone time, and this lake, the site of her troubles of so many years before, seemed the place to get it.

A flat stone skipped; he counted twelve times. Then he heard the car pull to a stop in the gravel roadway near his. He did not turn to look; he knew who it would be. It would be Juliette. Her work day had ended and he was not at home. "How did you find me?" he asked as she approached from behind.

"G.P.S," she said.

He did not need to ask. He knew what G.P.S. was from one of the many television shows he had watched to prepare himself for the job. And it reminded him that the shows hadn't really prepared him for anything, and that he needed to get a grip and start learning and applying real-life police procedures to his position before someone clever tagged him with the nickname, Hollywood Chief. "Do all our cars have G.P.S?"

"And our phones," she said and slid her arms around his neck from behind. The feel of her breasts against his back seemed to take some of the sting out of the day. He needed that. "Are you getting hungry?"

"Did you let Sis out?" he asked.

"I did. I brought her along. That's what you're feeling tugging on your pants cuff right now."

Mitch looked down. Sister Mary Elizabeth (Sis) weighed less than ten pounds soaking wet. He thought the tugging was something caused by the breeze off the lake. He smiled. "Is she going to eat me up?"

"She loves you. That's her way of showing you she missed you today. You did leave rather early, you know."

"What about you, Juliette? Do you love me too, or is this all just temporary?" he asked, and then wished he hadn't.

"Feeling a little vulnerable are we?"

"Maybe," he said and related Victoria's sad tale to her. At the end of it, Juliette told him that she understood where his mood came from.

"I do. I do love you. And this? This what we have going on? I don't think of it as some passing thing, so… well… it's only as temporary as you want it to be, I guess."

Mitch thought her to be a good time — almost too good for any permanence. He thought her to be the out-for-fun kind of gal, not serious.

"I joke a lot," she said. "I'm playful, but it's only with you. I haven't had a relationship in years and I thought I might not even have one in my future, Mitch. That is until you came along. I may not look or act serious, but let me explain something to you, Bucko. If I wasn't serious about you — about us, well… you wouldn't be getting any." She squeezed him tighter and kissed the back of his neck. He shivered. She laughed.

"I don't have a good track record," he warned, thinking back to three ex-wives.

"But you have a big house," she said as though it somehow compensated. "Why is that, anyway? You have no children, do you?"

"Not a one. Don't want any either. Sis, here, is enough for me."

"Does that mean we get to keep her?" Juliette asked.

"I don't see how we could make it without her. Who'd keep you warm on a cold morning when I have to leave the house early?"

"So tell me."

"Tell you what?"

"Tell me why the big house." Juliette said.

"Family heirloom," Mitch told her.

"It was left to you?"

"Not exactly."

"You bought it from the estate then," she reasoned.

"The first time," he said.

"The first time? How many times did you buy the house?"

"Two and a half. I bought it from my father's estate; he died without a will and I had to purchase it from the other heirs. Then I bought half of it back from three ex-wives. Seems I'm a slow learner. That makes two and a half times."

Juliette let go of his neck, stepped to his side, bent and picked up a stone — that's when Mitch noticed she had worn the short skirt uniform that day. She parted her feet and hiked the skirt further up so she could pitch the rock side armed and make it skip across the water. Sis dove in and swam after the rock. "Did you want to try for an even three? Two and a half seems an unlucky number," she said. She bent to pick up another stone.

He watched her do it. Those enticing legs. What the hell? Why not? "I wouldn't mind," he said. And he wasn't sure if he'd just jumped from the frying pan, or where he had landed if he had, but after all was said and done, the sting of the day had gone.

***

Ted Mayfield had taken the day off. His wondrous wakeup with his wife, Karla, that morning, led to a phone call in which he cancelled a meeting he had planned for ages. It was Saturday, after all. And it had been a long time, a very long time, since he had felt wanted at home. He would not trade that feeling for more work.

He and Karla had played in the bed keeping Homer awake in the study below. They played in the shower afterward, taking up all the hot water so that Homer's shower was cold. They lay back in the bed, skipping their morning meal and fondling one another, when they should have been providing Homer with breakfast, then lunch. And when they finally came downstairs in mid-afternoon, Homer was gone. "Shit," Ted said.

"Yeah," Karla agreed. "What do we do now?"

"I'm tempted to let him go," Ted said, then thought he shouldn't have.

"I'd agree," Karla said, "except for his recent suicide attempt. Who do you suppose these Jews are, the ones he's so afraid of?"

"I have no idea. He won't say more than that."

"We have to do something," Karla said.

"What should we do?" Ted asked, although he wanted to do nothing.

"Find him," Karla said. She looked at the disappointment in her husband's eyes. She had given far too much of herself to her father's needs since her mother passed away, and far too little to Ted's.

She knew that. Time for a change. "If he's all right, or if he seems all right, we'll see to it that he's settled in and safe. Then we'll come back home — alone."

Ted Mayfield silently thanked her with his eyes for her consideration of his wellbeing, then, "And if we don't think he'll be safe?"

"How about that home where Victoria Outing lives?" she suggested. The time had come for her to get on with her life. She determined to become less Homer Jenkins' daughter and more Ted Mayfield's wife. And again, Ted's eyes thanked her.

They checked the hospital first, then Homer's house, drove the neighborhoods (theirs and his), the downtown (searching the pool hall and Homer's favorite pubs) and finally landed back at the mining company's office where Homer had worked for decades. And that is where they found him, buried in the task of reorganizing after the mess Mitchell Polovina had made of the place. The police chief had touched little in the office, but to Homer Jenkins, it had been desecrated like a robbed grave.

The Mayfields thought him safe, so left him to his fantasy.

***

It was a small police force, but then, Farwell was a small town. Consequently, one officer would be assigned to overnight duty each evening, not that there was anything to do, just in case something might come up. Royal Parker was pleased that Willy Hobbs had returned to the force to take one of those nights this weekend. He was worn out — three such shifts under his belt already. "Whose plan is this anyway?" Hobbs asked Parker. Business under Randy Newell, their former boss now deceased, was not like this. All that happened on an overnight is one officer took home a radio and all calls were rerouted to that officer's home phone by the phone company.

"Our new boss," Parker told him. "Sucks, don't it?"

"You bet your ass it does. I think I'll have words with somebody about this."

"I wouldn't do that," Parker warned. He had learned. This new chief was no pushover. He was clearly in charge and those who did not know that soon learned it.

"And what's he gonna do?" Hobbs asked.

"He put me on dispatch for questioning him. If old Mrs.

Cherry hadn't died, I'd still be there."

"You ever put a name to her killer?" Hobbs asked. He had heard in the wind that the Cherry woman had been poisoned.

"Nope." Parker admitted. "Waiting on lab work. Doc Nason's in charge of it now."

Hobbs made up his mind right there and then. He would dig into the Cherry murder on his own, break the case wide open, become the next police chief for it. Hell, Polovina couldn't last long. He didn't have the heart of a cop, or the character. He was just some rich guy trying to be something he wasn't, just to feel like he had value in society. That's all Mitch Polovina was. His wealth was stolen anyway. Him and his daddy supposedly came up with an invention, a panel that could be attached to mining equipment and grease that equipment at regular intervals automatically. Mitch's daddy and Hobbs' worked together way back when, and Hobbs' daddy swore they stole the idea from him. Hobbs was only eight at the time, and the invention had been created in the Polovina family's garage and not at work, but Hobbs doubted his own father would lie about any of this. *Mitch Polovina? Hell, he ain't nothin'*. "Doc Nason, eh! What's he doin' in this?"

"He's been sworn in. He's a police officer just like us. And he's the coroner now too," Royal Parker said. "Look, Willy, you have yourself a good night. I'm going home. I'm whipped."

***

The little dog Mitch and Juliette were about to inherit from Victoria Outing was all play. Each rock the couple skipped atop the glass-like surface of the lake traveled one more bounce it seemed. And each extra skip seemed to motivate the little dog another step. She chased them all, until, finally, she wore down like a windup toy whose spring had run out. Unfortunately, that happened, not on shore, but far out into the lake. Mitch had to swim after her — to save her from drowning. And Juliette had to get involved to help Mitch — to save both of them.

At home, they toweled Sis to just damp, not soaked to the bone, and placed her in her bed (Juliette had purchased it along with a vast array of stuffed toys when she found all of Sis' former toys beheaded and dissected in Victoria's apartment), then pealed wet and stuck clothing from one another. The odor of dead fish washed up on the shore of the pit clung to them like the flies they had seen clinging to the fish themselves. They needed a shower — not standard for Mitch this time of day, but welcomed by Juliette as there was a lesson left from the morning that she needed to teach. She started the water and let it warm. He admired her body while they waited.

Inside the shower, Mitch grabbed for a washcloth. Juliette snatched it from his grasp and tossed it over the top of the ice-glass shower wall. "That's not how we'll be doing things from now on," she told him. He looked at her, her skin so soft and shiny from water running over it, her hair, the dampness causing a slight curl that seemed to fall magically onto her round breasts, their nipples standing firm against the shower's spray, and he could not think to argue with her. She began to rub the bar of soap to a rich lather in her soft hands, then set the soap aside and used her palms to wash his body — head to toe, lathering from the bar as needed. And when she had finished, she handed him the soap, straitened her body, shoulders back, breasts out, and said, "Your turn." And he took his turn without objection.

When he had finished washing her, a task he stretched out as long as he deemed reasonable, he stepped back to let her rinse. "Uh-uh," she said. "That ain't the way this works, Stud." And she pushed her soapy body on his and squirmed until he could stand no more. He kissed her hard and long on the mouth, tongues probing, anticipation building, bodies sweating, expectations growing. And they made love, standing, her back against the wall, the soap providing a lubricant that allowed them glide up and down one another in an erotic dance that brought them both to a climax, and to exhaustion. Then it was time to wash again. "That's how this works?" he asked.

"That's how this works," she told him.

"I don't think I'll shower alone again."

"That's the plan," she said.

CHAPTER TWENTY-TWO

Victoria Outing's little dog, Sis, snarled at the telephone then scurried under the covers between Mitch and Juliette. It was not yet five a.m. on Monday morning and, apparently, she did not wish to be up and around. Mitch grabbed the phone.

"She's taken a turn for the worse," Doc Nason said.

"What? Who is this?"

"Henry Nason."

"It's...," Mitch looked at the clock. "It's the middle of the night, Gray Eagle. What the hell do you want?" Mitch Polovina asked.

"Victoria Outing has taken a turn."

"A turn? What kind of turn?"

Juliette sat up and rubbed her eyes. Sis licked her on the ankle, and then rubbed against her leg. Juliette, not even considering their dog, screamed and jumped out of the bed.

"You're not alone, are you? Lucky bastard," Nason said.

Mitch pulled the covers back, exposing the ankle licker and settling Juliette's nerves. He helped her back into the bed. "Again, what kind of turn?" he asked Gray Eagle.

"She's had another stroke. Worse than the last, but not the end for her."

"Will she be able to continue talking with me?"

"I'm afraid not today, not for a few days. That's why I called you. To tell you not to waste your time coming here today," Nason said and hung up.

Mitch stretched. Sis poked her head out from the covers and looked at him. Time to go out.

Juliette wasn't sure she wanted coffee when Mitch and Sis returned, outdoor business taken care of and steaming cup in hand, but the aroma told her otherwise. She sat up against the headboard, bed sheet slipping down, exposing her bare breasts. "Is it shower time yet?" Mitch asked and grinned cynically.

"Coffee first."

"What'll we do today?" he asked. "Victoria's not available. She's suffered another stroke. Nason says she'll be down for several days."

"Poor thing. She can't have much longer," Juliette observed. "Will we be able to question her at all?"

"According to Nase we will, but not for a couple of days."

Juliette took a long sip of coffee. "Maybe something's come in on Michael Decker. We have a number of feelers out. Something's bound to turn up."

"Maybe," Mitch said.

***

Gordon Cherry awaited Mitchell Polovina in the police stations outer office when Mitch arrived at work. He held out a large brown file. "You'll be wantin' to take note of this," Cherry told him.

Mitch leaned over for Juliette to remind him who the man was and Juliette whispered in his ear.

"Mr. Cherry," he said. "I'm sorry for your loss."

"You'll be wantin' to look at this," he said again and pushed the file closer.

Mitch grabbed it and unwound the string wrapped around a button and folded the top back. He peered inside at what appeared to be some legal documents. What is it?" he asked.

"A will, I reckon."

Juliette stood on tiptoe and whispered in Mitch's ear again. "Gordon can't read," she told him.

"Mrs. Cherry's?" Mitch asked.

"Nope."

"Tell you what, Mr. Cherry, why don't you come into my office and we'll have a look at this."

"Just as soon not," Gordon Cherry said.

"I know. But do me a favor. Come in anyway, just for a minute, in case I might have a question or two."

"All right, but I can't stay long. Gotta see the funeral director and it's a long walk."

"I'll have someone drive you, Sir. Juliette, you come in too.

Let's have a look." And when Mitchell Polovina settled into a chair behind his desk, Juliette hanging over his shoulder while he dug a stack of papers out of the envelope, Gordon Cherry took the seat across from him. He opened a packet stapled inside a thick blue cover. *Last Will and Testament*, it read. He read aloud. "I, Sister Mary Elizabeth," he began. Mitch looked at Gordon Cherry and Cherry shrugged his shoulders, "also known as Victoria Marie Outing." He looked at Gordon Cherry once again. "Where did you get this, Mr. Cherry?" he asked.

"My Missus had it in a drawer for years. Victoria give it to her a long time back, told her not to give it to nobody should they come lookin'."

"Who did she think would come looking?" Mitch Polovina asked him.

"Don't know. Didn't nobody say. Can I go now?"

"Do you know what this says?"

"Nope. I reckon the girl there whispered it to ya already. I can't read."

Mitch read on silently for a moment. "You can go, Mr. Cherry," he finally said. "Thank you for bringing this in."

Mitch read further. It was a simple will, executed properly it appeared, by a known attorney of good reputation. And it seemed to leave all the old woman had to a home for unwed mothers, appropriate considering she had no one but a man claiming to be her son, no other family, and also considering how the so called son came to be. What baffled the mind though was an amount of money named in the document. According to what Mitch was reading, and Juliette (still glancing over his shoulder), the old gal was wealthy — filthy rich, some might say. The home would inherit fifteen million and change, plus any interest accrued between the date the document was initially executed and the date of her death. "I think we'd better find the money," Mitch told Juliette. "Then we need to find out where it came from." It could be a lengthy search. Victoria was a mystery. She hadn't come from money, not that anyone on the department had knowledge of, and she lived a frugal life. Finding the cash itself wouldn't make things add up. They had to follow it back. That's where, Mitch bet, the answers lie. "You think maybe Edith Cherry might have been killed because of this?" he asked Juliette.

"I don't know. But I do think we need to question Michael Decker."

"Not until Gray Eagle gets results back on the rat poison. If he gets a match, we can hold Decker. We bring him in prematurely, and he'll be out of here in two hours and out of town in four."

"What TV show did that come from?" she asked.

He smiled at her but said nothing. He couldn't. They were all running together now, those television cop shows.

***

Peter Casey, one of the deputies who had been laid-off by County Sheriff Marion Kuhn, it turned out, was a trained and skilled investigator. He and Royal Parker would take the lead on the Cherry murder, as soon as Doc Nason's lab results were back from the state lab.

A young and relatively inexperienced female officer named Lila Hartman, another of Sheriff Kuhn's out of work staff, would partner with Willy Hobbs, and the two of them would see to the general operations of the town's police force, chasing kids on stolen bikes, investigating shoplifting accusations, locking up drunk drivers —those many day to day tasks that take up a local police department's time.

Paula Bloom would stay on dispatch, however, she would also see to the general workings of the office, overseeing scheduling and the new secretary who had been placed with the department by a temp agency on a trial basis.

When Mayor Mayfield stopped by and saw all the activity at its best, he had but one comment for Chief Mitchell Polovina. "You've got this place running like a real police force, Mitch. I'm impressed. And amazed. It seems you can quarterback more than just a football team."

"I'm glad you stopped by, Teddy. I need to ask you something."

"It's Ted, or Mr. Mayor, and what is it you want to ask?" Teddy asked.

"Where's Homer?" Mitch asked.

"Why?"

"I need to ask him some questions pertinent to my investigation."

"Pertinent to your investigation? What'd you do, Bugsy, take some night classes at the community college?"

"All right then, Homer knows things, and I need to know how much he knows. That alright with you, Teddy?"

"He's out at the mine. Go gently, will you Mitch?"

"I will."

So Mitch, partnering of course with Juliette Moore, would take on the portion of *the bodies in the lake/girl in the drum/Victoria Outing connection/Edith Cherry murder/ Homer Jenkins mystery case* that had to do with Homer himself. They got into Mitch's personal car (the city was running low on cruisers with the added staff) and set out for the mining company office. Homer did not welcome the intrusion, but did not fire on them this time.

"What the hell do you want now?" he asked when Mitch and Juliette stepped through the doorway.

"Sit down, Homer. This is going to be a long visit," Mitch suggested.

"I'm busy."

"We could do this at the police station if you wish," Juliette warned. It was due to her caution that Homer settled down and took a seat. He had no respect for Mitchell Polovina—never did. But Juliette Moore? Well, he didn't need to respect her to do what he was told. She was a real dish and he was a man, albeit an old man, but a man just the same.

"Where do you want to start, Chief?" Juliette asked.

"Tell me about the Jews, Homer," Mitch said softly.

"What Jews?" Homer asked and looked down at his hands in his lap.

"Were they the Cohen brothers, Allan and Abraham?"

CHAPTER TWENTY-THREE

"I remember them, the Cohen brothers, from when I was just a kid," Homer Jenkins told Chief Polovina. "They were friends of my daddy's, well... not friends really, but he knew them and they used to come to the house back then, sometimes to talk, sometimes to drink, and sometimes they'd even stay with is for a night or two. But my daddy never seemed to like them, or them him. They all just kinda tolerated each other because of Arthur Shaw. Now Shaw, he was a friend to us. A real nice guy. Too bad what they done to him."

"You mean the brothers?" Mitch asked.

"I'd rather she asked the questions," Homer said.

Mitch looked at Juliette. The last time he and his brothers came out to the mine, back when he was in tenth grade and just getting started in football, full of piss and vinegar and all the mischief that accompanies that, Homer had caught him in the act of desecrating company property. At least to Homer Jenkins, a man who revered the company above most other things in life, it was desecration. And it was that boy Homer saw nowadays when he looked at Mitch Polovina, not the police chief of today. Mitch nodded at Juliette, his cue that she should ask the questions.

"You mean the Cohen brothers?" she asked.

"That's them."

"They did something to Arthur Shaw?"

"You saw him. He was one of them in a barrel at the bottom of the pit. You seen him when you brought him up. Did he look all right to you?"

"He looked dead," Juliette told him.

"It was more than that," Homer said. "He didn't die slow."

Juliette looked at Mitch, who shrugged his shoulders. "We didn't see anything," she told Homer.

"Take another look," Homer said. "The man don't have

fingernails."

Mitch Polovina pulled out his cell-phone, stood, and walked to the other side of the room. He called Doc Nason. "Gray Eagle," he said. "You take those bodies to the undertaker for cremation yet?" It was the most cost effective way for the town to deal with their disposal, and since few had been identified and those who had been had no relative claiming them, well... it had been decided that the town wasn't equipped to sit on them forever.

"Just getting ready to do it," Nason said.

"Hold up on that. I want you to pull out the corpse Virginia said was Arthur Shaw. Look him over real good, and then call me back."

"Are you saying the Cohen brothers tortured, and then killed Arthur Shaw?" Juliette asked.

"They did."

"Why?"

"Don't know. I was just a kid — six I think — hiding in the bushes. They didn't tell me anything," Homer insisted. "Don't think they even knew I was around. Nobody did, I reckon."

"How do you know it was the Cohens who killed him?"

"Told ya. I was hiding in the bushes. I watched 'em do it."

***

Henry Nason pulled the stainless steel drawer open and looked down at Arthur Shaw's body. "I don't know what our friend, Mitchell Polovina, hopes to find out about you, but let's have a look," he said to Arthur Shaw's corpse. He unzipped the body bag and viewed Arthur's face. Bruise on a cheekbone, one eye swollen, lip split open, a couple of teeth missing and another broke off. "I'd say you had a bad night," Henry told the corpse. He pulled the zipper further down to reveal his waist. He pulled Shaw's clothing open and checked his ribs — a couple broken, many bruises. He looked at the man's hands. "My God," he said and stepped back. "You must have known something somebody wanted you to tell." Shaw's fingernails had been removed — all of them — not gently. "Jesus," Henry said and closed the body bag. He had seen enough. He called Mitch Polovina back and confirmed Homer Jenkins' claim to be true.

When Polovina got off the phone, he began putting two and two together and hoped he was coming up with four. One, Arthur

Shaw had stolen money from the Cohen brothers. Two, the Cohen brothers beat and tortured him in an attempt to learn the whereabouts of the stolen cash — unsuccessfully, no doubt — then killed him. Three, Victoria Outing ended up with the Jewish mobsters' money. And four, well... Mitch couldn't quite get a handle on number four yet. But he'd bet on one through three being pretty damn close to the truth, and he'd put money down that he'd discover number four before this was over.

"That's enough for today, Juliette," Mitch said. "Homer thanks for the time and the answers. You've been a big help." He chose not to tell him that this would begin again tomorrow, or that it would begin again every day until this puzzle was solved — entirely.

***

Peter Casey, ex-sheriff deputy, now an investigator for the Farwell Police, felt it was not in anyone's best interest to wait for some lab report, which may or may not come, to pick up the pace on the investigation of Edith Cherry's murder. He had heard many stories over the years about this town and why it had always carried the nickname Little Cicero and this was his opportunity to dig into those rumors and either prove them or dispel them. If there was truth in those rumors, they had something to do with Edith Cherry. If there wasn't, this all would, at the very least, satisfy his curiosity about the place. Thank God for a layoff, or he may never have a chance like this. He would begin with a talk with the coroner, not the county coroner, he had never been called in (another rumor had it that the locals, the chief and the mayor particularly, wanted things hush-hush, at least for a time, something about draining the lake for whatever reason). He hadn't been told all the facts as yet. But when he walked in on Doc Nason and found four or five drawers open, Doc looking for damage to other bodies like that found on Arthur Shaw, at least some of the mystery would clear away. "What the... Jesus Christ," he said. "Where the hell did they come from?" he asked not concerned with whether he was asking the coroner or his partner, Royal Parker.

Parker answered. "The bottom of the lake," he said, for which he received a curious look from Henry Nason.

"And who would this be?" Nason asked Parker.

"I'm Peter Casey, the town's new chief investigator," he informed Henry Nason, not wanting to leave important introductions to someone like Parker.

"Chief investigator? By whose authority?"

"I've been brought in by the County Sheriff's Office."

"I thought you were laid off by that office. As a matter of fact, I know that," Doc told him.

"And how would you know that?" Casey asked, to which Henry Nason pulled out his own badge and flashed it at him. "You're a cop?"

"And a close friend of Mitchell Polovina."

"Christ! Another old guy," Casey said.

Royal Parker shook his head and mouthed *no* silently to him. But it was too late. Henry Nason's Indian blood came to a rapid boil and Casey was quickly slammed, back first, into a wall of stainless steel drawers that made up the entire south end of the makeshift morgue, Nason's grip closing around his throat, closing off all of his ability to speak and much of his air. "Now you listen to me, you little prick. The old guys you'll find in this town will kick the shit out of you in a heartbeat. And you are chief nothing. Parker here is. Isn't that right, Parker? You see, new blood, Parker is a veteran officer with more hours behind a badge than the likes of you will ever see. And you and me? We answer to him, and he answers to the chief. That's the way it is. Disagree with me and I'll kick your bony ass all the way back to the county seat where you can continue to collect your unemployment and food stamps. You got that, Boy?" And he turned him loose to fall to the floor in a heap.

"You're my witness," Casey shouted to Parker. "That was an attack on an officer of the law."

"I didn't see a goddamn thing," Parker said. "Thanks for your time, Doc," he added and left the morgue.

"Don't screw with these guys, Casey," Parker warned him out in the hall. "They'll have you for lunch. Now... I suggest we have a talk with Edith Cherry's widower. Maybe his son, Arnold, will be there and you can get yourself a second ass kicking for the day."

***

Juliette Moore checked her watch. One p.m. "What'll we do now?" she asked Mitch Polovina as they turned from the dirt pathway to the mine onto tar.

"Eat. I'm famished."

"Then what?"

"Then we look up Victoria Outing's old address."

"She had a little house on the west end. I know where it is," Juliette told him.

"Not that address. The convent."

***

"Mother Superior will be out shortly," a young nun, dressed primarily in street clothing and sensible shoes, told Mitch and Juliette. Mitch looked her up and down.

"What are you thinking?" Juliette asked Mitch.

"I was just thinking, when I went to Vietnam, I had been raised Catholic, and the mass was in Latin and the nuns wore habits. The only thing you saw of them was eyeballs, lips, hands, and rosary-beads. I came home from Nam and the mass was in English. Nuns had hair, elbows, bony knees, and rosary-beads. And in the first service I attended in my old church, the congregation sang a folksong written by a pop singer who now claims to be a Buddhist monk, accompanied by a six-string guitar strummed by a hippy transient. You think that's why I gave up my religion?"

Juliette chuckled a bit, and then said, "I have no idea why you gave up the church. It's enough for me that you did."

"What about you? Do you have a religion? Or did you ever?" Mitch asked.

"Me? I was raised Baptist."

"And you gave that up?"

"I did," Juliette said.

"Why?"

"The skirts were too long."

Mother superior, top nun of nuns, at this convent at least, approached Mitch and Juliette, her cane tapping the floor in front of her as she hobbled, effectively putting an end to their conversation, the most religion either of them had had in recent years. Juliette, upon noticing her gaze, tugged at the hemline of her skirt trying to cover more exposed thigh. Mitch pulled his sunglasses from his face and let his eyes meet the nun's. "What can we here at Saint Agnes' Convent do for the police?" Mother Superior asked.

"We're here about Victoria Outing," Mitch told her.

"Who?"

"That's right; you'd probably know her as Sister Mary Elizabeth." Color drained from the aging nuns face. "Are you all right?"

"Yes. I'm fine. It's just been so long since I heard that name. Is she all right? Is she still alive?"

"She has some issues," Mitch explained. "She's in the hospital over in Farwell. Old age kind of stuff mostly, heart weakening, strokes, that sort of thing." Juliette kicked him on the shin and threw her head in the direction of the old Mother Superior who looked to be Victoria's age herself. "But she's still with us," he quickly added. "How well did you know her?" he asked.

"Quite well, many years ago. Not so much since she left the order. I regret not having kept in contact with her."

"Then you did know her well when you were young?"

"I just told you I did."

"Did you like her?" Mitch asked trying to get a feel of how useful she might be to his investigation.

"I loved her," the elderly nun said.

Of course she did. Nuns had to love one another. It was part of their code, like cops sticking together — right or wrong, like crooks not ratting each other out — even to save their own skin, like cowpunchers watching each other's backs on the long trail drive — even though they didn't necessarily like one another. A creed. "Why?" he asked expecting something scriptural for a reply.

"Because she saved my life."

CHAPTER TWENTY-FOUR

Henry Nason usually, being a single man because his wife had left him years ago and he, unlike his friend Mitchell Polovina, was not a slow learner, spent his Monday evenings in a neighboring town getting sexual gratification from a tart he had known forever. He loved her, actually, and her him. But they entertained no thoughts of going another step up that relationship ladder, neither of them. They were, however, monogamous, and therefore safe. Condoms were not even used since menopause had already removed the threat of pregnancy from them. This Monday, though, Henry would alter his plan. Two things of urgency would stop him. First, there was Virginia Outing to see to. He did not feel right in leaving town when one of his patients was critical, and she was. Then there was his friend, Mitch, and his badge. Had he lost out on his part of the investigation? Had he been replaced, now that the diving was over, by Juliette Moore? Not that he could blame Mitch. Juliette had a great ass, and way better legs than he did.

He called the hospital. The head nurse informed him that Victoria had come out of it somewhat, that her vitals were close to where they were before the stroke. Then he called Mitchell Polovina.

"I was thinking, Bugsy," he told Mitch, "that I might spend more time with my practice, you having Juliette to fill my part."

"Nope," Mitch said bluntly. "I still need you, Gray Eagle. And you don't want to get off the band wagon just when things are getting interesting, do you?"

"What do you mean, getting interesting." For Doc Nason, the case had gone boring. His part seemed to be all lab work and stiffs. The lab work was new and interesting, that provided some solace, but the stiffs? He could certainly do without them.

"We're going into the tunnels. Me and you and Juliette. I

need your experience down there and I don't think it's an opportunity you'll want to miss."

"What're you planning, Bugsy, digging our way through three or four feet of concrete?"

"Not exactly. You heard Victoria. Arthur Shaw took her into another tunnel that led to a stairway that led to the warehouse at the bottom of the mine. We'll dive. Maybe the entry is still down there."

Adrenalin pumped through Henry Nason at the thought. He wanted to go that minute. "When do we dive?"

"As soon as we clear up a couple of things."

"Like what?" Nason asked.

"Like where did Victoria get the cash, for instance? Like who are the Jews Homer Jenkins is so afraid of? Like who the hell is Michael Decker, really?"

"Hold on. Slow down the information train. What money? What's this about Jews? And I was under the impression Michael Decker was Victoria Outing's son."

"You are a bit too far out of the loop my friend." Mitch said, and then he spent the remainder of their telephone conversation, about twenty minutes, bringing him up to speed as well as assuring him that he would be updated with future developments as they happen. Mitchell Polovina still considered Henry Nason, the man who stood alongside him above the water of the mine pit watching bodies pop to the surface, his second in command on the case. Aside from Juliette, who else could he trust? Who else had his back?

***

"Jenny?" Henry Nason asked when his phone call was answered.

"Henry?" Jenny asked. "I thought you were going to be tied up tonight."

"It appears not. Busy?"

"Yeah, but I can run him off."

"Wise ass."

"But a nice one. You even said so yourself," Jenny reminded him.

"When? When did I say that?"

"Last Monday night. In your sleep. Coming over?"

"On my way," Henry Nason said and hung up.

Jenny Cartwright was happy now. Her man would soon arrive. It had been a Monday night tradition, it seemed like… forever. They had known one another since kindergarten, and she had been in love with Henry Nason since those days. Too many problems though, for a full scale relationship. Always had been, always will be she suspected. Her parents objected to her hooking up with a half-breed, put a stop to their dating in high school, and discouraged any in college, forcing the young and ambitious Henry to look in another direction when it came to choosing a wife. She knew he was making a dreadful mistake marrying some slut just so he could call himself a family man. But would he listen? Hell no. And she had been on target with her estimation of less than a year before divorce reared its ugly head. So now she punished him. He got a little shot of leg, and hugs and kisses, and a warm bed with a warm, soft body to snuggle up to once a week and that was all he got. And that was all he was going to get. At least until she was satisfied that he had suffered enough for his error. Then she might marry him. Time would tell. But for now, Jenny Cartwright always looked forward to their toss in the sack on a Monday evening and back on it all week long in fondness until the next Monday comes around. It had become tradition. It had become their relationship.

***

"Is he all right?" Juliette Moore asked Mitch Polovina when his phone conversation with Henry Nason came to an end.

"He's fine. Just feeling a little left out. That's all."

"I didn't mean to interfere in your friendship with Henry," Juliette said.

"You didn't," Mitch assured her. "Henry just gets insecure now and then. He's been that way for years, since his divorce. I don't even think it was the divorce so much as it was rejection by Jenny Cartwright afterwards."

"I'm not sure I understand."

"I don't either. Gray Eagle's a bit tight with information about his personal life, prefers everyone guesses what's up. My guess is this: Henry and Jenny have a thing for each other, her folks didn't care for Henry, Henry runs out and marries another girl, the girl divorces him a year or so later, Henry sets himself to sniffing around Jenny again and Jenny gets pissed. Then Jenny, who really does love the guy, lightens up a bit but not enough to marry him. That's it in a nut shell."

"That's a lot to fit in one nut shell. So... do they see one another?"

"Every Monday night."

"But not this one," Juliette observed.

"Oh, he'll go. She don't give no rain checks. It's Monday night or a week without for him."

"Really?"

"Really."

"Poor bastard," Juliette said and straddled him in his easy chair. A lap dance struck her fancy. She liked the control, not as much, she suspected, as Jenny Cartwright though.

***

As Tuesday morning began at the Farwell Police Department, Royal Parker had to admit that his new partner, Peter Casey, knew a whole lot more than just a little about police work. Casey showed up, warrant in hand. His plan, to toss the Cherry home in search of rat poison. One couldn't simply assume that the first located item containing arsenic would point to a murderer, could one? So... off to the Cherry home Parker and Casey went. And toss that home, they would.

But before they arrived, they spotted it. A 1967 Buick Gran Sport driven by Michael Decker. He was parked less than a block from the Cherry place.

"We need to talk to that man," Casey said and pulled the car to the curb. He had been apprised of the Michael Decker portion of the investigation before hand, so thought his presence in the vicinity justified an approach.

"He's hands off by order of Chief Polovina," Parker warned.

"To hell with Chief Polovina," Casey said and opened his door.

"Casey. Get in here. We're not to talk with Decker. Those are the orders. You screw with this and Decker blows the country, which he probably will, and you're back on the street hunting a job. Now, I don't give a good goddamn if you blow your career, but you'll take mine with. I don't want mine ended because *you* don't think *you* should have to follow orders. Now get back in and let's go do what we came here to do."

Casey did as he was told, and soon, the two policemen were busily searching for rat poison, or anything else that might contain arsenic, in the Cherry home, Arnold Cherry chomping at the bit over it all and held back by his father. "Just let them look," old man Cherry had ordered. "They won't find nothin' in here. And he was right. They found nothing in the house. But they did, in the garage. Rodent poison. A different brand.

"What now?" Casey asked.

"Note it in your report, and we'll take it to Doc Nason," Parker told him.

***

"I think we talk to the penguin first," Mitch Polovina responded to Juliette Moore's query as to whether they were to question Homer Jenkins this morning, or visit Victoria's convent home.

"The Penguin?" she asked.

"Yeah. Isn't that what she looks like?" Mother Superior still believed in the original habit of a nun, and wore it religiously.

"You get that from a Batman movie?"

"Blues Brothers," Mitch told her.

"I guess I'm a bit young for them," she said, unable to make the connection.

Polovina slowed his walk and let her get a step ahead of him, then tilted his head and checked out the side to side action of her sensually formed firm ass. "Yes you are," he said and got back in step.

Before long, Mitch Polovina and Juliette Moore were sitting in a lobby at Saint Agnes' Convent, waiting the customary twenty minutes until Mother Superior would hobble in.

"Yesterday, you said Victoria Outing saved your life. Tell us about that, would you please?" Mitch asked Mother Superior.

"Did you ask her why she left the order?" the elderly nun asked.

"Yes. She said it had to do with her little dog, and how Catholics believed they had no soul."

Mother Superior chuckled a bit at Mitch's answer. "That couldn't be further from the truth. Sister Mary Elizabeth had no dog. Pets aren't allowed on premises I'm afraid."

"Why would she tell us that?" Mitch asked.

The old nun leaned over and touched Mitch's knee. She patted it a couple times. "To keep from telling you the truth, I should imagine."

"Why?"

"Sometimes the truth can be too painful," she said.

"Enlighten us, Mother," Mitch said.

"I don't know that I should. Maybe I should leave that up to her."

"I'm afraid you'll have to answer," Juliette threw in. "This is an investigation. You really have no choice but to answer all of the chief's questions truthfully."

"Well… I guess I can't very well answer your first question without telling you the whole story. I can't recall just how many years ago it was. Is that important?"

"No. That won't be necessary." Mitch knew how long ago it was from hearing Victoria's story, one of those pieces of truth Henry Nason insisted would fall through the cracks.

"We were both novices. That's like a nun in training."

"I know what it is," Mitch said. "Go on."

"Victoria was this little button of a girl, very pretty, so much so, most wondered why she wanted to be a nun. I was younger than her by almost a full year so she kind of looked after me. We had a priest, Father Hennasy was his name, anyway, Father Hennasy thought her pretty as well. He was always looking her over, lust in his eyes, sweat forming on his brow like she lit a fire within him. One night when we snuck out to the courtyard, we often did that because Victoria smoked. She wasn't supposed to of course, a habit she had picked up earlier in life when she frequented speakeasies. Oh that girl. To hear her tell it she led an interesting and dangerous life before she joined the convent. I often wondered how much of it was truth. But the smoking, there was no doubt that part was true. Anyway, that night Father Hennasy caught us. He sent me to my room and took Victoria to his office over it all. And when she finally returned to the dorm, she was in tears, the arm of her uniform torn loose. I asked her what happened, but she would not speak. It would be months before I would find out, and it was a night when Father Hennasy took me to his office. He tried to do things to me, unspeakable things. Victoria barged in just as the priest overpowered me and was about to have his way — her and a young man, I don't recall his name or even why he was there now. But the boy's presence surprised the priest and caught him off guard. That's when Victoria hit him on the head with a paperweight. Blood spattered over all of us and soon, Father Hennasy lay still on the floor."

"Was he dead?"

"Oh, heavens no. He was just knocked unconscious and in need of medical attention. He left us shortly after that. Rumor was that the Monsignor discovered the truth about that night, although nobody knew that for sure, but Father Hennasy was transferred rather quickly and we heard later that he died from a brain hemorrhage not too long afterward. Could a blow on the head cause such a thing?"

"I really don't know," Mitch admitted. "But I surely will find out. So…what were the unspeakable things the priest did?"

"Well… he sodomized that poor girl. Many times."

Silence filled the room, no one willing to speak. Mother Superior had been right. That truth was a painful truth no one wanted to hear.

But finally, Mitch had to continue. "I have one final question, Mother Superior. Then we'll be done here," he said. "You claimed Victoria Outing saved your life. If the priest was abusing young nuns, that's one thing, and a very bad thing. I'm not trying to make little of it. But I have no indication that he would have killed you. So how does this boil down to her saving your life?"

"I would have killed myself, Mr. Polovina, if Father Hennasy had done that to me. I wasn't strong like Sister Mary Elizabeth. I always felt she took my place."

***

Mitchell Polovina remained silent for most of the trip back to Farwell. It was Juliette who broke that silence with a question. "Why do you suppose Victoria Outing remained a nun several years after something like that happening to her?"

"I don't know. I don't know if I want to know." He tightened his grip on the steering wheel and glared at the road ahead for a moment. Then he said, "Juliette, I don't think I like this job anymore. I'm not even sure I like Little Cicero anymore."

CHAPTER TWENTY-FIVE

Mitch and Juliette, as luck would have it, happened by the office between lunch and their planned visit with Homer Jenkins. They walked in the door as the call came in, a request for wants, warrants, or priors on a license held by one Michael Decker. Paula Bloom was about to radio the results to Lila Hartman and Willy Hobbs, the team on standard patrol. Mitchell Polovina placed a hand over the microphone.

"Dispatch, are you there?" Hobbs' voice came over the speaker.

"Tell him you're checking," Mitch said.

"Still checking. Won't be but a minute," she said and looked at the chief.

Mitch placed a hand over the mike once more. "Tell them you came up with nothing."

"No wants, no warrants, no priors," she radioed.

"Well... he'll have a prior now. We got him for seven over," Hobbs said.

Mitch grabbed the mike. "Negative, Willy. Is Mr. Decker in the car with you?"

"He is."

"Turn him loose. This police force, and both of you are new so not aware of this, but this force doesn't ticket speeds less than ten over. It's a waste of time and paper. The judge just kick's them back."

"A warning then."

"Nope. Not even a warning. Let Mr. Decker go. Tell him to have a nice day. Then I want the two of you at the station as soon as you're free." He went into his office to wait. It would not be long.

"Michael Decker is hands off until I say otherwise," he told the two recent additions to his staff, Willy Hobbs and Lila Hartman.

"The two of you got that?"

"Why?"

"He's a suspect in our investigation. The name, Michael Decker, is an alias. We run his license, it comes back there is no Michael Decker. We ran his plates. Guess what. One time it shows up as belonging to Decker's Buick, the next time it comes up there is no such plate number registered to any car in the entire State of Minnesota. Apparently he's got friends in high places, whoever he is. What do you think of that?"

"I think we should run him in." Hobbs said.

"Wrong. I checked. We can't hold him. He gets a good lawyer, and just like that, he's gone, probably for good. We leave him alone until we find out who he is."

"But Chief, it's an old man in an old car. How fast and how far can he run?"

"Here's my guess," Polovina said. "That old man is about my age — with a great Hollywood makeup job. And that car? It's supposed to be a GS-340," he said referring to the size of the engine that came with it new. "340 my ass; I'll bet against that. I'd hate to even guess what's under the hood of that thing — probably wouldn't see taillights more than seconds if he hammered down. Now I want team Hobbs and Hartman back out on the street doing the job you've been assigned. Leave Michael Decker to me for now. I'll let you know when there's a change." The team left, heads hung low, still… something else shone in their eyes — anger maybe, or possibly embarrassment. Either way, it might spell trouble further down the line.

Royal Parker entered Chief Polovina's office as soon as Hobbs and Hartman left. He needed to catch the chief before he got away. With all that was going on, a moment with him one on one was at a premium. "I confirmed the things you wanted me to. Ms. Outing's will is legitimate and, her original attorney being dead now for some time, I took it to the county attorney. He says it's not only valid, it's airtight."

"Did you find the money?" Polovina asked.

"Still working on that one. The cash is in the bank over at the county seat. The rest is in bonds and who knows what else. There's a box in the vault listed under Sister Mary Elizabeth — probably where the rest of the stuff is," Parker said.

"How much cash?" Polovina asked.

"The bank won't tell. I interviewed tellers, loan officers, all the way up to the bank president himself. Even flashed a badge at them. No one's talking. The bank president says we need her signature, or her, or a court order to see anything. I could tell though, from the look on the first teller's face when she pulled up Ms. Outing's account on her computer, it was sizable. She looked twice, even pulled in close to the screen to be sure she was seeing right, if you know what I mean."

"Anything else, Parker," the chief asked.

"Yeah. That Decker fellow, he must know about all of this too. We spotted his car just up the block as we were leaving. Saw him walking toward the bank in the rearview as we drove off. He won't get nothing. If we can't, he can't," Parker told him.

"Unless he had Victoria's signature," Polovina said and shook his head.

"I'll call. Right now."

"You do that."

Mitch altered his plan. He'd put his interview with Homer on the back burner; maybe get to it later in the day — maybe not until morning. If Decker was already sniffing out the money, he'd best get with Victoria Outing — quick.

***

Henry Nason, in order to make certain he was back in the loop, left his Monday night sleepover with Jenny Cartwright early, and waited for Mitchell Polovina at the hospital. Should Mitch chose to continue talking with Victoria, he'd be ready. As it turned out, it was not a wise move. It would be after the lunch hour when Mitch Polovina, Juliette Moore in tow, would show.

"How's she doing?" Mitch asked Henry outside Victoria's door.

"I think she'll be able to talk some, if that's what you're asking," Doc Nason said.

"She on any drugs?" Mitch wasn't asking so much out of concern for Victoria. He was for thinking about the case pending, the bodies, the Cherry woman, Michael Decker, but mostly about Virginia's will and the large sum of money she apparently possessed under her former Benedictine nun name. A few of the right doses and she might surrender permission for the local police to access bank records.

"Nothing that'll help you," Henry Nason said, knowing

what the chief was thinking. "Shall we?" he asked waving a hand at Victoria's open door.

"Mitchell Polovina and Henry Nason," Victoria Outing said as they entered. "Just the two boys I wanted to see."

"Are we now?" Mitch asked her. "And why's that?" He *was* pleased to see her much more chipper than he thought she would be.

"Time is running out. That's why. But before we begin, how's that little dog of mine?"

"She's wonderful, Ms. Outing," Juliette answered. "She's real good company for both Mitch and I."

"So… the two of you *are* shacking up, then," Victoria said.

"Okay, Victoria, let's get started, all right?" Mitch suggested.

"Fine by me. Only you'll have to remind me where we were."

"You had just arrived home after your ordeal in the warehouse. It was the night your mother passed away I believe."

"That was a night that stands out as clearly in my mind as the faces of the three of you right now. I can even see myself, standing at the bottom of the stairs looking up at my father, one sleeve torn loose from my pretty dress, tears pouring down my daddy's cheeks, it was awful, just awful. And my father's words will remain audible as long as I live."

***

"You couldn't even make time for her on her deathbed," Mr. Outing told his daughter. He didn't see, or just didn't care about her tattered dress or how it had become that way. "What kind of daughter are you?"

Young Victoria sat on the bottom step and cried. She did not go up to her mother's room. She did not speak to her father when he scooted by her. She did not speak to the doctor who had been with her mother all evening and now looked at her as if to judge her, sniffed for alcohol on her breath, and passed her by like she was a nonentity of sorts. She felt small. She felt alone — abandoned.

Victoria rose from those steps and went out into the night air. She walked to Nancy Bjorquist's place over the café and knocked on her door.

"Good Lord, Girl. What's happened to you?" Nancy said and tugged up the sleeve as if it would somehow reattach itself to the soiled dress if she did.

"He raped me," she said and began to cry uncontrollably.

Nancy pulled her close and into her apartment. She shut the door against the cool night. "Let's get you cleaned up. Then we'll get you home to your mother."

"Mama's dead, Nancy. She died while this was happening to me," she said and pointed out a small spot of blood on her dress, centered below the waist. And the torn sleeve fell again. She yanked it off and threw it to the floor. She cried harder.

"Was it Arthur Shaw?" Nancy asked.

"Yes," she said. "It was awful, just awful."

"I know, dear. I know. Come. Let's run you a bath. We'll get you all cleaned up and you'll feel a little better. I have something to help you sleep. You'll rest, and then we'll do something about that horrid Mr. Shaw in the morning."

"No, Nancy. I love him. Please don't tell anyone. Please."

Nancy Bjorquist settled her guest in on her sofa, a spoon of bitter medicine and a strong shot of Canadian whisky to help her sleep. She would try in the morning to convince her that any man who did this to a young girl was not a man in love.

***

Victoria Outing fell back against the pillow of her hospital bed and shut her eyes.

Mitchell Polovina remained silent. There were things to ask. There was much to know. But now was not the time.

Juliette Moore wanted to run to the old woman and hold her. She wanted to go home and get her little dog to comfort her. She dried tears from her eyes, but to no avail. They would not stop coming.

Henry Nason hoped this hadn't been too much too soon. He had her health to think about, to shield him from his own emotions at that moment.

Then Victoria opened her eyes. "That was the last time I ever saw Nancy Bjorquist. I heard she had gone out that night after I fell asleep to confront Arthur Shaw, but she never returned. No one saw her again. Not until you pulled her from that barrel."

"What about Arthur Shaw? Did you see more of him?"

"I did," she said. "I saw plenty of him. You know, he took to treating me like a wife after he found out his seed took. It was the strangest thing. Just when I thought I was in it all alone, along he came."

"I have to ask you about the money, Victoria," Mitch said.

"The money?"

"The money. The money parked in the bank under the name Sister Mary Elizabeth."

"Dirty Money," she said. "Blood money. It was that very money that took Arthur Shaw from me. It was that very money that ruined my life. I only hope that, by leaving it to someone who'll do some good with it, it changes something for the better for a few lucky ones. That's my hope. That's my prayer."

"How much money is there?" Nason asked.

"Too much. A lot. I'm not exactly sure. It's in the millions now, though, with interest over all these years. I never touched a dime of it myself. I couldn't."

"Where'd it come from?" Mitch asked.

"Arthur Shaw, of course. He left it to me and the baby. He stole it from the brothers. It cost him his life."

"The Cohen brothers?" Juliette asked.

"Yes," Victoria said.

"He stole it from the Cohens and left it for you and the baby," Mitch said just to make sure his facts were in order.

"That's correct," Victoria confirmed.

"And your will says it all goes to a home for unwed mothers," Mitch said.

"That's correct."

"You're not leaving anything to your son, Michael Decker?"

Victoria crooked her finger and signaled him closer to the bed. As soon as he was near enough, she reached out and slapped him on the arm. "What kind of policeman are you, Mitchell Polovina? Haven't you guessed by now? Michael Decker isn't my son."

"Then who is he?" Henry Nason asked.

"I should imagine he's a Cohen, looking to get the family money back," Victoria Outing said and smiled.

"Victoria, I'll need your authorization to get into your accounts, and your safety deposit box," Mitch said.

"Why would you need that?" she asked.

"My officers have seen Decker over at your bank already. I think your money and your will needs protecting. And you'll need protection as well after we move the money and Decker no longer knows where it is."

"Don't you worry about Michael. He doesn't know that I'm on to him. He'll be the perfect gentleman thinking he'll inherit. I'll tell him it's in the hands of the lawyer along with an updated will and that I had the police move it for safety. I know," she said and donned a sinister smile, "I'll tell him I heard in the wind that those sneaky Cohens were after his inheritance." She looked into Mitchell Polovina's eyes for a moment. "Do you have something for me to sign?" she asked.

CHAPTER TWENTY-SIX

"Working late tonight, Gray Eagle?" Mitch Polovina asked Doc Nason. Henry's concern for his patient cut their visit shorter than Mitch would have liked it to be, but, all in all, he had to admit the session had been informative. And he did have Victoria's permission to dig into her financials. Just in time too, what with Decker nosing around.

"I started my day early, Bugsy. I've had it."

"Got plans?"

"None," Henry Nason said.

"We got plans?" Mitch asked Juliette.

"Nope. Why?"

"I thought it might be nice to do a cook out in the back yard. I haven't used the grill all summer," Polovina said.

"You sure it works?" Juliette asked him.

"Oh, I cleaned it and fired it up once… not too awful long ago."

"I'm for it," Juliette said. "Just the three of us?"

"I hoped Henry here would call that lady of his and invite her."

"What lady?" Nason asked.

"C'mon now, Gray Eagle. Just because you Indians are good at sneaking up on folks, don't mean others know nothing about you," Mitch told him. He frowned when Nason did not say more. "Jenny Cartwright, you boob. It's high time you took that girl out in public. You've been sneaking over to her place every Monday night for years."

"How the hell do you know that?"

"I'm a trained detective," Mitch said.

"It's true. He learned it on television," Juliette said. "Give her a call."

***

Willy Hobbs was a self-assured shit. That's what he was. And when his shift was done he'd do as he pleased without permission from that want-to-be police chief, or his partner — old number two on the force — Royal Parker. He considered himself above rules once he was out of uniform, and Parker? Well Parker, he considered a bit too much of a suck-ass anyway. So there Willy Hobbs sat, his own car, out of his jurisdiction, smoking a cigarette while he idled away his own gasoline — watching the '67 Buick belonging to Michael Decker. If Decker went anywhere, he would follow. He'd bust this case wide open if no one else had the balls to do it. Then they'd all see who's the number two man around this town, maybe even number one. "Fast car, my ass," he told himself and took another drag off his cigarette. "This here," he patted the dash of his Grand Am, "*this* is fast, V-6, supercharged. That son-of-a-bitch runs, and I'll show him fast."

It wasn't long until Hobbs got his wish.

It was dusk — the sun dropping in the western sky, moon rising in the east. Michael Decker walked out of his building. He looked directly at Hobbs, sitting there, a few car lengths up the street, motor running, and he smiled. Then the gutsy old bastard had the audacity to wave as he got behind the wheel of the Buick. He fired up the engine, floored the accelerator and racked off the dual glass packs. The crackle as the motor settled, impressive to be sure, was nothing when compared to the twist of the car's body due to the torque of its engine.

"Holy shit!" Willy Hobbs said. He threw his butt out the window and pulled his shifter into drive.

Decker pulled cautiously into traffic and watched his mirror. He saw Hobbs pull out behind him. He eased up the street and headed for the outskirts of town. A few blocks and — lights on. Dark was coming on fast. Hobbs' car remained unlit. "Hide, you fool," Decker said. He picked up the pace a bit. Hobbs followed suit. Then when Decker hit the city limit sign, he said aloud, "Hold on, Mr. Policeman." And he stuck his foot in it. He saw Hobbs' lights come on, but then? A blur.

"Jesus Christ," Willy Hobbs said as Decker's taillights faded into the distance. He pulled to the shoulder. He turned the car around and headed for home. He had been made. He hoped the chief had been wrong about the old coot running and never returning. He would not mention this to anyone on the force.

***

Juliette Moore found Jenny Cartwright a bit stuffy at first — thought it might be an objection to her style of dressing, something she only did to keep Mitchell Polovina heated up in the first place. Later though, she discovered Jenny's apprehension had a whole lot more to do with the fact that she and Henry Nason never went anywhere outside of her own apartment together. She didn't even know where Henry lived. And as the evening progressed, a few choice beverages to lighten the mood, and Jenny and Juliette became friends — sisters even. Soon they were in an upstairs room together, hemming up Jenny's skirt to match the length of Juliette's, Jenny's reasoning being, it had caused Mitchell Polovina to step aside and share his home with Juliette Moore; perhaps the same principle might have a similar affect on Henry Nason. Not that she'd accept, but it had been a long time, too long, since Henry's last proposal. And who knows? Maybe a few more of whatever she had been pumping into herself — she honestly couldn't recognize the flavor — and she might surprise all of them including herself and say yes.

When the two girls came down the stairs, both men cocked their heads to the side, trying for a sneak-peak, the short skirts and booze egging them on. Mitch unbuttoned the top button of his shirt. Too hot. Henry loosened his tie. "You better be looking at yours," Henry said.

"Same to you," Mitch said. "Mind just one tiny observation though?"

"Go ahead."

"It looks to me that you, my friend, are about to start feeling much younger."

"It looks to me like I had better start acting it," Nason added.

***

On his way to bring Jenny Cartwright back to her home, Henry Nason kept crossing the centerline of the two lane highway. "You that drunk?" Jenny asked him.

"No," he said and took another peek at the lovely pair of legs beside him. He crossed the line again.

"That's it. Pull over," Jenny said.

"What for?"

"I can see that you're not going to pay attention to your driving until you get some, so pull over. Head up that road." She pointed to a dirt road.

"That leads into the mine," Henry told her. He turned. Why not? Should be private enough if it isn't packed with teenagers by now.

Homer Jenkins watched the car drive slowly up to and then pull around behind the building. "Damn teenagers," he said. He sat in the dark. He waited ten minutes. Then he grabbed a six-volt lantern and headed out into the moonlight. He turned the beam on as he neared the car and there they were, him sitting in the seat, her with her skirt hiked up around her waist, riding him like a bull at a rodeo. The couple looked at the light in shock, like deer caught in the sealed beams of an oncoming automobile, eyes wide open, not blinking. "Doc Nason? That you?" Homer asked.

"Get your ass out of here, Homer," Doc shouted.

"Get your *bare* asses off mining company property," Homer shouted back.

***

Two adults with two hangovers, and one little dog so stuffed with last night's outdoor cooked juicy steak she could not get out of bed at her usual five a.m. finally stirred at eight sharp. The first point of order for Mitchell Polovina after seeing that Juliette Moore could scarcely focus without sunglasses was to telephone Henry Nason.

"I'm going to interview Homer Jenkins this morning. Want to come along?" he asked Nason. Silence followed silence. Then, "Gray Eagle?"

"I'm here, Bugsy," Henry said.

"So… you wanna come along?"

"No."

"Why not?"

"I have my reasons," Henry said. Jenny awoke and stretched. She let out a scarcely discernable moan as she tried to sit up.

"You're not alone, you dog," Polovina said.

"No. I'm not. Go away, Bugsy," he said and hung up.

Mitch took a look at Juliette sitting on the edge of their bed, her, totally naked, and him, utterly unable to do a thing about it. He decided if he were to talk with Homer Jenkins on that day, it would be alone. Even Sis, their little mutt, or Victoria Outing's little mutt — whatever — would not come out from under the covers to join him. He kissed Juliette on the top of her head, patted a small lump in the bed, and said his goodbyes.

***

"Did you know I had company last night?" Homer asked the chief of police as he got out of his squad car.

"I did not," Mitch Polovina said.

"It was that doctor friend of yours, the one that dove with you. He had some floozy with him, and they was goin' at it in the car like I never seen before. That car was a-rockin', windows all a-steam, him — pants to his ankles, and her — skirt pulled up over her hips. I tell you, it was a sight to see, all that snow white skin glowing in the moonlight like that."

"Is that a fact?"

"That's a fact," Homer said. "If I was one of those youngsters with the cell phones that take pictures, I'd be able to prove it."

"I bet you would," Polovina said. He looked Homer over for a moment. "How about you and me have a little talk about those Jews this morning, Homer?"

"I told you before; I don't wanna talk to you. I'll talk with that pretty lady of yours though, the one with the legs," Homer said with a sparsely toothed grin.

"I'll bet you would at that," Mitch said. "I'm afraid I'll have to do today, though. Juliette is a little under the weather this morning. Now... did we decide those Jews who might be after you were the Cohens?"

"I don't know that we did," Homer said. "But we can, cause it would be them, not the originals — I'm guessin' they're good and dead by now — but their kin, I'd say."

"So why would they be after you?"

"I told all this to your girl. You was on the phone."

"That's right, Homer. I was on the phone. So you tell it again so I can hear it," Polovina told him.

"It was likely because I watched those boys kill Arthur Shaw. That's why." There was more to it than that, but what the chief of police didn't know by then, he may never come to know. And if he already knew, Homer would know about it soon enough.

Mitchell Polovina didn't understand. Why didn't they kill Homer back then? Was it because he was so young? Still... why wait until now? Then came the answer.

"My daddy worked with them back in those days, knew all about those stiffs in the drums. Had proof hidden away to protect us. That's why they left us alone until now."

"So why are they coming for you, I mean, you have that proof, don't you?" Mitch reasoned.

"The proof, whatever it was, died with my daddy. He never gave it to me. Those Cohens just found that out," Homer explained.

"How do you know that?" Mitch asked.

"I got a phone call."

CHAPTER TWENTY-SEVEN

"Your ass looks to be dragging this morning, Hobbs. Rough night?" Royal Parker asked. Willy Hobbs had been hanging out at the coffee counter in the station, drinking cup after cup, strong coffee, no sugar, no cream. Still, his eyelids were heavy. He had changed his mind. Rather than go home he had looked for the Buick most of the night, unsuccessfully, finally giving in to exhaustion at thee-thirty. "Too much barley-pop?"

"I don't drink, Parker. You know that. We worked together long enough to know that."

"Thought maybe you started," Parker said, filled his mug, and started back to his desk. He had an investigation to conduct. Hobbs was just small talk before he got going. He didn't give a damn if Hobbs was hung over or not, or if he drank or not—just small talk, that's all.

"Now, why the hell should I start drinking?" Hobbs came back.

Just like the old days, Hobbs always on the defensive. It had happened under the former chief and it was happening now. Parker thought Hobbs an adequate cop, but this one bad flaw of his, this incessant need to defend himself to the point of out and out argument was annoying and would be if Hobbs was the best cop in the office. It got him in trouble before and with Parker still considering himself Deputy Chief, it could again if Hobbs didn't control it.

"Nobody gives a shit if you drink, Willy. Just making conversation," Parker said and hoped it would stop there.

It did. Hobbs walked away. And lucky for him, he did so prior to Mitchell Polovina entering the office. Polovina had just dealt with Homer Jenkins, and other than knowing who the Jews were and why they were after Homer at this late stage in the game, he had pretty much left Homer feeling like he had run into a brick wall, an unpleasant and mood altering experience on a hangover.

"Morning, Boss," Parker said.

"Is it now?" Mitch asked.

Suck-ass, Hobbs thought but held himself back from saying.

"I'll be in my office. When Juliette Moore gets in, have her join me," Polovina said and closed the door behind him. He picked up his desk phone and called Henry Nason. "You get that second sample to the lab, the rat poison Parker and Casey found in the Cherry garage?"

"I did, but we won't need it. We got a match. The sample from Michael Decker's trunk is chemically identical to that found in the Cherry woman's blood. Decker's our killer."

"Pretty amazing for a dead man," Polovina said. He had been reading a report Paula Bloom had tossed on his desk earlier, a death certificate on a seven-year-old Michael Decker, a boating accident victim.

"Dead man?"

"Dead boy. He died at age seven. Doubt he was old enough to kill anybody, don't you?"

"Now what?"

"Now we haul the fake Decker in. Now we got reason, plenty of it."

"Can I come along? I've never been on an arrest, except Homer of course. But his didn't stick. I want in on a real desperado's capture. Know what I mean?" Nason asked.

"Why not? It'll be my first, ah… *desperado,* too. We'll bring Juliette. She has experience. She'll keep us from doing it wrong and having him walk on us." He hung up and dialed his house. No answer. She must be on the way.

***

Michael Decker's '67 Gran Sport was not parked in front of his apartment building when Mitch Polovina, accompanied by Juliette Moore and Henry Nason, arrived to arrest him. Had he parked somewhere else? Had he skipped on them? "What now?" Mitch asked.

"The manager must know something," Juliette offered, looking over the bank of mailboxes in the building's entry. "One-A," she said as her finger slid to a tag on one of the boxes. "Marion Gustafson,

Manager," she read aloud.

"Did you see Mr. Decker leave his apartment this morning?" Mitch asked the manager.

"Who?"

"Decker. Michael Decker. Three-C."

"Vincent Corelli lives in Three-C," Ms. Gustafson said.

"It says Michael Decker on the mailbox," Mitch told her. She stepped into the hallway. She walked to the bank of boxes in the entry and found Three-C. "Well I'll be damned," she said. "I never noticed that. He used Vincent Corelli on the lease."

"Does your lease show a previous address?" Juliette asked.

"It does, but I never checked it out. It was in Farwell, though. Will you need it?"

"That won't be necessary," Mitch Polovina told her. He was a lifetime resident of Farwell, and he knew the man did not come from there. "You don't check previous addresses out when people lease from you?"

"Sometimes, but that young man looked so honest, and what a nice smile," she said.

Mitch cautioned her that her tenant may not be who she thinks he is, and asked her to say nothing about them looking for him, and then left. He would station a couple officers nearby to watch for Decker's return.

In the car, Juliette asked, "How old would you say Ms. Gustafson is?"

"I make her to be around seventy," Henry said.

"Me too," Juliette said.

"Why?" Mitch asked.

"She referred to Decker, or Corelli, or whoever he is, as an honest looking *young* man with a nice smile." It confirmed Mitchell Polovina's previous conviction that Decker was a younger man with a Hollywood makeup job. He picked up the microphone and radioed Paula Bloom.

"Yes, Chief?" she answered.

Polovina thought for a moment. What if this Corelli had a police band radio in his car? "Nothing, Paula. We'll talk when I get back in. Ask Hartman and Willy Hobbs to join me at the station in a half-hour."

"Will do, Chief."

Polovina thought things too serious. A suggested change in

the program for the day might lighten them all up. "I'll drop the two of you," he began telling Juliette and Henry Nason, "at the station. You guys go out and see what more you can get out of Homer. He clammed up on me this morning."

"I'm not going to Homer's," Henry Nason objected.

"Why not?" Mitch asked.

"No reason, I'm just not going."

"There must be a reason," Mitch said and smiled.

"That little son-of-a-bitch," Henry said. "He told you, didn't he?"

"What?" Juliette asked. "He told you what?"

"It seems old Homer Jenkins caught a certain couple at the mine last night. That couple was in very peculiar position doing unspeakable things, according to Homer. Pants around the ankles, skirt hiked up considerably — that sort of carryings-on."

"Ah… the mine. That's a great place," Juliette said.

"Not when Homer's out there," Henry corrected.

Mitch pulled the car to a stop in front of the station. Inside, he set Paula Bloom to running the name Vincent Corelli past any and all law enforcement agencies, state and federal, that she could think of. It was not long before she had several hits and was able to compile a rap sheet longer than anyone in the town of Farwell had ever seen, (Mitch suspected) even back when the place first got its nickname of Little Cicero. He studied it. Arrests for anything and everything it seemed: illegal gambling, loan sharking, breaking and entering, drug dealing, murder. *Murder?* No convictions — none! "Run him through the DMV," he told Paula.

"I did. He holds a valid license. Address is St. Cloud."

"That figures."

"Why? Why does that figure?" Royal Parker asked. He and his new partner, Peter Casey had just entered the station.

"Because the Cohen brothers were from St. Cloud. This whole thing stems from the Cohens: the bodies, Edith Cherry's murder, Victoria Outing's money, Homer Jenkins' fear of Jews coming for him, everything. And Michael Decker, or Vincent Corelli, or whoever the man in the '67 Buick Gran Sport is, he's the key to solving all of it. Paula, you got a drivers license photo on this guy?" Polovina asked.

"I do," she said and handed him a sheet of paper.

He looked it over briefly, then handed it back. "Can you enlarge it?"

"The whole thing or just the photo?"

"Both." He looked around the room. "Make a half-dozen copies." He scoped out the room again. "The rap sheet too. I want everyone to have copies. And I want everyone in this office right after lunch. Everyone." He rose, motioned for Henry Nason and Juliette Moore to follow him, and walked out the front door.

***

Homer Jenkins knew who was coming. He watched the old Buick rolling slowly up the drive. He wondered what had taken so long for this. Why did the Cohens allow him to talk to the police at all? Why didn't this guy just do him first, on the day he arrived around Little Cicero, and get it over with. It might have even been better. He was old anyway, Homer was. What's the difference? Maybe the Cohens' hitter didn't know about Homer until now. Had that goddamn Polovina tipped him off? Homer wouldn't put it past him. The Buick stopped twenty feet short of the office. The hitter got out. Should Homer sit tight, let it happen? Or should he make a run for it. It was tempting. Get it over with. But no, time to go. And Homer Jenkins slipped quietly out the back door of his office and into the thick brush beyond. He had, years ago now, set himself up with a plan for this day, a hideout dug into the bank of an ore dump. Could he still find it?

Vincent Corelli threw open the door to the mining company office. "You in here, old man?" he shouted. "We need to talk. I got a message for you from the Cohen Family. C'mon out. I won't hurt you. All the family wants is what's theirs, the money the old woman stole from them years ago, and of course, any interest she's made on it since. They know she still has it. They know you know about it too. Best you come out and we'll have this little talk. You got answers, and if you give me the right answers, you can go on your way. How's that. Homer? Homer?" Corelli began searching, pistol in one hand, tossing things aside with the other. No Homer Jenkins anywhere. He saw the back door, hasp slid back. "You clever old bastard. You were ready for me, were you?" And out into the brush he went.

***

After a lunch at Mick's Café, Mitchell Polovina and Juliette

Moore headed back to the office. Henry Nason took his lunch hour at the hospital conducting rounds, and then joined the rest of the police force in their meeting. Paula Bloom handed out printed material on Vincent Corelli for all to reference. "This," the chief began, holding up Corelli's enlarged driver's license photo, "is the man we're looking for. And this," he held up another photo, one of Michael Decker, "is also the man we're looking for. He's the same guy — made up to appear elderly. Parker, I know you've questioned the Cherrys about Michael Decker. Try showing them the other photo, see if Decker without the makeup rings any bells. Now the rest of you, find this man. Do not, I repeat, do not approach him on your own. If you need a reason, look over his rap sheet. He's a killer. So… let's do some teamwork so none of us ends up in Doc Nason's morgue, shall we? Be on the lookout for his car as well."

"What'll we do if we spot him?" Willy Hobbs asked.

"Call it in. Use cell phones, not the radio. I'm guessing he'll be monitoring the police band."

"Who do we call? You?" Hartman asked.

"Paula," Chief Polovina said. "Paula, you have everyone's cell-phone number I assume." Paula Bloom nodded. "Keep those lines open. When that call comes in, I want everyone there for the arrest. We'll only get one chance at Corelli, so let's not blow it. Team work." He dismissed his people. He had one more visit planned for the day.

***

Gravel had been scattered everywhere. Ruts had been carved in the hard-pack by angry tires. And the mining company's office looked deserted, in a hurry, doors — both front and back, standing wide open. Mitchell Polovina drew his sidearm before he opened his car door. He wanted to ask Juliette to wait in the car, but, considering he was green at his job while she was experienced, rethought his impulse. "Be ready," he told her. "Be ready for anything." He was ignoring his own order that no one approached Corelli on their own, and Corelli might well be between those open doors waiting for them. Who knew? But since he was being fueled by pure adrenaline and not by reason at the moment, he would examine his actions at another time. For now, he considered only that Homer Jenkins might be in there — in serious trouble.

At the door he signaled Juliette Moore that he would enter

first and that she would cover him. Then he dove, keeping low to the floor, rolling behind an overturned cabinet. No gunfire, no noise what so ever. Juliette entered. "I think he's already gone," she said and holstered her weapon.

Mitch got to his feet and made his way to the back door. "Think we'll find Homer out here? Maybe with a bullet in him?"

"Doubt it," Juliette said.

"Why?"

"The ruts. Whoever was here left angry. Had he found Homer, he would have left here pleased with himself. Homer got away. I'd bet on it."

"I hope you're right," Polovina said. He stepped into the brush. They searched for nearly an hour before giving up. Perhaps Homer had made his way through the woods and off of mining company property, back into town. He pulled out his cellular and pushed the preset for Ted Mayfield's office, once again ignoring one of his own rules, the one about leaving the line open. Oh, well, Juliette would get a call should anyone spot Corelli.

"Mayor Mayfield's office," the feminine voice answered.

"Put me through to Teddy," Mitch demanded.

"Who's calling?"

"Chief of Police Polovina," Mitch said. "And it's urgent."

"Mayor Mayfield," the next voice announced.

"Teddy, you heard from Homer?"

"Karla just called, Bugsy. He's made his way to my place. Scared shitless"

"I'm going to bring him in. It's the only way I can protect him. That alright with you?"

"Karla's going to fight you on it." He didn't know, considering recent events at the Mayfield home, if that was still true, but the warning wouldn't be a bad idea either way.

"Call her. This dude who's after him, he's a genuine hit-man. He'll plow right over Karla to get to Homer. I'm taking him in, Teddy. That's all there is to it," Mitch said and hung up before further argument could come.

CHAPTER TWENTY-EIGHT

"Yes sir. That there's Reverend Mudd," Mr. Cherry told Royal Parker and Peter Casey after studying Vincent Corelli's driver's license photo for several moments. His hair's longer in this picture, but I'm sure it's him."

"Did he visit you folks often? Parker asked.

"Me? Never. I don't hold much with preachers. Always handin' out pamphlets. Hell... I can't even read. Always suspected they knew that and just did it to embarrass me. He come 'round now and then to pray with the missus. She was a real prayin' kind, you know."

"When was the last time you saw this... ah... this Preacher Mudd?" Casey asked.

"The week Edith took ill. He come several times that week, just to check on her. They'd talk, they'd pray some, then they'd have tea."

"They'd have tea?" Parker asked. "You drink tea with them?"

"Nope! I be a coffee man. Tea's for women and children."

"The preacher drank tea though," Casey said looking for clarification.

"Nope. He'd have coffee. A couple times he even had a shot in it. Saw him put it in out of a flask he kept in his coat pocket. I wonder where that preacher got off to. I tried findin' him to give the funeral service seein' as how she was so fond of him."

Parker looked into the kitchen. He spotted a rather troubling stack of dishes. It appeared nothing had been cleaned in the room since Mrs. Cherry had last tidied up. "You got a maid, Mr. Cherry? Someone who helps out with the cleaning for you?"

"Can't afford one," he said and looked at where Parker had focused. "Maid wouldn't be allowed to work the kitchen anyway."

"Why's that?"

"My missus. She'd not allow nobody to mess with her dishes, not even the kids."

"When was the last time your dishes were done?"

"Two days before she died. I need to learn how to use that dish cleaning machine of hers. One of the kids is gonna teach me one of these days."

"Is the cup she last drank tea out of in that stack?" Parker asked.

"I reckon."

"Casey, gather all the cups" Parker ordered, then to Mr. Cherry, "It was a cup she drank out of?"

"It was," Mr. Cherry answered.

"All the cups, Casey. We'll bring them to Doc," Parker said. "Wear gloves. There might be prints."

***

The wild eyed Michael Decker, the eighty-year-old version of the sixty-two-year-old Vincent Corelli (according to the driver's license), glared at Doctor Henry Nason when he asked him to settle down a bit. He had been working into a heated argument with Victoria Outing over the location of her will. "None of this concerns you, Doc," he said.

"Anything and everything that might affect one of my patients concerns me," Henry Nason told him.

Decker's eyes softened. He'd try a less hostile approach. "Of course. Forgive me. It's just that my mother can be... well... let's just say somewhat stubborn these days. I suppose it's her illness. I really should be more cautious with her."

Nason nodded, and then went into the hall. He'd go to the nurse's station and phone Paula Bloom as he had been instructed. Their suspect was in just the right place for an arrest. It was unlikely he would resist and blow the cover he had worked so hard to create and maintain in front of the woman he wanted to convince she was his mother.

And so far as Decker knew, his cover hadn't been blown. Sure, there was the cop or private eye, whoever the hell that was who tried to tail him the other night, but he felt certain that joker had only been on a fishing expedition. The disguise was too clever, the two characters so far apart in age. Don't discount the third persona either, the one used on old Mrs. Cherry, the one he liked to think of as the preacher gig. Too bad about that old woman. She almost got to him, reminded him of his own mother even more so than Victoria Outing. The more he interacted with her, the more he came to admire her. She had a strength that seemed to outdo most others. Even as she slowly died from arsenic that unmatchable strength shined through. If only old lady Outing hadn't made her the protector of her will. If only as protector of that will she hadn't been so resolute about protecting it. Maybe he could have spared her. Not likely though. She'd still be a loose end. Oh well, why kick his own ass over it? Why kick his own ass over something that had to be done? At any rate, the local law would never figure him as the preacher; they were far too busy watching Michael Decker. He smiled at the thought as he walked into the hall outside Victoria Outing's hospital room and saw the doctor, no longer dressed in his standard white coat, along with the police chief and two officers — one male — one female, approaching at a purposeful pace, a scene reminiscent of Wyatt Earp, his two brothers, and Doc Holiday, all headed for the OK Corral. His smile grew. It was time for questioning. *Watch this,* he thought.

"Vincent, Corelli," the chief said. "You're under arrest for the murder of Edith Cherry." And he began putting hand cuffs on Corelli's wrists while Hartman read him his rights.

It's okay, he thought. They're smarter than they look, but that only meant he'd need a different approach to get past this one. He'd figure it out. "Don't worry about a thing, Mother," he shouted into Victoria's room. "It's all just a misunderstanding."

***

"The chief wants an airtight case, Doc," Royal Parker told Henry Nason. "I'm betting on one of these teacups having the match to that poison you sent to the state lab, but I'm also betting we'll find Corelli's fingerprints on one of them. Mitch wants the test for poison first, and then he wants to run the prints against the prisoner's." The state had sent a test kit for this very purpose, one which would detect the presence of arsenic. The process, a relatively simple one, included swabbing the inside of the suspected cup with a solution. The solution, if it came into contact with even the most minute sample of arsenic, would change from clear to a light to dark purple — the darker the color the heavier the poison content. But color, any color, would need to be sent to the state for verification that it came from that previously submitted sample.

Nason pulled surgical gloves over his hands. "I won't spoil your prints," he said.

"How long before I should come back, Doc?" Parker asked.

"This is quick, might as well wait. If I find something, I don't need the cup. The state lab just wants the contaminated swab. You can take the cups and run them for prints."

***

"I'm afraid, Mrs. Mayfield, you do not have the right to stop this. Homer is being brought in for protection, it's true. But he also has information that might well implicate him in criminal activity," Juliette Moore told Karla Mayfield. They did not honestly know that Homer was involved in anything illegal, but used it as leverage, little twist of the law that it might be. To not do so, would stop them from protecting someone who did not wish to be protected. And that would describe Homer Jenkins to the letter. But despite his daughter's agreement with her husband to leave her father on his own instead of sacrificing their marriage to protecting him, when it came to watching Homer being cuffed like any common criminal, Karla could be trouble. She'd need watching.

Mayor Ted Mayfield pulled up in front of the house to see his father-in-law leaned up against the siding and being frisked by Juliette Moore. She did not want another incident like they had last time—Homer stabbing himself with an overlooked knife. He got out of his car and rushed across the front lawn. "Is all that necessary?" he asked. The look of disdain on his wife's face told him he *should* ask.

"You saw it last time, Mr. Mayor. I don't want him bleeding all over the car again."

"I mean, I'm sure we can see to him right here," Mayfield said, his tone an attempt to usurp authority over the female officer in the situation and impress his own wife and father-in-law in the process.

"Your police chief disagrees with you," Juliette said. "He's convinced at least one person after Homer is a professional hit man, and he's certain that you and your wife are no match for him."

"We'll decide that, Officer Moore."

"No, Mr. Mayor. Chief Polovina decides that. As I explained to your wife, this action is to protect him, but it's also an arrest— with cause. Now you, Sir, do not want to interfere with an arrest," Juliette said and unsnapped the flap of her holster.

"What're you going to do, Miss Moore? Shoot me?"

"If necessary. But only to wound. Step aside please." And Teddy Mayfield did.

"Do something, Ted," Karla shouted out.

"I will, Karla. Just not here. Not now."

Without further incident, Juliette Moore helped Homer Jenkins into the backseat of the police cruiser, her hand protecting the top of his head as he sat. She wished Doc Nason was nearby. She wished for Homer to be sedated. It was only a mile to the cop shop, but it would be a long mile.

***

"I get a phone call, don't I?" Vincent Corelli asked as Royal Parker and Peter Casey stuffed him into the cell next to Homer Jenkins.

"After you're booked," Parker told him.

Homer Jenkins studied the newcomer for a time, deciding that he recognized him from somewhere. *But where?*

"What're you staring at, you old fuck?" Corelli said, tiring of Homer's glare.

"All right, Corelli," Mitchell Polovina said. "Enough with the language."

"What the fuck are you going to do? Lock me up?"

Homer recognized the voice and began to shake. It was the voice of his warning phone call a number of days earlier, the call telling him someone would be around shortly to collect for his crimes against the Cohan family so many years before. He cowered in a far corner of his holding cell. He pointed a bony finger at Corelli and opened his mouth to say something. Corelli slid a finger across his own throat as a warning. He smiled cynically and flipped Homer off. Homer did not speak.

"As soon as you guys get the paperwork done," Mitch told Parker and Casey, "Take him downstairs and clean the makeup off him. Let's unwrap this package and see what's inside."

"You going somewhere, Chief?" Parker asked.

"I'm going to see to his car — get it to the impound. Then I'm going to lunch. After that, I'll be seeing Doc Nason and continuing my interview with Ms. Outing."

"Oh, I almost forgot." Parker said. "Doc found poison in one of the cups Casey and I gathered from the Cherry home. We brought them all in to check for prints."

"There'll be a match. You find it, Parker. You find it and then you call me." He looked at Parker, a steely stare, then motioned him aside and whispered in his ear. He told Parker he didn't care if he had to hand Corelli a cup, then take the print from it. He concluded with, "He's a killer." Then Mitchell Polovina walked out of the station, Juliette Moore on his heels.

Mick's Café was crowded at lunch time; concentrating, with the extra noise, was difficult. "Where'd all these people come from?" he asked Juliette.

"It's welfare payday. They eat out the week of welfare payday."

"Really," he commented.

"I swear. It's true. Try the Vet's club tonight. It'll be full of 'em."

"Really," Mitch commented again. He had never been one to hang out in bars. He didn't like the noise. He didn't like the smoke. And he didn't have a need to go out to pick up women. On that plane, he always seemed in demand — had a gaggle of ex-wives to prove it.

"Really," Mitch repeated. "How do you know all of this?"

"I had a life before police work," she said. And when he said nothing, just appeared to have sunk into deep thought, she asked, "Something gnawing at you, Mitch?"

"Corelli's driver's license," he said. "Was it a commercial?"

Juliette pulled out a cell phone and called the station to check. "It was," she said, still connected.

"Have Paula find out how that lawyer who handled Sister Mary Elizabeth's will died." Mitch recalled something way back in his memory. He wondered if it had been that attorney he was remembering. The details were cloudy, but something rang a bell.

"She'll call back," Juliette said and ordered the noon special for both of them.

"How do you know that's what I want?" Mitch asked her.

"Might as well get used to it. Your future doesn't include choices, not when it comes to eating. I've had an eye on you. You don't eat healthy."

"And you're going to fix that?"

"You bet your ass I am," she said and smiled. She flagged the waitress off to get their food, the argument being short lived. "Now, what is it you're thinking?"

"How do you like being a cop?" he asked.

"It's okay," she said.

"Just okay?"

"It beats going out to lunch in the first week of the month, then going to the VFW." He shot her a curious look. "What? I told you I had a life before police work."

"I'm wealthy, you know," he said.

"Yeah, the invention for mining company equipment. So?"

"We wouldn't have to work," he said.

"Is this your way of saying you want something more permanent?"

"I... I guess it is," Mitch admitted.

"I thought you were kinda set against marriage," Juliette said.

"No. I said I was a bad marriage risk," he corrected.

"And just why is that?"

"Well... I had a mother who seemed to think of me as unwanted. I fought in Vietnam at too early an age, so my first experience with authority had me pointing a gun at other living beings — something I really never came to grips with. And when it came to choosing women, I chose poorly, always someone who considered themselves far above me."

"Anything else?"

"Yeah. I was raised Catholic."

"What's that got to do with anything?"

"If you're raised Catholic, you're raised on superstition and guilt," Mitch said.

"So why am I different? Why me?" Juliette asked.

"You're above me. That makes you somewhat the same. But you don't think you are. That's what makes you different." He dug into a pocket and came out with a small package. He flipped it open. It contained a full karat diamond. "I'd like you to be with me forever," he said.

"Will you love me forever?" she asked.

"I will. So?"

"So, what?"

"So… will you?"

"Will I what? Say the words, Mitchell Polovina," she prompted.

"Will you marry me?"

"Yes," she said. She got up. Walked around to his side of the table, pulled his chair out with him still in it, straddled him, snatched the ring box, and kissed him passionately while the crowd in Mick's Café applauded.

CHAPTER TWENTY-NINE

"What would you like to learn today, Mitchell Polovina?" Victoria Outing asked when Mitch, Henry Nason, and Juliette Moore entered her hospital room. Her eyes seemed a bit too sunken. Mitch hoped it was from medication and not death approaching. Henry Nason knew it was the latter and there was little he could do about it. Juliette Moore was too engrossed in the look of her hand, new diamond in place, to notice.

"I'd like to know why you became a nun," Mitch said.

"Do you want the convenient answer?"

"Excuse me?"

"The convenient answer. The answer my father would give if he were here."

"I want the truth," Mitch clarified.

Victoria closed her eyes for a time, gathering her thoughts, and then approached the subject from her usual stranger's point of view.

***

Victoria lived out the next couple of months after her mother's death a total stranger to her father, and as a mate rather than a casual companion to Arthur Shaw. They spent their days together, her helping him deliver his wares to the various underground speakeasies beneath the town's main street and to the mining company locations where his more legal product was occasionally needed. Their nights, they spent in celebration of whatever they had done that day. Life was a party. Life was glamorous. That is, until she discovered she was pregnant.

That one fact bore down on them like an approaching storm, causing them to hide, to seek shelter from the truth, neither of them having an intention of letting the lifestyle they had been enjoying be altered. But altered it would be. They fought, words at first, then bruises and broken bones. Abortion had been suggested and quickly declined, the couple finally coming to grips with the idea of family over partying. And it was this that eventually became the downfall for Arthur Shaw and for Victoria Outing and the baby growing within her.

Arthur went to Victoria's father. "The hell you will," was his answer to Arthur's asking for permission to marry his daughter. It seemed his loss of a wife took with it his fear of Arthur Shaw's power in the community. And when Shaw decided to press the issue with the news of Victoria's pregnancy, Victoria's father came at Shaw with a stick of firewood, nearly beating him unconscious before he could get away. "And I don't ever want to see you or that little bitch around here again," he yelled as Shaw made his escape.

The couple set up living quarters in the back section of the warehouse, their bedroom being the same place he had taken her virginity from her earlier in the summer. Their relationship faltered — often — and in its faltering, Arthur found reason to be gone more and more. And young Victoria found travel from speakeasy to speakeasy alone at night when Arthur was away more and more enjoyable. She became every man's favorite dance partner, most of them copping the occasional feel from time to time as liquor quieted the moral fiber that was otherwise in them. But she stopped them always, before a hand slid below her waist. And when the occasional dance partner tried to follow her back to the warehouse at the end of the evening, they would be met by the business end of a colt pistol she kept under her pillow.

But sooner or later, it was bound to be. Arthur Shaw caught wind of the goings on in his absence and more fighting came, violently at times, finally culminating in a decision on Shaw's part that they would, with or without her father's approval, wed and raise their child together. But that decision brought only temporary happiness.

Shaw began to steal from his St. Cloud partners in the illegal booze business, the Cohen brothers. The Cohens were mean through and through, and had no qualms about ripping a man's liver out if they felt it necessary to solve a problem or set an example. Theft was all right so long as one was stealing for them, but to steal from them was an entirely different and inexcusable act. It brought out the worst in them. And it was that worst that Arthur Shaw would come to know.

It happened on a fall evening, one where a heavy frost caused the breaths of the three men in the woods to billow like smoke from a campfire. Arthur Shaw begged for his life but would not give up the location of the hidden stash of stolen Cohen money. They removed fingernail after fingernail trying to loosen his tongue while young Victoria helplessly watched from a distance. Shaw never weakened and even as he screamed out in pain he protected her and the future he had gathered for her and their unborn child. The Cohen's would not get their money, and would finally put an end to Arthur Shaw's miserable life. But even that, they did not do in haste. They poked a tiny hole in his carotid artery and spat on him and kicked him while he slowly bled out. And then the Cohen brothers walked away feeling as though their money had at least brought them some pleasure.

Victoria Outing approached the lifeless body of her love as soon as the brothers disappeared, and stared down on him for a long time. Then she went home to her father.

"So...," Victoria's father began, "the slut of the century returns, her man as dead as her mother, her options thrown into my lap like so much dirty laundry. Go to your room. Sleep. We'll deal with you tomorrow."

Victoria went to her room but she did not sleep. She saw the gruesome sight she had witnessed over and over again, and wished that she had gone to the tunnels to drink enough shine to make her blind so she would not see it anymore. Perhaps tomorrow night she would do just that. But she would not see tomorrow night, at least not as a free person. For her father, before she had food in her young belly to keep her unborn child company, hauled her to the convent where she would deliver her baby, give it up for adoption, and become a nun for at least the remainder of her father's life. She would never see him again. She would hardly see anyone from her past again, for before she broke free from that place — from that life — all who she had known she would scarcely recall. But the money that rightfully belonged to the Cohen brothers, she would keep — as payment for the lives they had destroyed. And she would see to it that it did enough good to make up for its evil.

***

Victoria Outing laid back and closed her eyes, their lids

squeezing tears free to roll down her cheeks one after another until they began to pool on her pillow.

"I think she's had enough," Henry Nason said.

"So do I," Juliette agreed.

Mitchell Polovina agreed with them in silence, but felt compelled to clear up one thing that troubled him. "Was Homer Jenkins with you the night Arthur Shaw died?"

"Heavens no. Homer was but a tyke. Did he tell you he was there?"

"He did."

"Well… if he was, I certainly didn't know it." It was all she had to say for the day.

On the sidewalk outside the hospital Mitch Polovina looked at Juliette Moore through pity filled eyes. Tears welled. "I can't do this," he said.

"She really gets to you," she observed.

"Yes, she does." He paused briefly and looked down. "I can't do this job."

"Let's finish this, then we'll go away for a time," Juliette suggested. She hooked an arm through his and guided him toward the car. "I'll drive," she told him.

A long motorcycle ride and a fabulous home cooked meal did little to break his mood that evening. His thoughts hung on Victoria's account of a horrible youth spent by someone his admiration grew for as each day passed. This whole thing from bodies popping from the water, which, by the way, he still knew little about, was wearing him thinner and thinner. And he saw no end to it, no hope of escaping it.

Juliette Moore admired her ring as the night went on. It helped her cope. It helped her forget that the man she loved had a dark side she knew little about. But as she looked at that ring she knew he loved her. That was enough for now. She would figure out the rest as they went along.

Doctor Henry Nason spent the entire night at the hospital. He slept in a chair beside Victoria Outing's bed. He felt someone should be there, someone who would protect her.

CHAPTER THIRTY

Parker and Casey managed to get Michael Decker transformed into his real character, Vincent Corelli, hit man for the Cohen family, by removal of his Hollywood makeup job. Unfortunately, the battle that ensued while the process played out left Royal Parker with bite marks on an ear and Peter Casey with a black eye and a swollen lip. Corelli, at the ripe old age of sixty-two, proved to Casey one more time, that the sixties were not old enough to be counted among the elderly where fighting was concerned. It made him wish he would age a bit himself, just so he could be as tough. But all said and done, Corelli was finally contained in his own cage next to Homer Jenkins again, and the two officers were off licking their wounds. And so long as they were out of the room and beyond hearing distance, Corelli chose to wake Homer and have that talk he thought of more than anything since his arrival at the police station. He threw things at Homer and called out to him. Homer finally opened his eyes.

"Hey there. Little weasel," Vincent Corelli said.

Homer tried to ignore him.

"Talk to me, little weasel, or I promise I will kill you first chance I get."

"What you want from me?" Homer asked, his voice — strained — shaky — nearly an octave too high.

"Silence, little man. Question is, do I have to kill you to get it?"

"No!"

"You just remember, you say anything, and I'll slit your throat and watch you bleed to death," Corelli warned. Then he lay back on his bunk and closed his eyes just as the two policemen who were to guard them for the night walked back into the office.

Homer Jenkins did not sleep any more that night.

***

"You know what we're missing in all of this?" Mitch Polovina asked Juliette over coffee at the table in the morning.

"In all of what?" Juliette asked.

"The bodies, Mrs. Cherry's murder, Victoria's story, Homer Jenkins part — whatever that is," he said.

"What are we missing?"

"All the bodies. That's what started all of this and we know nothing. All we have is that one of them is Arthur Shaw and one of them is Nancy Bjorquist. Other than that, we're in the dark. We seem to have a mass murder and no mass murderer or even a clue to his identity."

"I think we have a clue. I think everything points to the Cohen brothers," Juliette said.

"Maybe so, but I want to know that, not think it," Mitch said.

"I thought you wanted out of all of this," Juliette reminded him.

"I do, but you said finish it. I've never left anything undone and I'll never forgive myself if we don't come up with all the answers."

"So let's come up with them. Where do we start?" Juliette asked.

"Homer. Get dressed. Let's interview him."

"What about Victoria?" Juliette asked, knowing she had more of the story than Homer. It had been her, after all, who told them that Homer was too young in the days of those murders. "Wouldn't she be the one to ask about all of this?"

"Homer knows something. He may or may not have seen anything, but he knows something. Besides, I'm curious. Why did he want us to think he was aware of what went on? Why did he say he saw Arthur Shaw die? And did he really, or is it as Victoria says, he wasn't there?"

"Interesting questions," Juliette admitted.

"They are. We need to find out if the answers are as interesting."

***

Paula Bloom handed Mitch a paper as he entered the office. It was a fax from Sheriff Kuhn over at the county seat, a report of an automobile accident more than a decade old, in which the attorney who drafted the original will for Sister Mary Elizabeth, according to the report, had been run off the road by a semi. It was what Mitchell Polovina suspected he'd learn after seeing that his new prisoner, Vincent Corelli, held a commercial license. Another piece of the puzzle. Corelli, the hit man for the Cohen family, the missing money, a dead lawyer who prepared the will to keep the Cohen money safe, it was beginning to snap together like it had been written for a television detective show. He handed it to Juliette Moore.

"Amazing," she said a moment later.

"Yeah!"

***

Homer Jenkins never made it to an interrogation room when he was last arrested. He spent his entire incarceration in a hospital room, with his daughter, Karla Mayfield for company. This time would be different. The police chief himself took him to a small room in the basement of the station, next to the shower where Michael Decker had been stripped of his makeup and transformed into Vincent Corelli. The floor of the shower, visible from where Mitch Polovina placed Homer Jenkins, was covered in flesh colored poly fragments of Corelli's former facial features. It looked as though a wild animal had devoured a human being in there. Homer felt sick. Mitch saw it in his facial expression. He left the room to let Homer stew for a time in the heat of the scene. He had seen the technique used many times on television and thought it worth a try.

Mitch Polovina returned to his office and sought the advice of his staff. This was, after all, the first official interrogation by a totally inexperienced and untrained chief of police. He received offers from everyone in the room but Juliette Moore to take the task on in his stead, but thought it too time consuming to go through the process of explaining just what he wanted in the way of results from a talk with Homer Jenkins. Besides, he thought it might be fun. He returned, armed with the best of advice from everyone, to interrogate Homer. He pulled a chair to the table across from Homer and slapped a file folder down between them. He opened the file and fumbled through the papers within for a time in silence, shaking his head from side to side for no particular purpose other than to make his subject nervous. He looked up occasionally at Homer. It was working. Time to begin.

"Nothing to be nervous about, Homer," he said and looked at the file again. "Just a few questions to clear things up." He flipped a few pages over, settling on one, which he picked up and pulled close to his face. "Why'd you say you're manager of the mine?"

"Because I am," Homer answered.

Mitchell Polovina tossed the paper he had been studying on the table. "No you're not." It was Homer's last communication from the company, letting him know he had been pensioned off and that there would be no further need for a manager at the facility.

"It's wrong. Once in a while they're wrong."

Mitch flipped another page at him, this time his first pension check, dated one month after the letter.

"That place needs me."

"You weren't there when they killed Arthur Shaw either, were you."

"I was there," Homer insisted.

"Victoria Outing said you weren't. She said you would have been too young." Mitch pitched Homers birth certificate on the table. "I believe her. You'd have been far too young."

"So what?"

"So you need to level with me, Homer. You need to tell me the truth about what took place way back then. I need to find out why you say the Jews are coming for you. Why is that, Homer?"

"Because I buried one of 'em. That's why. And they think I had something to do with killing him," Homer admitted.

"One of the Cohen brothers?"

"Not the brothers. But a Cohen just the same."

"Tell me about that," Mitch said.

"Can't."

"Why not?"

"I wasn't alone, and I promised to keep quiet no matter what," Homer said.

The interview went on more than an hour longer with few results. Mitch did learn, or at least pumped sufficient information out of the old man to make him believe, Victoria Outing was somehow connected to him. Maybe it hadn't been in the early days when Arthur Shaw met his end at the hands of the Cohen brothers, but a connection just the same. Mitchell Polovina chose to let Ted and Karla talk to Homer, to see if they could loosen his tongue a bit. He'd set up audio without their knowledge. He left Homer in the little room, went back upstairs, ordered Royal Parker and Peter Casey to clean up the mess they had left in the shower before the Mayfields arrived, and sent Willy Hobbs to the District attorney with Vincent Corelli's case file to seek an opinion on whether or not charges of murdering Edith Cherry would stick, or if the Farwell Police needed more evidence.

"I… I seem to have misplaced the keys to the squad car, Chief," Hobbs said.

"You did?" Mitch asked. "How'd that happen?"

"I don't know. I gave them to Casey yesterday. He needed the cruiser for a time. He claims to have put them on my desk. But I can't find them anywhere."

"Paula," the chief yelled out. Paula tossed a ring of keys in his direction. "Spares," he told Hobbs. "Don't lose them."

Mitch went into his office and called the mayor. He invited him to bring Karla and talk with the stubborn Homer Jenkins. "See if you two can get him to tell all. I can't very well protect him unless I know what to protect him from."

"He's not a criminal, Bugsy," Ted Mayfield said, still strongly objecting to his father-in-law being arrested.

"Ah… but he is, Teddy. He's admitted to burying somebody. And that's a crime. Now maybe if that's all there is, we can talk with the DA and get him some sort of bargain, maybe even immunity from prosecution for the truth. If that's all there is." Mitch had seen that done on TV and was certain it would work in real life. "Talk to him. That's all I ask."

"We're on our way," the mayor told him.

Police Chief Mitchell Polovina sat back in his chair and sipped a cup of coffee while Paula Bloom escorted the mayor and his wife to the interrogation room where Homer was being held. Juliette Moore entered with sandwiches. There was no way a lunch at Mick's would fit into their tight schedule today. Mitch could blame Homer for that. Had he given up the goods earlier, there'd be no need for all of this.

"You'll be glad to have this behind you, now won't you?" Juliette observed.

"You bet your cute little ass I will. Shut the door, will you?" And Juliette shut the door.

She started to speak, but was shushed. Voices began across a small intercom speaker on the desk. Mitch cranked up the volume.

"Why won't you tell him what you know?" Karla Mayfield asked her father.

"Because I'll never see daylight again."

"Why," Ted asked. "Mitch has agreed to get an immunity grant for you if you'll speak out about the body you helped bury."

"There's a whole lot more to it than that," Homer insisted. "I haven't exactly told you all of it."

"So tell us, Daddy," Karla said. "It's just us here. No one else. Tell us."

"I lied to you. I lied to everyone. I was too young to have known anything when Arthur Shaw got hit."

"You told me you were six, and you saw it," Karla said.

"I was six. But I didn't see it. I just know from rumors what happened. I thought if I said the Jews were after me because I witnessed a murder, Polovina would leave me alone. He's not buying it, is he?" Homer asked.

"No, he's not," Ted Mayfield said. "So what really happened?"

"It was later. I was an adult. My daddy made me do it."

Mitch Polovina jotted in a note pad, a reminder to himself that the only rumor Homer could have heard had to come from Victoria. He turned the volume up another notch.

"Granddad made you do what?" Karla asked.

"Help Victoria bury the body. Only he didn't know," Homer said and hung his head.

"Know what?" Ted asked.

"He didn't know I helped kill him."

Mitch's eyes grew in size. "What'd he say?"

"You heard him right," Juliette said. "Homer's just admitted to murder and we can't legally charge him."

"Why not?"

"It'd be thrown out as hearsay, or entrapment, maybe both. Mitch, we have to get Homer to talk to us. We have to get a confession out of him."

"How? We don't even know who he killed."

"It was that priest, the one who sodomized Victoria Outing at the convent," came Homer's voice over the speaker.

"Jesus Christ," Mitch said and flipped off the volume.

"Why'd you do that?" Juliette asked.

"I want Homer to stand trial. This is too much. And I think I know just how to make it happen."

"How?" Juliette asked.

"I'll get Victoria to implicate him."

CHAPTER THIRTY-ONE

A backyard campfire was something Mitchell Polovina never would have expected, but the latest addition to the long and varied string of women in his life, Miss Juliette Moore, was different from the rest by miles. She dressed as she pleased (and as pleased him), she worked a job alongside men (all the others wouldn't have been caught dead working at all), she rode motorcycle with him (and whatever else she could come up with on two wheels), and she liked camping and campfires. And one in the backyard of Mitch's upper class home in the middle of a drought with friends like Henry Nason and Jenny Cartwright suited her right down to the ground. It would not be long until it suited Mitchell Polovina equally.

"This is nice," Henry Nason commented, Jenny Cartwright leaning back on him in front of the fire.

"You would like it. All Indians like a camp fire, don't they?" Mitch said.

"Not the casino Indians," Henry said. "Their ancestors maybe, but not them."

"What you suppose they like, Gray Eagle?"

"I would think them to be rather fond of bells and sirens and the clatter of coins, Bugsy."

"Do these two spend all of their time trying to out-piss one another?" Jenny asked Juliette.

"Don't all men?" Juliette offered.

"When are you planning a dive, Bugsy?" Nason asked, more to get the women off the subject of the playful banter he and Mitch often engaged in and had done so since high school. Jenny, he knew, did not understand it, and therefore, was somehow intolerant of it.

"What dive?" Jenny asked. She didn't approve of diving in the pits — thought it dangerous.

"There's treasure under the streets of Little Cicero, Jenny.

Mitch has found us a way to get to it," Henry Nason told her.

"Little Cicero?" she questioned. She had heard Farwell called that on occasion, but it had been long ago. It didn't register at first. "Farwell's nickname, of course, the tunnels," she answered her own question. "And Mitch knows how to get in them? I thought they had been destroyed years ago."

"Not destroyed," Mitch told her. "Sealed off. Three feet of concrete covers the openings nowadays, so kids can't get into them and get hurt."

"So how do we get in them?"

"We?" Henry asked.

"Well… don't I deserve to see?" Jenny asked.

"Well," Henry started.

"Well, Nothing," Juliette Moore interrupted. "She goes if she wants to."

"Do you dive?" Henry asked.

"Only if there's treasure involved," Jenny said. "It's been some time though. I might need a refresher course."

"You know," Mitch said, "we're not talking real treasure. We're talking historical knowledge — that kind of treasure."

"I realize that, Mitchell. I just want to see," Jenny said.

"Then it's settled," Juliette said. "Henry will take you on a dive to freshen up your skills. So when do we dive?"

"Now wait a minute," Henry said. "I haven't agreed to anything."

"You will," Jenny Cartwright told him. "Juliette, here, has been instructing me on the techniques of modern dance, the kind you'll want to see, and so, considering the price for that show is diving lessons, well… you see where this is going."

"Want me to explain?" Mitch asked Henry.

"I think I got it," Henry said. "When do you want your lesson?" he asked Jenny.

"See how nicely that works?" Juliette asked Jenny.

"You mean how easy they are?"

The phone in the house began to ring. Mitch excused himself to answer it. When he came back, he looked as though his whole world had caved in on him. "Vincent Corelli got a hold of Homer Jenkins — tried to pull him through the bars. I best get to the station. Doc, you better come along too. Homer might need medical attention. We'll be as quick as we can, ladies."

***

The team of Hobbs and Hartman had chosen the short straws. They were the officers stuck with nightshift, the holding cells at the station having been filled to capacity. Mitchell Polovina, even though he had been told by the city council that any prisoners charged or to be charged with any serious offence, should be immediately transferred to county, opted to keep both of his detainees right there in Farwell for a time. One of them, after all, was the mayor's father-in-law, and the other, well… maybe he should have gone, but Mitch felt it better to keep him close until he could figure out what in the hell to charge him with. He knew there was more to it than poor Edith Cherry's recent demise. The floating bodies still demanded an explanation, and his connection to that and God knows what else remained very much a mystery. That mystery needed solving and Mitch thought it a waste of valuable time to drive back and forth to the county seat to interrogate the man whenever he or his inexperienced staff might come up with a question. And there was that other thing, the thing he and Teddy Mayfield and Henry Nason thought of when this all began. Go spreading this much beyond Farwell city limits, and how long would it take the feds and the hazmat geniuses to get here and begin draining the lake? The town's nickname, Little Cicero, kept it on the radar scope of those groups of fellows anyway. Give them a reason, everyone agreed, and they'll waste no time getting their hands in it up to their elbows.

Hartman looked worse for wear, sitting at Mitchell Polovina's desk when he came in. A nasty cut over her left eye, bleeding held off by a pressed down handkerchief, a bruised cheekbone, a split lip, and her clothing in tatters, told a tale of the struggle that must have taken place to subdue the aggressor. Hobbs, less battered but battered just the same, was cleaning wounds on Homer Jenkins' head, likely caused by his head hitting the bars of his cell. He was barely conscious. Doc Nason stepped in and took over while Mitch saw to Hartman.

"What the hell happened, Hobbs?" Mitch demanded.

"Homer got too close."

It made little sense to Mitchell Polovina. He had seen the look on Homer's face when he first recognized Corelli. No way. None at all. Homer wouldn't have gone near enough to Corelli for Corelli to touch him with a broom handle. "Where were you when this started, Hartman?" he asked.

Hartman, due to her now swollen as well as split lip, murmured barely audibly, "In the bathroom."

"Where was your partner when you came out of the bathroom?"

"He was trying to pry Homer loose from Corelli's clutches."

"Which cell was he in?"

"Homer's."

"And you? What did you do?" Mitch asked.

"I… I opened up Mr. Corelli's cell and tried to help," Hartman said.

"Brave," Henry Nason observed. "Brave but stupid. Why didn't you shoot him?"

"It happened too fast. Hobbs was pulling on Homer, trying to free him, and all I could think to do was to get in there and try to stop Corelli from beating him to death or strangling him."

"I hadn't thought of strangling the little fucker," Corelli yelled out.

"Shut your mouth, Corelli," Chief Polovina shouted back. "You keep it up and I'll personally come in there. Believe me, tough guy, that's something you want to avoid." Mitch Polovina rarely used his size, speed, and experience against any other human being, but in the case of Vincent Corelli, he'd gladly make an exception. And his threat wasn't mere boasting. He was a large man, mass and height more like a lineman than the quarterback he played in his youth, but fast — a lightening speed runner, odd for his size. And his Vietnam experience? Special Forces, not supply or office clerk. To sum up, Mitch Polovina was an adversary to contend with. His natural gentleness sometimes hid that from others.

Vincent Corelli was not stupid. He could read faces and in Mitch Polovina's he saw the truth of his words. Corelli doubted Polovina would say anything he couldn't back up. He leaned back in his bunk. If the need came, he'd require an advantage, and that took planning.

"I think we'd better take Homer to the hospital, Bugsy," Doc Nason suggested.

"You're the doctor. Better give Hartman a once over. She might need care too." But Nason cleared her, her wounds looking far worse on her pretty feminine features than they really were. Chief Polovina sent her home, and then called for an ambulance for Homer. He instructed Hobbs that he was not to go anywhere near Corelli until morning when someone else was in.

"What if I have to go to the bathroom?" Corelli asked. The holding cells had no facilities of their own. Detainees had to be escorted when a need arose.

"Piss your pants," Mitch said. He felt it just, considering what the man had done to Homer Jenkins.

"Will he be all right, Doc?" Hobbs asked about Homer Jenkins.

"I can't tell yet," Nason said.

"You'll have a guard on him, won't you?"

Henry Nason shot Mitch Polovina a glance. "He'll be guarded," Polovina said. "You give this piece of shit a phone call yet?"

"No, Sir," Hobbs said.

"Don't. I'll see to it in the morning, personally," he said and looked at Corelli for any reaction. There was none.

***

"Did you mean what you said in there, Gray Eagle?" Mitch asked once they were in the car and away from the station. He was referring to the doc telling Hobbs he couldn't tell if Homer would make it or not.

"Nope!" Henry said. "You?" Nason referred to the placement of a guard on Homer. Mitch hadn't called anyone.

"Nope!" Mitch remained silent for a time. "You got an out of the way room where nobody can find him, maybe a small staff to watch over him discretely?"

"I have a male nurse built like a linebacker. He'll stop anyone at the door, cops even if you wish."

"Everyone," Polovina ordered.

"You got a feeling about that Hobbs, don't you, Bugsy?"

"Why would he let little Lila Hartman go into Corelli's cage alone?" Mitch asked. "That's dumber than her doing it. Her, I understand. She's relatively green at the job. Him, though, a ten year veteran? It don't add up, Gray Eagle."

"You going to give Teddy Mayfield a call?"

"No. Don't you either. Think we need to cuff Homer to the bed?"

"He'll be too stiff and sore for a day or two. I don't see the need. Anyway, my linebacker nurse will keep him in his room."

"How do you think Homer's going to feel in the morning," Polovina asked.

"Like death is knocking on the door."

"Let's see him first thing. And let's not be too quick to tell him death isn't knocking," Mitch suggested.

"Why not?"

"The dying aren't so tight-lipped."

"You saw that on television," Nason commented.

"I did," Polovina admitted.

CHAPTER THIRTY-TWO

Victoria Outing's small dog who bore her name from when she was a nun, and who Mitch and Juliette had adopted and now call Sis, had been getting increasingly earlier with her wakeup calls. "You think there's something wrong with her?" Mitch asked Juliette at four-thirty the following morning. "Do you think we need to take her to a vet?"

"I read once that these little ones have an extremely keen sense of something gone wrong with their master. My guess is that Victoria is experiencing difficulty more and more during the night, perhaps toilet needs, maybe pain."

Mitch smiled at her explanation.

"What?" Juliette asked.

"Nothing, really. I just find it humorous that one of us takes his cues about certain things from television, and the other from magazines." He studied Sis as she walked laps around them in the bed for a moment, and then got up to take her out. He didn't mind. Sis was good company for Juliette and a fun scrapping and roughhousing partner for himself, activities that seemed to keep the kid in him alive. But it would mean a long day. Once up, he rarely went back to sleep. Oh well… he'd get an early start on things today. The rest of the world would have to catch up.

"Did she go?" Juliette asked when they return.

"She peed and pooped, big girl," Mitch announced in a high sing-song voice. He had taken to talking baby talk around Sis as it seemed to cause a wiggle in her that made it appear as though her aft half might come loose from the fore half. He personally got a kick out of watching her. Perhaps, Juliette thought anyway, he was the way he was with her because he had never had children. Pity. She sensed he would have made a fine father.

Sis jumped up on the bed and ran a few laps, then draped

herself across Juliette's midsection with a pounce. It seemed to let Juliette's air out. A fair payment, Mitch thought, for her making him be the one to hit the backyard every morning while she lay there under warm blankets.

"How did last night go?" she asked. He hadn't given her an update on the mishap at the station. The hour had been too late.

"Homer's in the hospital again. Hartman has a few bruises and cuts. How well do you know Hobbs?"

"Well enough to not like him," Juliette said.

"But, do you trust him?"

"I wouldn't want to partner with him, if that's what you mean."

"No. What I'm after is, can he be trusted? Is he honest?"

"Mitch, if I were the chief of police, I would not have that guy on the force," Juliette announced. "I know we're shorthanded, and crime is at an all time high for Farwell, probably even for Little Cicero, but I have my doubts that I would have him around anyway. I really question his loyalty."

"Me too."

"Will you fire him then?" she asked.

"No."

"Why not?"

"I think he's dirty. I think it's a better idea to keep him where he can be watched, Mitch said. "You hungry yet?"

"I could use coffee. You buying?"

***

Mitchell Polovina came face to face with Henry Nason's male nurse at Homer Jenkins' hospital room door. The nurse would not let him pass. Nason, inside going over the many contusions on Homer's head and breaks and bruises on his upper body, finally called out his permission for the chief of police to enter. "Linebacker my ass," Mitch told Doc. "The guy's a D-9 Caterpillar." His observation brought a grin of pride to Nason's face. "How is he this morning?" Polovina asked. He cocked his head and shot the doctor a warning frown.

Nason knew what he was to say. "Not good."

Homer looked up at him with curious terror.

"The chief needs to ask you a few questions, Homer. Are you up to it?"

"He's up to it," Mitch answered for the injured man. "Homer, you have to level with me," he said and dragged a chair to the bedside. He straddled it, the chair's back toward Homer. "How do you know Corelli?"

"I don't."

"Come now, Homer. I saw the look in your eyes when we brought him in and put him in the cell next to you. You were scared shitless." Mitch thought about the comment. *How could that be? Either a man had the shit scared out of him, or he was scared shitless. Was it the same thing?* "You're going to answer my questions or I'm going to put you back in that cell. That's the only two directions this is going to take. It's your call."

"He's a hit man for the Cohens," Homer offered.

"We already know that. How do you know it? Have your paths crossed before?"

"I seen him before," Homer admitted.

"When?"

"You ever hear about a couple women being found floating in the pit back when my dad was chief of police?"

"I did," Mitch said.

"I saw him then."

"He killed those two?" Mitch asked. This guy, this Vincent Corelli was the real deal.

"He didn't kill them," Homer said.

"Then who did?"

"My dad."

"Why?"

"They found Victoria's money and they were about to tell the Cohens. I guess they called in Vincent Corelli before my dad got 'em."

"Then your dad killed the two girls before Corelli got any information out of them?" Mitchell Polovina asked.

"Makes sense. She does still have the money," Homer said.

"Corelli's a hit man. Why didn't he kill your dad?" Mitch asked him.

"He was told me and my dad was off limits, 'cause of what my dad knew. Daddy had the goods on the brothers, information that would put them behind bars for the rest of their lives. They was afraid of my dad."

"But not afraid of you," Mitch observed.

"Why should they be? I didn't know nothing?"

"But they left you alone because of your dad?"

"Not Corelli. He found me back then. He held me out in the woods for two days, no food, no water, tied to a tree with bugs crawlin' all over me. He beat me with a hose now and then, just to see if I knew anything. I didn't. And he finally left the area; me still tied up in the woods."

"How'd you get away?" Mitch asked him. He thought over what Homer had just said. No wonder he was scared to death of Vincent Corelli.

"Victoria Outing found me. She took me to that convent she used to live at. The nuns nursed me back to health. They hid me for months, until the priest found me," Homer explained.

"The priest?" Polovina asked. "Hennasy?"

"No. Another priest. Can't recall his name. He sure didn't want me around there. Seemed almost afraid of me. Run me right out of there, he did."

"Tell me, Homer. Getting back to the two women found in the water… naked. You have any part in that?"

Homer Jenkins looked away for a time. "My daddy made me do it."

"What, Homer? Your daddy made you do what?"

"He made me undress those two, then he made me throw their bodies in the lake."

"Why not burry them? Why not try to hide them?" Mitch asked. It seemed the better thing to do, the less obvious. Why would someone murder two people and not try to hide the bodies?

"My dad wanted to leave the Cohens a lesson. Stay out of Little Cicero. Leave Victoria Outing alone. That sort of thing. And as far as hiding the bodies? Hell… all daddy had to do is order the coroner over at the county seat to call 'em drowning victims."

"Your father had that much power?" Mitch asked.

"My daddy was hooked up with the Cohen brothers and Arthur Shaw. Everyone around Little Cicero feared him," Homer said.

"But the coroner was county."

"He came from here," Homer explained. "He once worked for my dad."

Mitchell Polovina thought things through. Progress had been made. Now he had the story of the two women in the water, and it all added up. But there was more Homer knew. And Mitch needed it. "What do you know about the priest, not the one who ran you out of the convent after Vincent Corelli tied you up in the woods, the one who attacked Victoria?"

Homer became tight lipped. He clammed up. He wouldn't say more. Mitchell Polovina, even Doc Nason, tried to get him to give up more of the story, but no. Homer wouldn't budge. "You go ask Victoria herself if you wanna know more," was his staunch answer to their questioning.

"Ever kill anyone, Homer?" Mitch finally asked.

Homer Jenkins closed his eyes. Polovina thought he saw a tear slip from under an eyelid. Regret? Maybe. Maybe dust. Homer Jenkins refused to reopen them.

***

"What now?" Henry Nason asked.

"Breakfast at Mick's. Juliette is going to meet me there. Want to give Jenny a call and join us?"

"She won't drive the distance for breakfast."

"Gray Eagle?" Mitch questioned. "I'm a trained investigator. Don't you think I know where that girl spent the night?" Mitch was guessing, but considering the late hour at which Henry and Jenny left him and Juliette the night before, it was a safe bet.

"I'll call her. If she's up to it, we'll meet you at Mick's."

"Before you leave, warn your D-9 nurse that Parker will be by to guard Homer. I wouldn't want him to pound Royal Parker into the ground just for showing up," Mitch said. He punched in the station's number and spoke with Parker. He asked if Hobbs was still in the station, to which he was told the officer had gone home. He told Parker where he was to report and what to watch out for, mainly the linebacker. He instructed Parker to tell no one, not his partner, not even dispatch. "And, Royal. Be alert. Expect trouble. And if trouble comes, use your weapon. Don't let anyone get to Homer. And cuff Homer to his bed. I expect he'll try an escape before long."

"Corelli's screaming for his phone call, Boss," Royal Parker said.

"Tell him he'll get it as soon as I arrive."

"When will that be?"

"After breakfast. You got my cell number programmed into

your phone?"

"Yes, Sir."

"Use it at the first sign of trouble, even if it only looks like trouble. Anything out of place."

***

"Are you and Mitchell coming by this morning?" Victoria Outing asked Henry Nason when he stopped to check on her.

"I don't know," Nason said. "Why? Did you have something to tell us?"

"Ask him to stop sometime today. It's important," she said and rolled on her side, facing away from Doc Nason.

CHAPTER THIRTY-THREE

"Are you going to give Corelli his phone call?" Juliette asked. The waitress poured their coffee and handed them each a menu.

"There'll be two more joining us," Mitch told the waitress.

"Well?" Juliette asked.

"Well, what?" Mitchell Polovina's thoughts were too wrapped around what Homer Jenkins avoided saying. Something gnawed at him, something connected to the priest, the one who went after Victoria. The priest had a whole bunch more to do with things than anybody was willing to admit, or so Mitch's gut told him.

"Are you going to give Corelli his phone call?"

"I am. But I'm going to charge him first."

"We got enough to make charges stick?" Juliette thought not. Her experience in the field had taught her that it didn't take much for a clever criminal to skate by weak charges.

"Oh yeah. We got plenty," Mitch said. He studied his menu for a moment before going on to explain. "Maybe we can't make Edith Cherry's murder stick, but assault charges over that little incident last night, they'll stick to him like glue. Might even get an attempted murder out of it. We'll charge him first. Then we'll let him have a call."

"Charge who?" Henry Nason asked as he and Jenny Cartwright approached.

"You, Gray Eagle. We're going to charge you for being so late," Mitch said and stood. "Good morning, Miss Jenny. Sleep well?"

"Well. Not long though," she said and smiled.

"What's for breakfast?" Nason asked.

"That's the charges for your tardiness. Breakfast is whatever you buy, yours and ours. What kept you anyway?"

"Victoria Outing. She wants you to stop by. Says she has

something important to tell you."

"She say when I was to be there?" Mitch asked.

"Before the end of the day."

Mitch looked at his watch — nearing ten already. He had Corelli to see to, that should take him several hours. Then he wanted to talk more with Teddy Mayfield. He thought Teddy and Karla might get Homer talking one more time. Then he would have time for Victoria. "Will you be going with me, Henry?"

"I can't. I have diving instructions to see to. I'm guessing it'll take up most of my day."

"Don't you two go in that warehouse, not until we're all together," Mitchell Polovina ordered.

"Why not?" Nason asked. Not that he had any intention of entering the place without them, he just wanted to know Mitch's reason.

"First of all, it's dangerous. We need to work it as a team."

"And second?"

"Second, it's a crime scene. You and I, Gray Eagle, are the only two in there so far. Other than removing the barrels, nothing's been disturbed. We go as a team, Juliette leading us so any evidence we find isn't compromised."

"You're not leading?" Juliette asked. The direction Mitch had taken surprised her. She was unaccustomed to men who turned something of importance over to a woman.

"Let's face it, Baby; I don't know the first thing about what's evidence and what's not evidence. You do. You lead. The rest of us touch nothing until you give us a sign it's all right to do so. Everybody clear on that?"

Nason raised his hands in a sign of surrender and Jenny smiled and winked at Juliette with pride for her gender, she too, being accustomed to taking a backseat to her in charge medical doctor beau.

The waitress brought food.

***

The interrogation room in the basement of the Farwell police station was little more than a closet with a steel table and a couple of chairs in it. It was dark — dank. It smelled of mold and must. And when its thick steel door was closed, its one bare light bulb hanging from a wire providing its only illumination, it was intimidating at best, tomb-like at worst. Mitchell Polovina hated going into the room himself. Imagine what a stranger to it felt.

The chief left his subject alone for a time, just as he had done with Homer Jenkins, but this suspect, he did not leave the door open for. And when he entered, Corelli, although he couldn't be described as putty, did seem more willing to talk than he had in his cell. "Are you here to charge me?" he asked Chief Polovina.

"Eventually," Polovina answered. "But first... I have some questions."

"Fire away," Corelli said. He was willing to talk. Why not? He'd answer anything so long as it wasn't about his personal actions. And he knew the chief would want to fill in the blanks about the long gone days of the Cohen brothers and Arthur Shaw. But that's not what the chief would ask about first.

"Did you kill Mrs. Cherry?"

"No."

"No?"

"No."

"We have rat poison from your trunk. It matches that found in Mrs. Cherry's bloodstream," Polovina said. He dug through papers in a file. He pulled out a copy of the license Corelli had in his wallet when he was arrested, the name on it being Michael Decker. He slid it across the table. Then he pulled out Corelli's Commercial License and placed it next to it.

"So?" Corelli asked. There was no real crime in it. It was just a fake license, nothing more: traffic court — a misdemeanor at best. So he had tried to convince an old woman he was related to her. A con is a con, only if it results in success. Until then, it's underhanded mischief. An apology and a fine would probably get him out of that one.

"Tell me what you know about the bodies."

"What bodies?"

"Let's start with the two floating girls back in the 'sixties."

"The police chief killed them. Homer Jenkins, Sr."

There was something Mitchell Polovina could claim as success, confirmation of what Homer, Jr. had told him. "What about the ones in the drums at the bottom of the pit?"

"I'm not that old," Corelli said.

"But you know, don't you?" Mitch asked.

"Rumors."

"Rumors will have to do, unless there's someone else alive who can tell us what went on back then."

"Do I get a phone call?"

"Soon as you answer my questions, you do."

"One of the Cohen brothers, the younger one, the story goes, killed all those women. He literally dumped his girls when he got what he wanted from them," Corelli said and smiled.

"That funny to you?" Polovina asked and glared in the suspects eyes for a time. He got no answer. He moved on. "And Arthur Shaw?"

"Shaw was a thief," Corelli said. "He deserved what he got."

"He deserved to have his fingernails pulled out with a pliers?" Mitch asked.

"He could have stopped it. He could have told the boys where he hid their money."

"They would have killed him anyway," Mitch suggested.

"Killed, yes. Tortured? Probably not."

"Tell me about you and Homer, Jr. Homer tells me you tied him to a tree out in the woods the last time you met, and that you tortured him. Is that true?"

Corelli thought it through. It had been a long time, too long. He hadn't killed Homer, so thought it not to be a capital offence. Surely there was a statute of limitation in play. He would admit to part of that. What could it hurt? "Some of that's true."

"Which part?"

"I won't say," Corelli said.

Mitch hit a dead end on this issue and knew it. He chose a different direction. "You don't like Homer, Jr., do you Corelli?"

"Nope!"

"Mind telling me why?"

Corelli placed his arms on the table and leaned over them. His eyes seemed to turn to stone. His brow wrinkled. "He killed my father," he said. And he would talk no more. His demand for a phone call filled the rest of their session, Mitchell Polovina finally yielding to his suspect's rights. He gave Corelli his call, and then formally charged him with assault. He would await Doc Nason's final conclusions, along with a report from the investigators and the final from the lab on the swabs Doc had sent down before charging him with Edith Cherry's murder.

***

"What'd you get from him?" Juliette Moore asked.

"We might have to charge Homer after all," Mitch told her.

"With what?"

"Murder. Vincent Corelli claims Homer killed his father."

"How do we find out for sure? It may not even be true considering the source. Corelli isn't what I'd call… reliable," Juliette insisted.

Her experience greater than his, Polovina had to agree. But still… he was ninety-nine percent sure he could prove or disprove the allegation. "We'll ask both Homer and Victoria. If they both say no, and their stories match, we can probably assume Corelli is lying. Should they disagree on how things went down, one of them is lying."

"Think it'll be that simple?"

"I think I can't read Corelli. That's what I think. The only time during our talk that I could read anything in either his tone or in his body language, was when he told me Homer killed his father, and that was pure anger. Homer is easy to read; so is Victoria. Confirm or deny, we'll see the truth in their faces. I'm sure of it."

"Where do we begin?" Juliette asked. She assumed she would be with him the remainder of the day. Henry Nason was out teaching diving to Jenny.

"Victoria. She wants to see me anyway."

***

"I received a visit from Mother Superior. She tells me the two of you have been snooping around the convent," Victoria told Mitch and Juliette.

"That's my job, Victoria. I'm Chief of Police. I snoop."

"She told you about Father Hennasy, didn't she." It was not a question. It was a statement. She looked only for confirmation, not answers.

"She did."

"Did she tell you what he did to me?"

It was not a question Mitchell Polovina was prepared to answer. Victoria was a mature woman and to be respected. That which had been done to her as a young lady, a child really, was unspeakable then and it is today. Mitch looked down at his shoes. Juliette stepped in. "Mitch, would you get us a coffee?" And he left the room in search of the cafeteria, glad for the errand. Juliette could field that question.

"He wasn't a priest at all," she told Juliette. "He was a thug for the Cohen brothers. He was there to spy on me, to see if I would lead him to Arthur Shaw's money, or, to be precise, their money Arthur had stolen from them. I let him do those things to me, you know."

"Why?" Juliette asked, one tear in her eye for the plight of a young girl and another for the awful memory bestowed on an old woman. "Why would you let him? Why didn't you report him?"

"Mother Superior and the Monsignor both thought the world of Hennasy. I would have been ignored as the girl whose father threw her into the convent as punishment for evil, a sort of prison, a life sentence. I would have been chastised as a slut who got herself pregnant and now was disgruntled and willing to accuse good men of horrible things. That would have been my plight had I turned Father Hennasy in. My best option, my only option really, was to turn off my emotions, suffer through the nastiness, and protect my friend who I know would not have held up to the abuse. My ability to do so, I can thank my life in the tunnels of Little Cicero for."

Mitchell Polovina had been outside the door waiting for the conversation to come to an end before he brought in coffee. Give them time for a woman to woman talk, was his design. A man in the room could dissuade Victoria from revealing the personal side of her tale, and in the personal, the truth lies. He waited a moment. Silence. He entered. "Did you want tea, Victoria?" he asked.

"I have some. Thank you."

"Have you finished, Juliette?" Mitch asked.

"Yes. For now anyway."

"What happened to the priest, Victoria? Mother superior told us that you hit him with a paperweight. Is that so?"

"I did. But what was I to do. He had the poor young girl's habit pulled up around her waist, her face shoved down on the desktop, and there he stood his trousers around his ankles. I had to do something."

"Why didn't you go for the Monsignor, or Mother Superior?"

"He would have been done with her before I persuaded either of them to listen to me." With that, she became silent. She was done for the day, not even enough left in her to say goodbye.

Mitchell chose to leave the question of Homer Jenkins killing Vincent Corelli's father for later.

CHAPTER THIRTY-FOUR

The big day of the dive had come. Mitchell Polovina, Sis having rousted him at precisely five a.m., had been ready for hours when Juliette Moore finally came around. Henry Nason had called three times since six, and each time, Mitch could hear Jenny talking in the background, trying to get him to ask for a time for the dive. Mitch could not give one. Fall had come to Little Cicero. The temperature would need time to rise. It had dropped into the forties during the night, common for the time of year. The day, however, promised the seventies and sunshine. Perfect.

"We eating?" Nase had asked.

"And dive on a full stomach? Have you forgotten that much?" Mitch asked. His memory trailed off to a time when the two of them had dived too soon after eating. He nearly died that day. Nase had nearly died that day. The cramps didn't hit them until they were on the bottom of Stilwell Pit, and they just about didn't make it back to the surface, and when they did, they had to tread water, it seemed for hours, before they had what it took to hoist themselves into the boat. "If we eat, we don't dive for two full hours." He checked his watch. Seven a.m. Breakfast at Mick's would take them until at least nine. "It'll be eleven at the earliest."

It was at the insistence of the ladies more than Henry Nason that they would join at Mick's Café and let the dive wait for eleven. But the two hours needed for food to settle would not be wasted. Mitch would talk with Homer, Ted and Karla Mayfield present.

"Vincent Corelli said you killed his father," Mitch told Homer.

"I don't think so," Homer said. "I thought I killed Vincent Corelli. Imagine my surprise, coming face to face with him like that in the jail, me thinkin' I had killed him once already — so many years ago."

"Has Doc Nason got him on heavy medication?" Mitch asked. No one knew for sure. He sent Karla to the nurses' station to check. It was quicker than hunting down Nason himself, who was somewhere in the hospital, checking on patients.

"The nurse says he's pretty doped up. Pain pills," Karla explained upon her return.

"Figures," Polovina said. "He sure ain't making sense now." He shot Homer a look, then Karla, then Teddy. "When he comes back to earth, see if the two of you can get him to be a bit more reasonable about this investigation." He started out of the room

"You can't expect him to implicate himself, Mitch," Karla objected, following Mitch and Juliette into the hallway. Ted Mayfield joined her.

"C'mon! We've all known Homer forever. Don't you think anything he's actually guilty of would have shown in his personality sometime over the years?" Mitch suggested.

"You don't think him a murderer then?" Ted asked.

"I think he had something to do with putting two girls' bodies into the water. He may have had something to do with killing someone, the priest from the convent, I suspect. I also think we'll find out he was coerced into disposing of the bodies by a father he feared and maybe a couple of brothers from organized crime. And the priest? Well… from what I've gathered so far, the priest, if he was even killed, it was done protecting Victoria Outing, maybe protecting Homer as well. That's what I think we'll uncover. Look, Karla, if it was my father, and I knew he had been troubled for so many years by something like this, I'd want the truth brought out just to give him a little peace."

"But what if it turns out he's guilty? What then?" Karla Mayfield asked.

Mitchell Polovina leaned and whispered something in Karla's ear. She nodded her understanding and said no more. Polovina placed a hand in the small of Juliette Moore's back and guided her away down the hall.

"What did you say to her?" Juliette asked when they walked through the main hospital entrance into the sunlight.

"I told her if it turns out Homer's guilty, I'd quit my job."

"Will you?"

"I will anyway," Mitch said and opened the car door for her.

***

Henry Nason and Jenny Cartwright had everything they would need — filled tanks, face masks, air regulators, swim fins — ready and on the barge by the time Mitch and Juliette arrived at the mine pit. They would dive without pressurized equipment this time since they had no topside man to see to the compressor. Their time underwater, if all went as they hoped, would be limited. They'd only pass through the old warehouse and be under long enough to find the stairway Victoria claimed was there. Mitch thought he knew pretty much where to find it from listening to her. He had been told it was close to the room Arthur Shaw raped her in, and he recalled seeing what might have been that room the day he and Henry pulled the drums out of the water. But to be certain, he felt he and Juliette should make the first dive alone, just to check things out.

"Would you prefer pressurized equipment for the first dive?" Henry asked, his concern that they might be under longer than planned scoping out the building, not fully sure of what they'd find. "I mean, if two of us are staying here where we can man the lines and compressor, why not take the safe way?"

"I think we'll go with the tanks. We might need the freedom down there. We'll keep it short. So don't you worry, Gray Eagle," Mitch said and pulled his tanks over his shoulders. Both he and Juliette grabbed an underwater lantern, checked to see they'd be bright enough, then slipped into the water.

Only moments passed, or so the divers thought, and they stood looking first at the empty warehouse, a few fish swimming about being the exception, and then at one another. Mitch gestured at the back wall of the building and motioned for Juliette to go first. A glass paneled door closed off a small room. A bed and a few pieces of furniture, most of it covered in weeds, took up much of the floor. Juliette grasped the knob — Froze, locked maybe — but whichever, she couldn't get past it. Mitch tried—no luck. He looked for something to break the glass with. That's when he saw it. At the very back of the building, beside and beyond the small room, a large sliding door covered a good section of the wall. It had to be the entrance to the stairway Virginia Outing told them about. A few moments of trying to gain access, unsuccessfully, and Mitch decided they had been under long enough. He signaled that they should surface. One more push, Juliette decided, and then she would go. The door moved, just slightly, but it moved. Mitch joined in, and soon it was open a foot, then two feet, then enough to squeeze by. Juliette shined a light around. Steps. This was it. She shined the light upward. The water looked somehow different, odd. Mitch looked up, and then began a climb of the old stairs. At the height of the building he broke into a pocket of trapped air. He pulled his regulator out of his mouth and tested to see if it was breathable. It was… stale… but breathable. He could smell the odor of fermentation. This was the place all right. He reached down and pulled Juliette to him.

"I wouldn't have believed it," she said.

"Me neither," Mitch agreed. He looked around. To one side was the conveyor Victoria had mentioned, or at least what was left of it. "Shall we go get Henry and Jenny?"

"Did you see the living quarters when you came for the drums?"

"I saw it, but other than a quick look for more drums, I ignored it. Is it something we need to take a closer look at?"

"I'm not sure. I do think we'll want to leave it undisturbed for a time, just in case," Juliette suggested.

"In case of what?"

"In case Victoria reveals something that leads us back down here, something that can be proven only from what's behind that door. Look, Mitch, you asked me to be sure we didn't compromise evidence. Near as I can tell, that's the only place we'd find any. Let's leave it undisturbed for the time being."

Mitchell Polovina yielded to the authority he had previously handed her. The two of them returned to the surface.

"You find it?" Henry Nason asked as he helped Juliette from the water.

"You bet your ass we did," Mitch told him. "Get ready, you two. Let's get in there."

"Not so fast," Henry said. The doctor served as safety for the team, and his word was law. "You get fifteen off before you dive. You know that." It was not a hard and fast rule for divers, it was just their rule, always had been. Henry had read a magazine in his youth, a sporting publication with much about diving. The author, his claim to be a highly experienced diver of fresh waters, suggested that a fifteen minute pause between dives was needed for inner ear health, especially if the dive was deep, over forty feet. Neither he nor Mitch ever knew if it was true or not, but had decided years ago, not to chance it.

"Fifteen," Mitch agreed and pulled up a lawn chair.

***

Willy Hobbs strolled into the police station a half hour after his shift was to begin. Paula Bloom had left for the day and Hobbs' partner, Hartman, was filling in as dispatch. Royal Parker, running late on the evening of a very important diner party his wife had planned weeks in advance and had warned him that it had better go off without a hitch, was furious. "Polovina sent me to check on something on my way in," Hobbs lied, knowing Polovina was nowhere he could be tracked down for verification and guessing that by morning Parker will have forgotten all about his tardiness.

"Really! What?" Parker asked.

"Polovina said not to tell anyone."

"Why?"

"I don't know. You'll have to ask him?"

"I will," Parker said, and began to walk out of the office.

"Think he's gonna tell you if he wants it to be secret?" Hobbs yelled after him. He turned to his partner. "Chief told me to send you to the hospital. You're to interview Homer Jenkins. See what you can get outta him. Then you're to stay there on guard duty."

"Why me? I don't know anything about conducting a suspect interview?"

"He thinks it's time you learned."

Hartman packed her things in a purse and walked out of the station. Willy Hobbs slid a chair over near Vincent Corelli's cell.

"I see you got your call," Corelli said. Hobbs had turned. He now worked for the Cohen's. The pay was so much better.

"You make your call, I get my call. That's how it works, Corelli."

"Unlock this door," Corelli demanded.

"Tell me what you're planning first."

"I'm planning to walk the fuck out of here. That's what I'm planning."

"You know what I mean. I want to know that you're planning to get your ass out of Little Cicero, and that you're not going to stick around here and do something stupid. That *was* the deal."

"I thought it was Farwell," Corelli said.

"You know what I'm talking about," Hobbs said. He almost always referred to the town as Little Cicero. He liked the name; he liked the history. "So, what's your plan?"

Corelli, sensing Hobbs was not going to open the door until he received an answer that suited him, said, "Don't worry. I won't do anything to tarnish your reputation or your town."

Hobbs unlocked the door and slid it open. Corelli walked into freedom, one hand in his pocket, the other reaching out to shake Hobbs', a gesture of gratefulness. "How we going to make this look like you escaped, rather than me just setting you free?" Hobbs asked.

"Like this, Corelli said. His hand shot out of his pocket, the missing keys to the police cruiser in it, one key protruding between his fingers, his hand in a fist. He jammed the key into Hobbs' right temple, then a couple stabs to the throat. Hobbs fell to the floor and convulsed for a time, then quieted in a pool of blood. Corelli pitched the keys on of Hobbs' chest. "That do anything to get your motor running?"

CHAPTER THIRTY-FIVE

An uneventful dive was followed by apprehensive exhilaration as the foursome broke out of the water and stood, masks and regulators removed, about halfway up an ancient set of stairs. "Wow," Jenny Cartwright said, looking toward the top of the stairs at the tunnel's darkness. "Wow," she repeated.

"I'd say," Henry Nason agreed. "I would not believe this if I wasn't seeing it for myself. I swear, I thought the old woman might be remembering some hallucination caused by an unhealthy quantity of shine consumed in a speakeasy. I saw us coming to a dead end at the back of a flooded warehouse."

"She's made sense so far, Gray Eagle," Mitchell Polovina said. "Why wouldn't you think this real?"

"Things like this don't happen to me, Bugsy. They just don't. How many times have you and I dove the waters of these old mines? We've never come across anything like this before."

"We never dove in Little Cicero's pit before. C'mon, let's hit the tunnels. Stay together though, we don't know how safe this'll be," Polovina said. "Juliette, anything we need to be concerned with, anything that might be evidence, you yell out," Mitch said. He began the climb to the top of the stairs, all lights pointed up. At the summit the stairs emptied into a narrow passage, a dirt floor gentle incline that seemed for a time to have no end. The stench of stale alcohol and, Mitch assumed, rotted vomit and excrement and urine, filled their nostrils at first, and then seemed to dissipate into thin air, the only form of air that existed in the city beneath the city. The first tunnel, no frills, no concrete, only hardened clay, ended at a thick style and rail door, half on its hinges, half off. Mitch and Henry had to tear it loose to pass. But beyond, the tunnel was more lavish. Lanterns hung from concrete walls, farmer matches tucked into a pouch nearby. The team lit lantern after lantern, bringing the tunnels to life, making them appear as normal hallways akin to those of an aging hotel, remarkably uncluttered and undamaged. They walked tunnels lighting lanterns until they came to the main passageway, the passage that led from the cellar of Mick's Café to the largest of the speakeasies, the one where Arthur Shaw first took Victoria Outing, the saloon under the Mercantile. It was that establishment the team wanted to see, for in it was history, the proof of the tale they had been hearing from the woman who lived it so many years in the past. And in that tunnel, no lanterns hung and no pouches of farmer matches. Instead, its ceiling was neatly lined with knob and tube wiring, a bare incandescent bulb every five feet, most of them still in one piece. Mitch searched with a light, following the wires to the café side of the street where they took a sharp turn and headed down the wall to a switch, a white, round, porcelain fixture with a brown turn knob. He turned it. "I wonder whose meter is running this?" he asked as the tunnel lit brightly.

"It has to be Mick's. The Mercantile burned down years ago," Nason said.

"I remember that," Mitch said.

"You ought to. You burned it. It was homecoming night in our senior year. The building was abandoned by then. Any of this ringing a bell with you? Or were you too wasted to remember?" Henry asked.

"I remember the night, but only fuzzy."

"Really? Don't you remember? You were just off a date with the delicious cheerleader, Karla Jenkins. You got laid on the bleachers that night I understand."

"Karla Mayfield?" Juliette asked. "That Karla? You laid Teddy Mayfield's wife?"

"That was a long time ago, and she wasn't Teddy's wife in those days. Thanks a bunch, Gray Eagle, for that unpleasant walk down memory lane," Mitch said. "C'mon. Let's explore."

"Wait a minute. We didn't get to the interesting part," Henry objected. "Old Mitch there, he was so out of it by the time he joined the rest of the team in the abandoned mercantile building, he run right into this mammoth linebacker from the opposing team. Why... he literally bounced off the guy and went sailing to the floor. He thought sure the linebacker did it on purpose, so he jumped to his feet and landed one right on the guy's jaw. The fight was on, half of the guys cheering Mitch on, half backing the other fellow. They rolled around, more wrestling than anything else, for a time, and then Mitch got loose and got to his feet. About that time, Karla Jenkins and a batch of cheerleaders stormed in, all of them yelling for vengeance against Mitch, calling him a dirty rotten two timing bastard and a whole bunch of other things that were not nearly as flattering. Anyway, Mitch goes to take off running from the team of vigilante cheerleaders, and the mammoth linebacker sticks a leg out. Mitch goes flying across the room and hits head first into a pole with a lantern hanging from it. The lantern falls. It breaks into pieces. Kerosene flows out in a giant puddle. The whole floor burst into flames and everyone scattered, screaming… boys as loud as the girls. It wasn't long and we were all sitting atop an ore dump several blocks away, nursing a beer and watching the fire department hose down the building, just barely able to contain the fire and keep it from taking the rest of Main Street with it. It was quite a night. Bugsy, you disappeared just after that. Did that vigilante cheerleader squad catch up with you? I do recall you having several lumps cuts and bruises in school the following Monday."

"Let's get on with it," the police chief insisted, ignoring all Henry Nason had to say. He took the lead, his stride filled with purpose as he made his way through the tunnel to the other side of the street. He stopped once in the middle to let the sound of a vehicle overhead pass. At the end of the tunnel a thick door blocked them. It seemed welded in place when he first tried to open it. Henry Nason joined in, both women adding their weight to that of the men. And swiftly, all of them were lying in a heap beyond, staring at a view so magnificent it held them from moving or even speaking. It was just as Victoria had described it, perhaps buried under as thick a layer of dust as eighty years would provide, but, otherwise, identical. Mitch Polovina wondered why no one, maybe teens of his father's generation, had gotten in and desecrated it. That's what generally happens. And to discover this find in this condition defied the norm. Had someone from the past treated Little Cicero's speakeasies like the Egyptians had treated the pyramids, as holy icons of a life passed? Or had the city fathers who ruled at the end of prohibition sealed the tunnels off before any desecration could take place, perhaps to preserve them, perhaps to protect those who might come down here and be injured, perhaps in an attempt to kill off inexorable and unflattering rumors of the town previously known as Little Cicero. Nobody seemed to know, at least no one Mitchell Polovina knew, exactly when the concrete was poured at the entrances to the tunnels. Maybe Victoria will know…

maybe Homer. "I'm... I'm speechless," he said as he stood. He took Juliette's hand and helped her to her feet, then Jenny, then Henry. He walked to the bar and brushed the dust away from a small spot. "Absolutely speechless," he added.

A glimpse of the time came to Juliette Moore when she gazed around the room: people at tables, a band on the stage and a couple dancing, bartenders pouring shine into spotless glasses. She closed her eyes, not knowing if she wished them away or wanted to prove their reality. And when she opened, they were gone... but the music... she still heard. "Can anyone else hear that?" she asked.

"Hear what?" Jenny asked, knowing Juliette was talking about the music. "I don't hear anything." She walked to the bar, swept dust from of a stool, and slid into it. It gave up a groan of protest, yet still turned. "Comfy, even for today. Elegant, I would imagine, for way back then." She turned and looked at a couple clothed in costume of an earlier time at one of the tables. "How long do we have to stay in here?" she asked.

"Not long, I hope," Henry Nason said. He felt more than he saw, a presence of sorts, seemingly unfriendly. Uninterested in having visitors, maybe even annoyed. "As fascinating as all of this is, I'm getting a bit claustrophobic down here. It's likely just a lack of fresh air." He looked up as glasses rattled from the vibration of a large vehicle, a truck or bus, from above. He looked on the floor, just a few scattered pieces of broken glass. He wondered what held them on their shelves all these years. Maybe the spirit straitened them now and then.

"You thinking we're in some kind of danger, Henry?" Mitch asked. *Henry. Why did I call him Henry instead of Gray Eagle?* He questioned. Then it came to him. He did that. His old high school football buddy was always Gray Eagle, until it came to a question or comment falling within his professional realm; then it was Henry.

"We will be if we overstay," Nason said.

"Then we go when you say."

"Then we go."

***

Vincent Corelli made his way back to his apartment. Makeup is what he needed. He'd get one last shot at convincing Victoria Outing to turn over the Cohan money to her son, Michael Decker, and only one. The law wasn't as stupid as he had judged them, even if they were inexperienced and unaccustomed to serious crime. They'd be all over him in no time at all. That new police chief over in Farwell, the man's a pit-bull. *Where'd they take my car?* He questioned in his mind. He missed it. It was hell keeping to a schedule and a jump ahead of the authorities by taxicab. He sat in front of his mirror, working his disguise to perfection. The old woman would pick up on a hurried job — more astute at ninety-six than most at fifty. He'd be glad for this to be over. He was tiring of her, of calling her Mother, of putting up with her crap and insults and lectures. *Fucking schoolteachers anyway.*

He walked to the living room. He glanced down at the body of his nosy landlady and wished she'd kept more to herself. He brushed at a bloodstain on the back of his hand, one in her blood, left there on purpose as was his custom whenever he had to kill someone, especially a woman. It had been his father, not him, who got into killing women. At first, so his dad had told him, he hadn't found it at all pleasurable, neither was it disgusting, simply his job. But after a time, the Cohen brothers both handing down their unwanted conquests for disposal after they moved beyond virgin and on to slut, he began to enjoy getting rid of them. There were so many, it became like slaughtering lambs, just a job and not a bad one either. But Vincent was not his father. Killing bothered him, unless of course, it was someone he did not like. His landlady though, he did like. He regretted having to kill her.

He called a cab and watched out his apartment window until it pulled up in front. He rinsed the bloodstain from his hand and headed out the door.

"Where to?" the cabbie asked.

"The hospital in Farwell," he said and jabbed the barrel of his pistol into the driver's temple. "And we won't be needin' to call it in, will we?"

"I'll get in trouble," the driver said.

"You already are."

***

"There's one thing I'd like to see while we're down here," Mitchell Polovina said. "That is, unless the doctor here has an objection."

"How long will it take?" Nason asked.

"Minutes… ten at the outside."

"I think we'll handle that all right," the doctor gave his approval. "What're we going to see?"

"The pub that was devoted to low-lifes, the one at the end of the tunnels under the livery."

"Under the livery? Now how do you know it was under a livery stable?" Jenny Cartwright asked. "Farwell doesn't have a livery stable."

"No, but Little Cicero did, and Gray Eagle and I know where it was," Mitch said. "Don't we, Nase?"

"I'd put it somewhere in the neighborhood of Comstock's front-end alignment shop," Nason said. The exact location was, of course, unknown and would remain that way unless they researched the earlier town from a historical point of view: old newspapers, books and photos at the local library, searches at the courthouse, things like that. But Victoria Outings accounts of that earlier day led them to believe research would prove them correct, so... why do it? Why waste time on it?

Mitch Polovina didn't expect to find anything in the dingy tavern under Comstock's but a feeling. He thought it important for all of them not to romanticize their adventure into the tunnels below their town and back into the day they represented, by excluding the less appealing side of the story. He felt it important to the process of investigation that all sides of a thing were included before a total picture was drawn. "I just want us all to see the entire scene. It's how we'll get the whole image of Victoria Outing and her story. This place is part of it." They were still in the doorway of the more elegant of the underground establishments. "Her father's home is another. Her home at the nunnery, that's another."

"Convent," Juliette corrected.

"All right, convent. But the place where the dregs gathered, that was also part of it."

"But all she talked about was one visit to the place," Nason threw in.

"No, I don't think that's true. Remember what you said, Gray eagle, back when you and I decided we'd be the ones to get her story. You said we get her talking and the truth would fall through the cracks. Remember that?"

"I do."

"Well… here's one of those truths. Victoria indicated there

was a time when Arthur Shaw spent days away from home. They were already a couple, her living in the back of the warehouse, pregnant, and as she admitted, everyone's favorite dance partner in all of the speakeasies down here." Mitch rolled the thought over in his mind. "I'm guessing the dirt-floored speakeasy frequented by that society's dregs was one of them. We need to see it."

***

Michael Decker pulled to the curb in front of the Farwell hospital. The cab's driver was no longer with him.

CHAPTER THIRTY-SIX

Virginia Outing struggled to focus. Michael. It was Michael. Or was she dreaming? Mitchell Polovina had seen to it that Michael Decker was under lock and key. Had something happened? Had something gone wrong, perhaps a tricky lawyer getting involved, perhaps a judge had turned him loose at an arraignment hearing, perhaps the arrest itself had been done incorrectly and they simply couldn't hold him. *Well... no matter,* she thought and rubbed her eyes, *there he is.* "Good evening, dear," she said and smiled.

"I told you it was all a mistake, Mother. And here I am to prove it."

Careful, Victoria, she warned herself. *Remember, he's a criminal. Don't let yourself get caught up in what you've allowed him to believe, that you see him as your flesh and blood.* She buzzed for the nurse. She wanted someone, anyone, to know she was not alone.

"Why'd you do that? I can get you anything you need," Michael Decker told her. He reached for her water glass. "Thirsty?"

"Hungry," she said. "I want the nurse to get me a snack."

"I could get you something, Mother," he offered. He did not want the nurse to see him, yet saw no way around it now, goofy old bat.

"Whatever for? They'll charge me for it no matter who brings it, Michael. You just sit tight and keep your old mother company. It's lonely here all day long by myself."

"And what can I do for you, Ms. Outing?" the nurse asked and adjusted her pillows.

"I'd like some ice cream if you have some."

"Certainly. I'll just skip out and get some for you," the nurse said.

Skip out. That's what I'd like to do. I've had it up to hear with this dying old creature and her undying bedsores, Skippy the nurse and the infantile staff of this smelly pit, this whole town. Corelli never saw what kept his father serving the Cohen brothers so long as he had to frequent this den of mental midgets in this God forsaken ore country. *The mighty and beautiful Mesabi my ass. Red ore, vomit of the earth, as far as the eye can see.* Only thing he saw good here was it was a great place to bury bodies. *They'll be sifting through orange dirt till hell won't have it, and they'll never come close to that cabbie after I plant him there.* "You comfortable, Mother? Can I get you anything? Books? Magazines?" *Can you even see anymore to read?* He wanted to ask but didn't.

"I'm fine," Victoria insists. *Where's Mitchell Polovina?* She silently asked. *I'm frightened.*

On another floor, Victoria's cheerful nurse having been on duty when the police first hauled Michael Decker from the hospital approached Homer Jenkins' room where she knew a police officer would be stationed. Hartman, after making sure Karla Mayfield had her cellular number programmed into her phone for fast access, left Homer in his daughter's care and took Ted Mayfield with her to check out Victoria's visitor.

The mayor, Ted Mayfield waited out of sight in the hallway. He knew the visitor, be it Michael Decker or Vincent Corelli, it made no difference. Either would recognize the mayor.

Lila Hartman went in. She had only seen the prisoner, Vincent Corelli, never Michael Decker. "Hello, Ms. Outing. Who's your visitor?"

God… was she glad to see a badge, even if it was pinned to breasts. "Why… this is my pride and joy. This is my boy, Michael."

"Really! I didn't know you had children," Officer Hartman played along. She saw the lines on Corelli's face relax. He had bought it.

"Not children, dear. Child. Michael is my only."

Hartman stuck out a hand. "Good to meet you, Mr. Outing." *That ought to drive it home.*

"It's Decker," Corelli corrected. *No threat here, no smarts either.* "Good to meet you, Officer."

"Please, Lila."

"Lila then," he said. It always felt better, more personal, if he knew the first name of someone he might later need to kill. He sat for a time. But when it occurred to him Hartman may never leave, he chose to excuse himself.

"Oh, I wouldn't hear of it. You want time alone with your

mother. "How thoughtless of me," Hartman said. She left the room. She had to before Corelli did or Corelli would run smack into the mayor.

***

Anything favorable from their dive would be wiped out by their visit to the remains of the tavern at the end of the tunnels, the dirt floor and hardened clay ceiling cave-like room with fixtures made from old crates and shipping pallets. It was a lamentable sight. It stunk of death. The air was thick — nauseating. It hung like a cloud of toxic waste. And in its dim distance the divers could make out what appeared to be shadows of men in bibbed overalls milling about without direction or purpose — humped at the upper back — ghoul-like.

Mitchell Polovina imagined Victoria Outing at sixteen years old, pregnant, drunk from Canadian whisky or rot-gut moonshine, being pawed by the likes of these creatures — no father there to protect her, and he felt acid filling the back of his throat, tightening his jaws. He turned and went back into the tunnel before it turned to vomit. He had had enough. He had all he wanted of the tunnels beneath Little Cicero. And he had had enough police work. It showed him the side of life he did not wish to see. "Let's get the hell out of here," he said.

***

"I know I killed him. That son-of-a-bitch. He had it coming," Homer Jenkins murmured and rolled to his side just as Hartman entered.

"He's been saying that over and over since you left," Karla Mayfield said. "I tried to talk back to him, ask him what he's talking about, but he seems in a trance. He just looks back at me and stares as though I'm not here. Could it be the medication?"

"I'd be the wrong one to ask that." Hartman said. "You should talk to his doctor."

"We can't. He's not here."

"I know I killed him," Homer mumbled. "You'd have killed him too if you had seen what he was doin' to those girls." And he rolled once more, onto his side. He stared at the wall for a moment, and then closed his eyes. "Why'd he come back?" he whispered.

Hartman stepped into the hallway. She called her partner at the station. No answer. She punched Chief Polovina's number into her cell phone. Nothing. She'd try again and again. Finally her phone would go dead. Should she go back to Victoria Outing's room? No, she should continue guarding Homer. Victoria was too close to the nurses' station for Corelli to do much. Corelli's dangerous. There could be no mistaking that. But he was smart — too smart to try anything with the staff right there. Homer Jenkins was the one to protect. Corelli had come once for him and where they put him, Hartman considered him vulnerable. She'd stay put, sidearm ready.

***

Juliette Moore was the first to pop out of the water, exhausted from the dive and ready for it to end. It shocked her to see darkness. Fall had arrived on the Mesabi, and along with it, an earlier dusk. She strained to see the barge as she treaded water waiting for the rest of her diving partners. Doc Nason was next to surface, then Jenny. They waited. They watched for bubbles from Mitch's tanks. Nothing.

"Should I dive?" Henry Nason asked her.

"Give him a minute. I saw him stop at the room," she said. She was talking about the old office for the warehouse, the room Arthur Shaw and Victoria Outing lived in after her mother passed away, the room she conceived in. Juliette felt Mitch was safe, thought sure she'd feel it if he weren't. They had become that close. But Mitch had another closeness develop along with theirs, his connection to Victoria Outing, the Victoria of today as well as the Victoria of the past. It had become almost an obsession, this need to know that had grown within him concerning the ninety-six year old woman and the innocent girl of her youth. Of course he would not pass the room without at least a brief study of it. Juliette hoped brief would be all that it was. And soon, relief of bubbles floating to the surface would come, then Mitch. It was over.

"Were we down that long?" he asked in the darkness.

"We were," Henry Nason answered.

***

Vincent Corelli unsuccessfully badgered Victoria Outing until Victoria closed her eyes and appeared as though she had fallen into a deep sleep. "Fuck!" he said softly. "I should just put a pillow over her head and be done with it." Victoria held fast to the button that would summon a nurse—just in case. She hoped he would go away. He might as well. She'd sooner die of suffocation than give up the Cohen money after all these years. Hadn't she paid? Hadn't she suffered sufficiently at the hands of Arthur Shaw and the Cohen brothers, with having been tossed out like last week's trash by her father, by undergoing the humiliation and physical pain of being sodomized by Father Hennasy at the convent? Didn't this money need to go to someone who would put it to just use? At least the Cohen money could cleanse itself, even if she couldn't. *Go ahead! I'm ready!* She thought. But the nurse showed up.

"I'm sorry, Mr. Decker. Visiting hours are over for today. You can come back at seven a.m., after she's had her breakfast if you'd like." She had just come on duty. She recognized him as the man the police had arrested in the hospital not long ago. She wondered, should she call the cops? Nah! He was probably released, not escaped. No one escaped from Farwell's station.

Michael Decker smiled and left the room.

He got in his stolen taxi. He headed for the police station. With luck, Parker hadn't come in early to relieve Hobbs. And luck was on his side. He entered the station, gathered up Hobbs' body, rigor already setting in, and carried him into the street, looking all around to see he wasn't being seen. Under cover of an earlier than normal darkness, it had clouded over, he hauled Hobbs to the taxi and stuffed him into the trunk alongside the cab's original driver. "You two wait here," he said and grinned. "I'll be back for you, and then we'll plant you together in the ore, for company." And he went back inside the station. He checked the clock. Plenty of time. He cleaned up Hobbs' blood, then removed his makeup and locked himself back in his cell, this time, the key tucked under his mattress.

Parker arrived to find Corelli asleep in his bunk, the building, other than its one prisoner, empty. "Corelli," he shouted out.

"Corelli opened his eyes and rubbed them. "What?" he asked.

"Where's Hobbs?"

"He went out about an hour ago. Said he'd be back with food. Never returned. You got something for me to eat?"

"Christ," Parker said and shook his head.

***

Mitchell Polovina hadn't thought to check his phone after the dive. Too much on his mind, too many visions. But in the morning, he saw that Hartman had called. He called back only to get her answering service. "She must be on her line," he said to himself. Then he left her instructions to go home. He hadn't sent her to guard Homer in the first place. Corelli was under lock and key, so where was the danger. But he had to admit, someone on hand in case Homer had come around and decided to talk wasn't a bad idea. One of his people was thinking. He wondered which one? He called the station and talked briefly with Parker who informed him about Hobbs' tardiness last night and his early disappearance this morning. He made a decision. Understaffed or not, Hobbs was all done when he showed next. He handed authority over to Royal Parker, his second in command, should that happen before he got to the station.

"You coming in first thing this morning, Chief?" Parker asked.

"Can you stay late?"

"Yeah. I got nothing going. How late you need me?"

"I should be done by ten. I just need to check with Ms. Outing first thing," Polovina said.

"Come up with something?" Parker asked knowing they had made the dive. "You find something suspicious?"

"No. Nothing like that. Just a hunch. That's all."

Juliette Moore had been listening in. "A hunch?" she asked.

"A hunch," Polovina confirmed. He had, just that day, given one of his people hell for using the term. He had insisted that hunches were not police work, not good police work anyway. Facts, facts were what he wanted to hear about, not hunches.

"A hunch," Juliette said and smiled. "What kind of hunch?"

"I think I might know who Father Hennasy really was."

"Care to share?"

"Not just yet," he said. He looked at her and smiled. "I only share facts."

CHAPTER THIRTY-SEVEN

Mitchell Polovina, in the backyard with his and Juliette's little dog, Sis, at just after daybreak, heard the electronic tones of his cellular on the table inside. He thought of rushing in, but chose to let it answer itself. After all, wasn't he paying for that service as well? And Sis deserved the time to finish her morning work. Whoever it was, they could wait until he could return the call.

Juliette Moore couldn't sleep. The sound of Mitch's cell had awakened her and now, no matter how hard she tried, she couldn't drop off. She swung her legs over the edge of the bed and slipped out from under the blankets. Cold. Fall was here, not heating season yet, but close. She shivered and reached for a robe.

Mitch and Sis came in the back door to see Juliette filling the coffee pot with cool water. Three minutes. That's all it would take. And fresh brewed would be chasing the cobwebs from their minds. Mitch kissed her on the back of the neck and she smiled. "Good morning," he said.

"Good morning," she said back. And Sis jumped into her arms. "Who's calling this early?"

"Don't know. I didn't pick up." He walked to the table and checked the screen on his phone. "Teddy Mayfield," he said. "I wonder what he wants."

"Call him. I'm sure he'll tell you," Juliette said. "Unless," she said and pulled her robe open, exposing her naked breasts to him, "Unless something distracts you."

Mitch tossed the phone on the table. Juliette put Sis back on the floor. Only seconds, and she would be sitting on the counter, him kissing whatever his lips came in contact with, the neck first, and then working down from there. The phone began to call out in its annoying electronic tones as he moved below her breasts. "Shit, Teddy. Go away," he shouted at the phone. But it didn't listen; it persisted. "What?" he said into it, the mood spoiled.

"Homer's awake. He wants to talk to you. He says he ready to tell you everything."

"Get dressed," Mitch told Juliette, and hung up the phone.

"Where we off to so early?" Juliette asked.

"Work. Homer wants to confess."

***

A Highway Patrol cruiser pulled up in front of the station. A trooper went inside. "Anyone know anything about the taxicab parked out front?" he asked.

Royal Parker looked at him curiously, and then opened the door to see into the street. "It was there when I came in for night shift," he said.

"You're on overtime, my friend," the trooper said after checking his watch and finding it just past seven. Day shift cops usually reported at six in most towns. The trooper knew that. He had served his time as town cop in three such little towns prior to signing on with the State.

"Filling in. We're a bit understaffed," Parker explained. "Why? Something wrong? I mean with the cab."

"Reported stolen. Listen, would you folks mind keeping an eye on it? I'm due in traffic court over at the county seat. I already called it in — wrecker's on its way."

"No problem," Parker said.

"I'm hungry," Corelli barked from his cell. "When's breakfast?"

"Breakfast is when breakfast is, Corelli," Parker said. "Not any sooner."

Vincent Corelli studied the room. A receptionist — a temp no doubt. She wouldn't be any trouble. She wasn't going to get courageous. Paula Bloom on dispatch. Chunky woman — no gun. Just smack her a good one if she gets stupid. Hartman, fresh in from hospital duty, rested. He wouldn't mind taking that little piece of tail along for the ride — except she'd probably shoot him. He might need to shoot her first. Pity. Then there was Royal Parker, Deputy Chief, the man with the title. Corelli would take him out first. Simple. Sneak up behind him, pull his gun from its holster, and smack him hard on the back of the head with it. He'd go down like a bag of garbage. He'd wait until they came for the cab. It'll be like turning on a movie, all faces smashed against window panes trying to see the wrecker hook up. He'd make his move then. Time to cut his losses. The old woman wasn't going to give it up. He could kill her, but why? He wouldn't gain from it. A little satisfaction, maybe, but that's it. Not worth the effort. But that Jenkins? He'd get that son-of-a-bitch before he blew this town. He had a score to settle. It was personal. It was that simple. He sat back against the wall, his legs stretched out on his bunk, and waited. He felt under the mattress for the key, just to make sure he knew exactly where it is. He wouldn't have much time to pull this off. *Be prepared,* was his thinking.

***

Mitchell Polovina pulled a packet of papers out of his car's glove box as he pulled to the curb in front of the hospital. He sifted through them until he came to the paper he wanted. That one, he folded neatly and placed in his shirt pocket, then stuffed the rest back where they came from. He opened his door to get out. "Ready?" he asked Juliette.

"I'm ready. I don't know what for, but I'm ready."

Inside the hospital, the couple nearly ran into Teddy Mayfield. He was on his way for coffee. He paid no attention to where he was walking. Exhaustion had him by the balls. "Jesus, Teddy," Mitch said, and grabbed his arms to slow him down. "You trying to kill us, or you?"

"Sorry," Mayfield apologized.

"How's Homer this morning, Mr. Mayor?" Juliette asked.

"Full recovery, it seems. He's chipper. He's talkative. He even seems in a good mood. He does want to talk to the chief of police, though. We'll see what that does to him. You two heading down there now?"

"One stop. I need to run something by Victoria Outing. I think it might clear a whole bunch of this mystery up for us. We'll get down there shortly."

Victoria Outing lay on her side, her back toward the door, when Mitch and Juliette approached her room. A nurse stopped them just before they entered. "Make it brief this morning, will you? She's a bit under the weather, up most of the night."

"We'll only be a moment," Mitch promised and slipped by

the nurse. He walked to the far side of the room and smiled down at her.

"I was hoping to see you," she said weakly.

"How are you this morning?" he asked her.

"I'm dying," she almost whispered.

"No you're not," Mitch insisted.

"But I am, Dear Boy," she said. "But I am."

A tear came to Mitchell Polovina's eye. Juliette saw it and it brought one to her eye. She moved closer to him.

"None of that, Mitchell," Victoria said. "An old lady passing on to a better place isn't a sad occasion."

"Of course not, Ma'am."

"Have I taught you nothing?"

"I'm sorry... Victoria," he corrected.

She smiled a small smile. "Did you have something to ask me this morning?" she asked.

Mitch pulled the paper from his pocket, unfolded it, and held it out in front of her. "Do you recognize this man?"

"Yes... I... I think so. It's been so long. But I'm sure of it," she pulled the paper closer, him still holding the top of it. She looked harder, squinted, "that's him. That's Father Hennasy," she finally said. She closed her eyes. She fell into a deep, peaceful sleep, from which she would not awaken.

Juliette hooked an arm through Mitch's and guided him into the hallway. She called a nurse. "I think she's gone," she said. She grabbed the paper from Mitch's hand and took a look at it. She looked at him. She looked back at the paper. "How did you figure that one out?"

"Lucky guess. That's all it was."

CHAPTER THIRTY-EIGHT

Vincent Corelli had been right. The wrecker no sooner pulled up in front of Farwell's police station and all faces, except his own of course, were plastered against windows like the first snow of the season had arrived.

He gently pulled the key from beneath his mattress and tiptoed his way to the cell door. He reached carefully through the bars and silently thanked the town fathers for not having the good sense to install electric locks on their holding cells like every other town in this day and age. He pushed in the key, cautious not to make a sound, and turned the tumblers.

Seconds later he stood at Royal Parker's back, looking over his shoulder, Parker paying no attention to him thinking he was one of his own people trying for a closer look at the goings on outside. Corelli reached around Parker's waist, unfastened his holster, pulled the gun from it, and smacked Parker on the back of the head one mighty blow. And Parker hit the floor, knees first, and then slumped into a pile at Corelli's feet.

Hartman turned. She looked into the barrel of Corelli's weapon, shocked at seeing him; still, she drew her sidearm. He fired — point blank — into the shoulder of her gun arm. She grabbed for the wound her gun falling with a crash to the floor. Corelli swung a foot out and swept the gun across the room. Hartman's eyes rolled back into her head. She slumped into Paula Bloom's arms. Corelli shoved them aside.

He lit out the door. He ran at high speed toward the wrecker operator who was standing between the wrecker and the cab, operating the rig with a remote. He hit the operator with the butt of Parker's gun; the operator dropped the remote to the pavement where it smashed into pieces.

The cab literally fell to the ground, its trunk popping open.

He ran to the rear of the cab, slammed the trunk once, then twice, then a third time. It would not close. An arm hung in its way, Willy Hobbs' arm.

Corelli looked back at the police station. The temp receptionist of all people stood aiming Hartman's gun at him. He fired at the door, the window smashing, the receptionist jumping back with a scream, and then he returned to his task.

He pulled Willy Hobbs out of the trunk and flopped him on the pavement. He turned back and did the same with the cab driver, then slammed the trunk. He got in behind the wheel, started the motor, cramped to wheels and put the car in drive. Not enough room to clear the wrecker. He threw it in reverse. He stomped on the accelerator and backed over the two bodies, threw it in drive again, and pulled into traffic, Willy's body being dragged along with him for half a block.

The receptionist watched until Willy broke loose from the car's undercarriage. Then she vomited.

***

Mitch Polovina sat in a tiny waiting room down the hall from Homer Jenkins' room for a long time. He thought over his time with Victoria Outing, not his time years ago as her student, although those days did flash briefly before his eyes. It was the more recent that he dwelled on, his mind going all the way back to the morning bodies began popping to the surface of the water filled mine pit. He recalled seeing her look down on them. He remembered asking if anyone knew who she was and he recalled wondering why she had been watching. Her life, over now, had been an interesting one, filled with memories like none other he knew of. She had lived the days of prohibition, seen folks go from afoot or horseback to driving automobiles, from outhouses to indoor plumbing, from dirt farming to industry then on to depression. She had lived the life of the speakeasies and the convent in the same decade, a time of contradiction beyond reason for Mitch Polovina. And he knew she had tremendous hardship in her time. He only hoped she had had a balancing of good and fun and adventure. He adored her, cherished his brief time with her. He would always remember her and he would miss her. She had changed him in many ways, but mostly, she taught him that he did not want to be a cop, a lesson he would endeavor to keep close forever, perhaps packed in with the memory of her.

"You ready to question Homer?" Juliette asked. She hoped to pull him from his depths and guide him to something better. Maybe doing his job was an answer. "He wants to confess. You might not want to wait until he changes his mind."

Homer Jenkins stared when Mitch and Juliette walked into the room. He did not look afraid; rather, he looked almost perturbed. "Pop," Ted Mayfield said. "Be nice. And remember, this isn't the teenaged Mitchell Polovina; this is our Chief of Police. Treat him as such."

Homer's eyes softened. *What the hell. What does it matter anymore? I give him what he wants and I get jail, most likely for the rest of my life. Can't be too long.*

"Teddy says you want to talk," Mitch started.

"I wanted to tell you what I did, me and Victoria. Only I don't want to get Victoria in trouble."

"Don't worry about Victoria. I give you my word, Homer. She won't be held accountable for any of this." He did not want to tell Homer she was gone. He didn't think it necessary or helpful.

"I killed a man," Homer said. "I know I did."

"Sounds to me like you question it," Mitch said.

"He's come back," Homer said.

"The man in the cell. The man who did this to you, is not who you killed," Mitch said and passed a picture in front of Homer. "This is the man you killed." It was, of course, Vincent Corelli in the photo, but Homer wouldn't know. Victoria hadn't. She had identified it as Father Hennasy. "Father and son, Homer. You killed the father, when he was playing a priest. Father Hennasy wasn't Father Hennasy. He was just a guy working for the Corelli family. Now, suppose you tell us about that killing."

"It was a real long time ago," Homer began. "I needed a place to hole up, my daddy, he was huntin' me for one thing or another, something he didn't like, don't even remember what it was that time it happened so often. Anyway, Victoria had me hid in the cellar of the convent till he cooled off. Well... one night she comes in and wakes me. The look on her face, oh... God... terror, frightful terror. "Come, Homer," she called. "He's doing it to her now." I didn't know who the her was, a young nun, a friend of Victoria's. I still don't know the girl's name. But I knew who was doin' the doin'. Father Hennasy. One evil son-of-a-bitch, that Father Hennasy," Homer said. Then he shut his eyes and lay silent for a time.

"You're doing fine, Homer," Mitch told him. "Keep going."

"Victoria, she grabbed my hand and pulled me out of the bed. We ran the halls of that convent that night, nearly run into a wall we was goin' so fast around one turn. When we got to the priest's office and threw the door open, he turned and looked at us. The poor girl was already bent over the desk, her habit pushed up over her hips, her underwear in shreds at her feet, him with his pants at his ankles." He went quiet again.

"What happened then?"

"Victoria ran to the desk and picked up a paperweight. She slammed him with it, right in the face, then on top of his head. The priest tripped on his pants and lost his balance. When he hit the floor, he must have hit his head hard, 'cause he went out like a light. Victoria pulled the girl's skirt down to cover her, helped her to stand up straight, and started to walk her out of the room. I turned to follow, but heard a noise from behind me. It was the priest, comin' back 'round." He fell silent and closed his eyes.

"What happened next, Homer?" Mitchell Polovina asked. "Homer?"

"I'll tell you what happened next. He went back into that room and finished my daddy off. That's what happened next. He bashed him in the head so hard and so many times that his brains leaked out all over that floor. That's what he did. Then he dragged him out into the night and buried him in the woods. Ain't that right, old man. You didn't know something though. You didn't know the monsignor knew all of this. You didn't know the monsignor was a friend to the Cohen brothers. And you didn't think about that man having a family, and that one day that family might come for you, did you? Well... guess what. Here I am. I am Vincent Corelli, son of the man you knew as Father Hennasy, the man you killed."

He stood in the doorway, his gun pointing at Homer. "I've come to even the score," he said. He pulled the trigger, one shot cleanly in the forehead of Homer Jenkins.

Mitch and Juliette pulled their weapons simultaneously and fired several shots into Vincent Corelli. He fell to the floor, his gun slipping loose from his grip and sliding just out of reach. He grabbed at it as Polovina kicked it aside. Mitch knelt on one knee beside him. "Do you know who the bodies were, the ones in the lake?"

"Yeah. My... daddy done... the killin'. There's... a... list."

"Where? Where's the list, Corelli?"

Corelli lifted his head. Mitchell Polovina moved his ear closer to listen to his weakening voice. "Fuck... you," he whispered. And he was gone.

CHAPTER THIRTY-NINE

Mitchell Polovina gave up his job. He didn't need it anyway. And he certainly didn't need to run into another situation where he'd have to deal with the kind of sadness and misery that plagued Victoria Outing all of her life. He wished he hadn't known her, ever heard of her, ever came in contact with any of this. His life hadn't exactly gone well before all of this, not with three ex-wives to his credit and a war that shouldn't have been fought to dream of most nights until Juliette Moore. But there *was* Juliette. He *did* get her in the midst of all of this. He'd keep her too. It was the rest of it he wanted to lose. And lose it he would. But to do that he had to lose a lot. The job would be only the beginning.

Mitch found he could no longer live in Little Cicero, not with all he knew. Let someone else romanticize about gangsters and prohibition and illegal booze and speakeasies in elaborate tunnels beneath the streets. They could have it, and they'd enjoy the stories. For they hadn't seen the ugly truth behind them like he had. But he did have Juliette.

The house had to go. He didn't want it anymore. It now belonged to the town and the job and the memories he did not wish to keep. He would take Juliette and Sis and he would go away.

Henry Nason gave up his badge. He gave up his connection with the police force, his side job as coroner. He'd go back to healing the living — let someone else see to the dead. He had his fill — like Mitch. But he did finally propose to and marry Jenny Cartwright, Bugsy Polovina as his best man, Juliette Moore as Jenny's maid of honor, and he whispered to Mitch during the ceremony a thank you for his not calling his new wife a squaw. Then he and Jenny settled into the home they purchased from Mitch and Juliette.

Victoria Outing's misery ended with her passing, and when Homer Jenkins died, his life-long feelings of guilt died with him.

No one felt for Vincent Corelli. The grave was where he belonged. Even the Cohen's rejected him in the end, as did, it's certain, everyone but Satan. And Willy Hobbs, well... Willy went with Vincent.

The Farwell police force is smaller these days, but then, so is the crime. Royal Parker was made chief, Lila Hartman his assistant after she recovered from her wounds. The rest is the same, except of course, no Mitchell Polovina or Juliette Moore. And the impound is emptier since Vincent Corelli's '67 Buick Gran Sport went at action to the highest bidder, Mitchell Polovina, for one hundred dollars, his last act as Chief. He and Juliette are towing their Gold Wing behind it on a Route 66 trip, their honeymoon trip, their goal, to find a new place to begin their lives together along the way, perhaps Santa Fe, perhaps near the Grand Canyon. It was on the first leg of their journey, in the middle of Wisconsin, that Juliette asked him, "Where do we stay the night?"

"At the start of Route 66," he answered.

"And where's that?" she asked.

"Cicero, Illinois," he answered.

"Perfect," she said, and smiled.

Mayor Teddy Mayfield would win no more elections. He and Karla would separate, her distraught over the loss of her father, but Ted would return to teaching as he had done before he was Mayor, and the couple would eventually become a couple again, the rough spots behind them.

The bodies? No. I'm afraid not. No one was ever able to put names to them. They now rest in numbered graves in the Farwell cemetery with identical footstones that read 'Victim of the Little Cicero Mystery'.

End

The Dead Guy has received Gold IPPY Award in 2009

The Dead Guy

A Novel

Author: Doug Hewitt
Publisher: Aberdeen Bay
ISBN-10: 0-9814725-7-5
ISBN-13: 978-0-9814725-7-7

Jack Thigpen works in Detroit, nicknamed The Motor City, the perfect place for a fraud investigator who specializes in car insurance scams. Ironically, as he is targeted for death because of his current investigation, Jack is diagnosed with a fatal disease that is untreatable, a disease that will end his life within months. And instead of killing Jack, the hit man shoots Jack's best friend.

Struggling to come to terms with his impending death, Jack vows to track down his friend's killer.

Jack plunges into the world of corrupt car dealerships, chop shops, and fraudulent auto repair shops. Death is staring him in the face, but he doesn't back down. Jack pushes ahead, plowing through perilous roadblocks planted by his enemies, propelling himself toward the finish line and a teeth-gritting, heart-pounding conclusion.

The Dead Guy is a high-octane, pedal-to-the-metal ride through the criminal underbelly of the automobile world. A murder investigation in Detroit uncovers an international crime ring that threatens widespread violence. Murder and mayhem in Motown—I loved it!

-- Lynn Chandler-Willis author of The Preacher's Son

One of my favorite mysteries of all time. Well written and tautly paced, the Dead Guy is impossible to put down. As his lifeblood ticks away, Jack Thigpen tries to track down his best friend's killer. The Dead Guy is funny, wise, and suspenseful.

-- Karin Gillespie

LaVergne, TN USA
29 May 2010

184328LV00002B/6/P